THE
FLOOD

BOOKS BY G.N. SMITH

Fiona MacLeish Crime Thriller Series
The Island

THE
FLOOD

G.N. SMITH

bookouture

Published by Bookouture in 2023

An imprint of Storyfire Ltd.
Carmelite House
50 Victoria Embankment
London EC4Y 0DZ

www.bookouture.com

ISBN: 978-1-80314-914-1
eBook ISBN: 978-1-80314-913-4

To my son, who is already a much better person than I could have ever dared expect he'd become.

PROLOGUE

Fiona saw eyes filled with hate.

As much as she knew it wasn't all directed at her, Fiona was compelled to recoil away from it such was the intensity of the anger streaming her way. As a police officer Fiona had seen killers before, but they were people who'd killed in the heat of the moment. Tonight she was staring into the eyes of someone who'd made a cold-hearted decision to take the lives of three people.

Worst of all, Fiona was looking into the eyes of a killer from the wrong end of a shotgun.

ONE

EIGHT HOURS EARLIER

Fiona MacLeish stepped out of her aunt Mary's cottage, and four steps later she turned back, her police torch having illuminated everything she needed to see.

In the kitchen Aunt Mary met her with fearful eyes as she shrugged off her coat, dripping water onto the kitchen floor. 'How bad is it?'

'It's starting to top the bank.'

Fiona didn't say anything else. She didn't need to. This was the fourth time she'd been out to check the river in the last hour. It had risen a foot in that time and, the way the rain was thundering down, it was going to keep rising. Fiona's best guess was the river would be in the cottage within half an hour.

As rivers went, the Scales Burn was no Ganges. It wasn't even a Thames or a Clyde. At the nearest point to Aunt Mary's cottage, it was around fifteen feet wide as it wound its way along the Scales Valley. In occasional places it would fan out to a section fifty feet wide, where it burbled over shallows. Fiona had swum in its pools during summer and never once had she feared it. Now the Scales Burn was filled with threat. Roiling, tumbling brown water swarmed downstream with a malevolence only nature can provide.

The back door of Aunt Mary's long, low cottage was a scant few inches above the level of the riverbank. This had never been a problem before tonight. The closest the waters had ever got to topping the bank was still three feet short.

Today was different from all those other days. Four days ago, when Fiona had travelled from her home in Lochgilphead to Aunt Mary's cottage in the Scottish Borders, there had been a thick coating of snow on the hills and grit on the roads. But the warm front carrying Storm Odin onto the UK's shores had dealt with the snow as surely as a hammer blow from the Norse God the storm was named after.

Storm Odin wasn't a normal winter storm; it was a mega storm, and the predicted rainfall from Odin, combined with the snow melt, was the reason widespread flood warnings were in place for all low-lying ground near water courses in every part of the UK north of Birmingham.

So far Storm Odin was living up to his name. Fiona and Aunt Mary had already seen news reports of floods across Scotland and northern England, and now the threat of flooding was here.

When it arrived at the cottage, the murky brown river would ruin everything it touched. The silt carried by the raging waters would seep into fabrics, leech itself into every area, and then settle, leaving behind a red-brown scum that would have to be swept and shovelled out.

Aunt Mary's lips thinned as she drew her mouth into a line. 'We have to try and save the cottage. All my things are here. Everything I hold dear is in this house.'

The desperation in Aunt Mary's voice cut through Fiona with the delicate ease of a surgeon's scalpel. Her aunt's reaction was normal. Predictable even. Except it wasn't possible to save the cottage. They had nothing to barricade the doors with.

There were vents around the cottage designed to let air flow behind the walls, which they wouldn't have time to seal.

Fiona knew she'd have to be the bearer of bad news, that in her current distress Aunt Mary wasn't her usual switched-on self. 'I know, Aunt Mary, I know. But, unless this storm totally changes direction or suddenly blows itself out, we won't be able to stop this flood. Let's concentrate on what we can save. You get all your paperwork together and into a bag, I'm talking insurance documents, your passport and birth certificate, everything important. Pack another bag with enough clothes for a few days. I'm going to get all the electrical stuff I can and lift it onto the cupboards. Once you have your bags packed, do the same with the things you most care about: put them somewhere higher. We can only hope the river won't come too high and ruin everything.'

'Right.'

The lone word was enough to tell Fiona her aunt's usual fortitude was back. Aunt Mary was tungsten strong, the despair at the thought of floodwaters ruining her home and possessions a rare aberration from her stoic norm.

Fiona busied herself, unplugging the TV, lifting it and other electrics to the top of the cupboards, as well as the precious Portmeirion crockery. Having unplugged the fridge, she stood in the middle of the galley kitchen, looking around to see if she'd missed anything.

In the lounge, the presents beneath the Christmas tree and the lamp were all she could see that might be easily saved. The six Lladro figurines on the mantle were scooped up, carried to the spare bedroom and wrapped in clothes from Fiona's travel bag, before being carefully packed back into the bag. The figurines had belonged to Fiona's mother, and after her parents were murdered, Aunt Mary had inherited them, as well as her devastated niece. Now the porcelain ladies were as precious to Fiona as the crown jewels were to the king.

'Are you nearly done?' Fiona gathered up the few things she'd brought with her and stuffed them into her bag.

'Five minutes.'

Fiona traipsed in and out of the cottage. First, she slung her own meagre bags into her car, then she set to bringing the bags and cases Aunt Mary was filling. When both her car and Aunt Mary's were filled, Fiona picked up her torch and went for another look at the river.

Ripples of brown water were coming up the garden. They came as inch-high waves. Each one propelled by an incoming tide that advanced on the cottage like a barbarian army.

They had maybe fifteen minutes, by Fiona's guess.

Three ideas came to Fiona as she marched back into the house, her wellies squeaking with every step.

'Aunt Mary—'

'Yes?'

'Gather up as many small precious things as you can. Use the steps and put them in the attic. They ought to be safe there. Don't try and go up there, just get high enough that you can push them in. We can sort it out when we get back.' Fiona stopped speaking long enough to make sure her face was arranged in a way that would give her aunt strength at what she was about to say next. 'I'm going to go check on Mr and Mrs Edwards, make sure they're safe. As soon as you're done and ready to leave, switch off the leccy at the main board.'

Aunt Mary's hand flew to her mouth. 'You're right, their cottage lies so close to the river those poor people are sure to be flooded by now.' Her hand moved from her mouth. 'Quick, get yourself along there. They'll need your help more than I do. As for the others, they're all young enough to look after themselves.'

There was no doubting Aunt Mary's logic, even if it was ageist. There were only a handful of people living in the remote valley. And Pierce and Susie Normanton, the property developers who'd bought some land and built a sprawling eco-friendly bungalow, would be fine, as would Tom the shepherd. He was a taciturn man who lived a lonely life, but he was as capable a person as Fiona had ever met. Fiona didn't know much about Leighton – the buff guy who'd bought the Andersons' place last year – but as he was around her age, she expected that he'd be able to keep himself safe, even if he couldn't protect his home.

There were just two more properties in the immediate vicinity. William and Elsie Green were the farmers who owned the surrounding land. Their farmhouse was built on the highest ground and would be the last to flood. That only left Craig Kinning, William's dairyman, whose home was a pair of cottages that had been knocked through to provide home enough for his pregnant wife and two kids. It was the lowest lying of all the houses at this part of the valley and would be the second to flood after George and Isla's.

The thought of young children being uprooted from their home so close to Christmas was a kick in humanity's teeth.

Fiona had taken three steps towards the door when the cottage was plunged into darkness. This wasn't good. It would hamper Aunt Mary, and if there was no electricity at the Edwards' house, Lord alone knew what she'd find.

TWO

Ever since moving into the valley as a bereft teenager, Fiona had always thought the Edwards' cottage idyllic. It was the home furthest along the valley and was surrounded by stunning views. George Edwards spent every moment of daylight tinkering in his garden, shed or greenhouse. In summer, such was the riotous display of blooms in every colour imaginable, the cottage looked as if it belonged at the Chelsea Flower Show, or on a chocolate box. At the back was a vegetable garden, and there were many occasions where the kindly George had delivered a few potatoes, a cabbage or, best of all for Fiona, peas, which she'd guzzled straight from their pods.

Fiona had seen first-hand the joy George took from his garden, and he'd admitted to her that, throughout his years working as an accountant, he'd dreamed of the day when he could retire and work his hands in the fresh air instead of an overfull office. For George's sake, Fiona was delighted to see his dream come true.

George's wife Isla was the opposite of her husband. A former doctor's receptionist, Isla Edwards would say nothing to your face, and everything behind your back. Like a collie, she'd travel a mile to sneak behind you just so she could nip your ankles unseen. Like all such people, she thought nobody knew what she was really like underneath the friendly demeanour she portrayed. Both of her children had left home at the earliest opportunity, and George had once admitted to Fiona that he was lucky if he saw his kids and grandkids more than twice a year.

Fiona had learned the hard way, the only truly jolly thing about Isla Edwards was the bright floral dresses she habitually wore. All the same, she was a human being and one who might need help, and there was no way Fiona wasn't going to offer that.

Tonight, with a rainstorm crashing torrents of water from the sky, their little cottage seemed to skulk and cower in the darkness. As she trundled along the track that hugged the side of the valley above the farmable land, the headlights of Fiona's car penetrated the gloom, but they didn't have the power to disperse it. After what seemed to be an age, she found the fork she was looking for. Down and to the left lay the Edwards' cottage, ahead, the track followed the valley floor.

Trying to escape the guilt and death that had forced Fiona on a recuperative leave of absence, she'd taken an early morning hike up to the end of the valley just a couple of days before. Aunt Mary had, of course, come along. Together they'd trudged through the melting snow, skirted the wood at the head of the valley, and watched as Tom the shepherd navigated a quad bike up the narrow track that gave access to the hilltops surrounding the Scales Valley.

Fiona eased her car down the slope that led to the Edwards' cottage. Her headlights showing a tale of destruction. Around the outside of the building, dirty brown water swirled back and forth, swamping plants, and washing against the front door. To see a forewarning of what was coming to the only place she truly felt relaxed left Fiona heartbroken for the fate of Aunt

Mary's home. How poor old George would feel about his beloved garden was beyond Fiona's imagination. She'd sometimes wondered if he devoted his time to being outside so he wasn't in the company of his wife, but there was a huge difference between keeping yourself busy and pouring your heart into a labour of love.

Their car was in its usual parking space, the brown water halfway up its wheels. Fiona could picture them inside the house doing what they could to preserve their home. By now their efforts would be beyond futile, but she knew that if Isla commanded it, George would keep trying, even if the water was chest deep. She had to get them out of the house and up to somewhere safe. At their age, the exertions of a doomed attempt to stem the waters, coupled with the emotional trauma of seeing their home destroyed, could prove disastrous for their health.

Fiona turned her car so it was pointing back along the valley, and climbed out, the toes of her wellies swamped with the waters running along the narrow track.

There were no lights showing in the cottage. As she walked towards it, Fiona flashed her torch at a window. Instead of curtains blocking the beam, it penetrated the house and skittered over the walls. She aimed it at another window, hoping to attract the attention of the elderly couple, to let them know help was at hand.

There was no reaction. No lined faces appeared at the windows. The front door wasn't opened so a plea for assistance could be made.

It crossed Fiona's mind that the house might have been deserted because the Edwards had seen the writing on the wall and left. Except their car was there. She knew from talking with George yesterday their daughter was in Manchester and their son had moved from Liverpool to Chester, and that neither of their offspring was visiting until Christmas Eve, a week away.

George's face had been full of sadness when he told her both children were only doing a flying visit.

The water at Fiona's feet was six inches deep as she banged on the door with the heel of her hand. It was the knock her first sergeant, Dave Lennox, had taught her; he had said it would get the best response. He didn't have any faith in pussyfooting around with knuckles issuing a gentle rap. The only time he'd ever connect knuckle with door was when he had bad news to break, or was summoned to the office of a superior.

There was no answer to her thumps on the door so she tried again, harder. As she waited she directed her torch downwards, not just at a window, so it was aimed at the floor inside the cottage.

The floor was dark and brown and moving in rippled waves. With confirmation the water had already breached the cottage, Fiona grasped the door handle – it was unlocked.

There was little resistance when Fiona pushed on the door. She'd feared George or his wife would have tried barricading the door to stem the flow of water, but there was no way that had happened. Her next thought was the Edwards had already evacuated the house, but they'd have locked the door behind them, and taken the car. They *must* still be in the cottage.

Fiona made her way inside, her torch beam scoring horizontal swipes as she searched the room. 'Hello? George? Mrs Edwards? Are you here?'

There were no answering shouts. No croaked answers. The only sounds were made by water. The splashes as Fiona's feet drove her forwards, the thrum of large raindrops colliding with the ground, and the hissing roar of fast-moving water.

Fiona's torch pierced the gloom as she searched each room. The hall, lounge and three tiny bedrooms were devoid of human form. It was in the kitchen where she discovered what she sought. Except what she found was something she never wanted to see. George Edwards lay on his back on the kitchen floor, a current of murk pushing and pulling his grey hair back and forth. His face was battered and bruised. A thin trickle of blood ran from his nose and across his cheek until it was consumed by the lapping waters.

It took Fiona two rapid steps to reach him. She grabbed his shoulder and shook it.

George didn't open his eyes. Didn't moan. Didn't respond in any way.

Fiona directed the full dazzling beam of her torch at his eyes. Even with the lids down, the glare would burn at the retinas enough to provoke a response.

There was no response, so, fearing the worst, she put a hand to his throat. Her fingertips seeking out his carotid artery.

The cold water numbed her fingers, but Fiona stuck to her task, afraid she might miss a sign of life.

She didn't. This wasn't the first time Fiona had seen a dead body. As a cop that was part of the job, but it was the first time she'd seen the corpse of someone she liked and respected. She had chosen not to see her parents at the funeral home.

Fiona cast her torch around the kitchen looking for Mrs Edwards. There was no sign of her. 'Mrs Edwards? Isla?'

As she waited for a response, Fiona took another look at George. She'd seen no sign of a makeshift flood defence. Nor had she seen any of the preparations for a flood that she and Aunt Mary had made. That didn't seem right to Fiona. George and Mrs Edwards weren't idiots, they were sure to have seen what was coming and taken steps to protect their possessions. Except they hadn't.

The beam of Fiona's torch scanned down George's inert body. She suspected a heart attack had killed him, but the teachings of Dave Lennox wouldn't allow her to accept the obvious solution without first checking for signs she might be wrong. George had been in good health when they'd spoken yesterday, and his regular exertions in his garden would keep him a lot fitter than other men his age.

The blood cascading down his cheek rang a warning bell, but Fiona faintly remembered George suffered from nosebleeds on a regular basis. No obvious wounds showed on George's body, and there was a chance the wounds to his face had been caused by colliding with a piece of furniture as he fell to the floor. There were no rents in his clothing that could have been caused by a knife. It was when Fiona's torch rested on George's throat her suspicions began to firm. There was bruising around his throat. It suggested George had been strangled. Taking care to be gentle and respectful, Fiona lifted one of George's eyelids.

George's normally clear eyes were bloodshot. A sure sign he'd died from asphyxiation.

Now she had this confirmation, Fiona was no longer a concerned neighbour. Instead she was back in her day job as a police constable. George was the second murder victim she'd seen, and she still blamed herself for the death of the first, a fellow officer, even if her actions at the time had saved the lives of a woman and child as well as her own.

The wounds on George's face now spoke of a violent death rather than a fall induced by a medical condition.

Fiona backed herself into a corner and scanned the kitchen with her torch once more. She was no longer looking for her neighbours. She was checking George's killer wasn't lying in wait for her.

THREE

As the torch traversed its way around the room, Fiona drew her mobile from a pocket and swiped in her passcode. There was no signal. There was nothing new about that. The hills forming the Scales Valley repelled mobile signals at the best of times. With the rainstorm having knocked out the electric, there was a good chance the mast supplying the signal was affected too.

She tried dialling 999 anyway.

Nothing happened.

Fiona's pulse raced as she cast her memory back over everything she'd seen in the Edwards' cottage. She'd found no human apart from George, which meant she'd not inadvertently stumbled across his killer, but that didn't mean they hadn't pressed themselves into a hiding spot and were waiting for a chance to pounce.

As she forced herself to think like a cop instead of a victim, Fiona mapped out the cottage and any potential hiding places, all of which she'd already looked through. Therefore any killer lying in wait would have had their best chance of attacking her. Except they hadn't taken it, which meant they probably weren't in the house. *Probably*.

With this logic easing Fiona's nerves somewhat, uppermost in Fiona's mind were two things: she had to find George's wife and apprehend his killer. It could be that Isla had killed George, of course, but Fiona doubted that. George had told her during their chat that his wife's arthritis had got worse, and that her hands were now so gnarled she struggled to grip anything. Her hobbies of needlework, knitting and crocheting had been abandoned due to her inability to grip the needles or hooks.

It seemed improbable Isla had been able to grasp the rope or wire that had left the ligature marks on George's throat. Being that Isla was a slight woman, neither was it credible that she possessed the strength to resist any efforts George would have made to free himself.

Fiona took a mental run through her training. How the hell was she supposed to preserve a crime scene that was flooding? And how was she meant to find Mrs Edwards by herself, when George's killer could be watching her at this very moment? Dave Lennox had taught Fiona way more than any of the courses at Tuliallan Police College, but she felt that even he, with all his experience and natural wisdom, would have to stop and think about what to do. There were only so many situations the rule book could cover before common sense had to take over. The bookshelves in her Lochgilphead home were stacked with every policing manual she could source. It was these tomes, in addition to her training, that Fiona now relied on to guide her decision-making.

Fiona ran through the meagre options available.

As much as she wanted to begin searching for Isla, Fiona knew her first duty was to protect herself. Another considera- tion was the fact she didn't know where George's killer was. But she had to scour the cottage. With luck she'd find Isla cowering in a wardrobe, and then she'd be able to get the woman to a place where she could keep her safe. For all she planned to call the murder in as soon as she could, she knew she shouldn't leave until she'd established Isla's whereabouts.

But, if she closed the doors and left George where he was until the flood subsided, there'd be only a tiny chance of forensic evidence remaining. If she could somehow haul George's corpse out to her car, his body could be kept relatively sterile, in forensics terms. However, she'd have to move him down the path and up the track to where her car was free of the floodwaters. By the time she got him there, the heavy rain would have finished the cleansing started by the floodwaters. And that was doing nothing to preserve the kitchen, which was also a crime scene.

With the torch's sweep not finding anyone lurking, Fiona crossed the kitchen and removed the largest knife from the block by the chopping board – her eyes picked up a pair of red spots on the counter. Both were teardrop in shape. This told Fiona they were blood spatter and that in turn confirmed someone had been beaten in the kitchen. The blood was still damp, which meant it was recent.

To Fiona, the threat of further violence hung in the kitchen like a malevolent aroma. She made her way towards the back door. The key was in the lock, so after a quick scan in case Isla was outside, she closed the door and turned the key.

The chairs by the kitchen table had rails as their backs, so she hooked her torch hand under a rail and stepped back to the hallway. Once Fiona determined it was empty of human life, she took the chair and splashed her way to the front door. There was no key in its lock, but she managed to jam the chair's top rail below its handle.

It was now impossible for the killer to breach the cottage without making a lot of noise. Noise that would serve as a warning to Fiona. She knew she had to work quickly, preserving George's body where he lay, as the crime scene was far less important than finding Isla, but Fiona knew that once she left the cottage, she wouldn't be returning until she had other police officers at her side.

With the knife gripped in her right hand, Fiona entered the bedroom nearest the kitchen and swung the wardrobe door open. Floral dresses hung by the dozen, but there was no killer, or Isla.

Fiona returned to the kitchen and pulled her mobile from a pocket. She knew it wasn't the ideal tool for taking crime scene photos, but it was all she had. So, using the torch to illuminate George and other key points like the drops of blood, Fiona snapped as many angles as she could before securing it back in her pocket.

'I'm sorry, George.' The words may have been whispered, but they were heartfelt.

Fiona wound her free hand into the top of George's jumper and hauled him upwards until he was in a sitting position. She kept a firm grip until she'd moved behind him and rested a knee against his shoulder blades. Only when she was sure he wouldn't topple, did she tuck the torch under one arm and use both hands to grip the back of his collar.

Step by step Fiona dragged George along the floor, sweat beading on her brow as she fought to haul his inert body. By the time she got to the bedroom she was panting and had to suck in deep breaths before she attempted to lift him onto the bed.

Fiona positioned George so one of his armpits rested against the bed's divan and reached down into the murky water to take a handful of his belt. Once she was satisfied she had a firm grip she bent her legs until she was squatting beside him; here, the mouths of her wellies were a fraction above the rising water. She kept her back straight and used the power of her thigh muscles to lift George. When her legs were straight she had to wrestle and roll George to get him onto the bed.

George's body was loose and his arms and legs flopped powerless as she manhandled him, but in her years as a police officer she had gained plenty of practice at moving unconscious drunks. George was now as high as she could get him, and she had to hope it was high enough to keep his body from being submerged by the rising flood.

Where was Isla? Had she also been murdered by whoever killed George? Or was she hiding out somewhere terrified of encountering her husband's killer?

Fiona gave a quick but thorough scan of the bedroom, in case there was anything that would be of use to the investigation. The dresser yielded nothing but underwear. The wardrobe, outer clothes. Three brisk steps got Fiona to the little bedside cabinet, where the top drawer was opened a little. She pulled out a diary. A quick scan of some random pages revealed spidery but feminine script. Fiona stuffed the diary into her jacket's inside pocket. When she had a moment, she'd go through it, in the hope its pages would offer up the identity of George's killer.

Fiona unlocked the kitchen door and stood in the doorway, her torch scything through the rain as she examined the rear garden for any sign of Isla. There was no trace of human life, just frothing brown waters, occasional bushes and shrubs, and rain thundering down from the blackness.

Back and forth Fiona swept the torch. Inside her mind an argument was raging. The blood on George's face had still been wet, therefore it wasn't long since he'd been killed. That meant his killer could be outside the house, waiting to ambush her if she stepped out. The suitcases on the bed spoke of George and his wife preparing to flee the flood, rather than staying to fight it with makeshift flood defences. Even in the short time Fiona had been in the cottage, she'd noticed the water level rising.

Isla could have already fallen victim to the killer as she was packing, or she could be hiding out somewhere else. If she'd even been at home. Fiona knew that, at least twice a week,

George would take Isla into Hawick, so she could meet with the few friends she had.

Fiona was aware one person couldn't search the valley alone and expect any reasonable odds of success. In this weather visibility was little more than a dozen feet, and when Fiona added in the dangers presented by the killer and the overflowing river, she knew that mounting a one-woman search party was a ridiculous plan. If Isla wasn't home, Fiona would be risking her life for nothing.

Fiona yelled Isla's name at the top of her voice and kept her torch moving, looking for movement that wasn't related to water. Finding none, she grimaced and made a tough decision.

Fiona locked the back door, walked through the cottage and removed the chair barricade. She teased the door open and once again shone her torch into the blackness enveloping the valley. The powerful light illuminated nothing but bare stalks, swirling waters and plummeting raindrops. Fiona couldn't make her mind up if that was good or bad. No way did she want the torch to reveal the body of someone waiting for the chance to murder her too, but she couldn't trust that she hadn't missed a hiding spot.

'Come on. Stop being a divot and get yourself back.'

The knuckles of Fiona's fingers were white as she sloshed her way to the car with the knife in one hand and her torch the other.

As soon as she got into the car, she locked the doors and twisted the key in the ignition.

She had to get herself to a place where she could report George's murder. There would be some detectives stationed at Hawick. They'd be able to lead the investigation, or at least begin it until a specialist team from Glasgow or Edinburgh could be sent.

Fiona had three priorities, now: getting Aunt Mary out of this valley during the worst storm in living memory, finding Isla

Edwards, presumably with a killer at large, and summoning help, so that the killer could be caught.

The sooner she got some officers from Police Scotland here, the better the chance of George's family having the closure of knowing his murderer was caught and convicted.

It was a closure she'd never had in the nineteen years since her parents were murdered in the family home.

BEFORE

Fiona pressed her lips together, to hide the yawn, as she filed into the assembly hall of Annan Academy. Instead of revising, as she was supposed to, last night had been mostly spent on the phone with Olivia. Fiona's best friend had been distraught, as she'd caught her boyfriend, Zane, kissing a classmate. Everybody knew that Whitney liked nothing more than causing trouble. She was the girl every boy at school fancied, a fact she was well aware of and exploited for her own amusement.

When Olivia told Fiona of how she'd slapped Zane and called Whitney a slut to her face, Fiona had delighted in her friend's courage. Whitney wasn't just the prettiest girl in the fourth year, she was also the hardest.

Fiona took a seat and scanned the assembly hall. Olivia, as always, was occupying the next seat, and she could see Donna and Naomi were two rows ahead. They were the best friends anyone could ever have and Fiona's fifteen-year-old mind couldn't comprehend how the four of them wouldn't always be in each other's lives.

Today was the day Fiona would sit her third GCSE. It was History, and Fiona was under no illusions as to why it was her favourite subject. Mr Daniels was soooo dreamy, all the girls fancied him. He wasn't a crusty old teacher marking time until retirement; he was young enough for this to be his first job, and when he spoke, his voice was layered with passion. His classes were disciplined, but not authoritarian, and even the loons like Psycho and Snecky didn't act up for him.

Fiona's pen danced across the page as she completed the final question. A look at the clock on the wall showed there were five minutes left before the exam ended. That was enough time to give her answers a quick check, and then she'd be free to go and get lunch.

The smell of macaroni and cheese was wafting in from the kitchen and it was enough to make Fiona's stomach growl. Olivia's head spun her way, and as Fiona reddened, Olivia shot one of her thousand watt smiles across the gap between them. It felt good to see Olivia smile again.

As the exam came to an end and everyone filed out, Fiona chattered with Olivia about the questions and what answers they'd given. Everything was good, and with a free period scheduled after lunch, things were about to get better.

'Excuse me, Fiona. Can you come with me, please?'

It was Mr Daniels. The gravity of his tone and the serious-ness of his face dropped a ball of dread into the pit of Fiona's stomach.

'Sir?'

'Please, Fiona, come with me.'

Fiona stood her ground. Not from any anarchic sense, but because everything about Mr Daniels suggested that something was very wrong. Fiona wracked her brain, trying to think of any exam rule she may have breached. All she could come up with was the look from Olivia after her belly rumbled, and surely that couldn't be classed as an attempt to cheat at the exam?

'What is it, sir? What's up?'

'I... I'm not sure I can tell you. I need you to come to the

Head's office with me.' He set off walking, turned and looked at her. 'Come on, Fiona, now please.'

The hesitation in his voice and the way he couldn't meet her eye spoke volumes.

Fiona gave a squeeze of Olivia's arm. 'I'll catch you up. Save me a seat.'

Mr Daniels walked ahead of her and even as the ball of dread was bouncing around her stomach, Fiona couldn't help but notice he was walking at a measured pace, far slower than his long legs normally achieved.

There was no delay between Mr Daniels's knock on the Head's door and him reaching for the handle, and while Fiona recognised the fact as significant, she couldn't work out why.

When Mr Daniels walked through the door and stepped to one side, Fiona saw three people in the Head's office. The Head, her aunt Mary and a copper. All wore sombre expressions.

Fiona could feel tears pricking the corners of her eyes before any of them spoke. Whatever they were about to say was sure to be far worse than anything she'd imagined.

FOUR

Fiona's windscreen wipers whipped back and forth at their highest setting, but such was the volume of water falling they didn't stand a chance of dispersing it fast enough. To Fiona it was like looking through a fish tank; she turned the blower on full to combat the condensation misting the edges of the windscreen. It didn't solve the problem, but at least it halted the mist's advance.

Each rut of the track was an overflowing stream of water as the landscape funnelled the massive amounts of rainwater down to the Scales Burn in the floor of the valley.

Fiona used numb fingers on the hands-free to try and call in the murder. Still no signal, so she fired off a text to her best friend, DC Heather Andrews, so that word would get out the second the signal was restored. Had this happened when she was on duty near her home in Lochgilphead, she would have had a police radio to make the call. Off duty, as she was, in the wilds of the Scottish Borders, she was just another civilian. Except she wasn't really off duty. She never considered herself to be off duty. Besides, her sergeant and inspector had listened to the wisdom of the police psychologist she'd been forced to see, and insisted she take not just some leave, but to put Lochgilphead in her rear-view mirror for at least a week. Fiona hadn't wanted to, but the inspector had told her to either take leave, or be declared unfit for duty. They didn't get it. The officer who'd been killed in the line of duty, right in front of her, was in her thoughts wherever she was. She could travel to the furthest reaches of the solar system, and she'd still not escape the mental images of his death. There was no distance great enough for Fiona to leave behind the guilt she felt.

As she crested a small rise, Fiona felt the car's wheels spin as they lost traction. Her instinct was to gun the engine, but she knew that wouldn't help. Instead she eased off the throttle, feathering the pedal with just enough power to make sure the engine didn't stall. For all her car was an SUV, Fiona's budget hadn't extended to the four-wheel drive model and she could feel the front wheels clawing at the sodden track. The back end started to slip sideways, but the front tyres gripped the track's gravel bed well enough to drag her car to the top of the rise, where she stopped for a moment.

Before she continued on, Fiona fished Isla's diary from her pocket and rifled through the pages, searching out entries from a few weeks ago. Isla's penmanship suffered due to her arthritis, turning her words into a near illegible scrawl, but Fiona did what she could to decipher the words. The more she read, the more she learned of Isla's fears for her and George's safety. They'd put their house up for sale and had struck a deal with an unnamed party whom Isla referred to as 'that infernal couple'.

Fiona's heart sank as she digested this. The fears George and Isla harboured had been strong enough to make them sell their forever home. For George to abandon the garden he'd so lovingly created would have been a terrible wrench, but he'd felt so threatened, he'd agreed to move.

The last line on an entry dated three weeks ago thrust a spear of dread into Fiona's chest.

I don't believe anyone in this valley is safe.

Fiona dropped the diary onto the passenger seat and gunned the engine. She had to get Aunt Mary out of the valley and summon help.

As Fiona neared Aunt Mary's cottage, the headlights picked out the little red VW Polo her aunt loved driving. It was parked at the junction to her cottage and its lights were on.

Good, Aunt Mary was safe. Not just safe, but ready to leave her home behind and strike out for the safety of a hotel in Hawick.

Fiona drew alongside her aunt's car and dropped the passenger window an inch. Aunt Mary did the same, her face behind the glass tense, yet stoic as always.

'We need to get to Hawick as soon as possible.' Should she tell Aunt Mary what she had found? While she'd never got on with Isla Edwards, her aunt always had time for George. But it felt like a conversation for a brightly lit room. It wouldn't do to scare her aunt out here in the darkness.

'Pardon?'

Aunt Mary's voice was drowned out by the thrumming of the rain on the car's roof. Fiona could see her lips move, but couldn't make out what she was saying.

Fiona repeated herself as loud as she could without fully shouting, but got the same blank look and lip-read *pardon?*

Rather than continue doing the same thing repeatedly and expecting different results, Fiona pointed at her chest and held up one finger, then pointed it at her aunt's car and raised two. Next, she pointed at the road which led to the A7 – the main artery through the Borders.

Aunt Mary gave a nod and wound her window up. Fiona allowed herself a grim smile; Aunt Mary might be in her seventh decade, but she was still as switched on as she'd always been.

Fiona had gone ten yards when her headlights picked out a human shape. Clad in orange rain-slicked waterproofs the shape waved her down. The first thing she did was make sure her doors were still locked. The size of the shape gave her clues as to who the figure was. Craig Kinning was the dairyman at Scales Valley Farm. He stood north of six foot and was big, capable, and possessed with a genial nature, or at least it was until drink was taken.

Craig was a likeable man, but Fiona knew plenty of tales of his younger days, when he'd rarely enjoy a night out without getting into at least one fight. Fiona always thought Craig was trustworthy, but with an unknown killer in the valley, she didn't dare trust anyone. Not someone she'd known for the best part of twenty years, even if he was the guy she'd shared her first kiss with.

'Are you okay?' Craig's eyes flitted past her shoulder and looked into her packed car. 'You leaving?'

'Yeah. The cottage is bound to flood, so we've got as much stuff out as we could. We'll get a room somewhere in Hawick tonight.'

'Be careful. I've been down with William; the heck beneath the bridge has caught so many trees and branches it's formed a dam.'

The heck was a timber fence suspended across the river from a wire rope, tied off at either side to a sturdy tree. It hung across the Scales Burn and stopped cattle and sheep escaping the fields by wading into the burn. Trees and other debris passed under the heck as its suspending wire rope acted as a hinge.

'I will. How come the heck caught a tree?'

'A big elm was washed down a few months back. One of its branches snagged the wire and it's been there ever since.'

The big elm would collect other branches and debris, which in turn would form a barrier for more trees to get caught up in.

'How's your place looking?'

Craig had a wife and two kids. His cottage was on higher ground than Aunt Mary's, but as there was a dam forming, the waters would continue to rise.

'It's okay for now. Becky and wee Jamie are packing some bits up, in case. We'll go to the farm and stay with William and Elsie, if we have to. I'm sure there'll be space for you two as well.'

The offer was good and made sense on a lot of levels, but Fiona knew she had to leave the valley and report George's murder. With Isla missing as well, Fiona had to summon help. She considered asking Craig to keep an eye out for Isla, but as soon as she did that he'd ask where George was and she didn't think it wise to broadcast there was a murderer in the valley just yet, not when there were so many tensions already running high before the flood came.

'Thanks, but I think Aunt Mary will be better off in a hotel. I think she'll hate to be in the vicinity of her cottage if it floods.' Fiona felt shame at blaming Aunt Mary for fleeing the valley. Still, it was a necessary evil, as she had to raise the alarm.

'Fair enough. Look after yourself.'

It was as Craig stepped away from the window that Fiona turned her mind to the valley's other inhabitants. As well as Craig and Becky, and William and Elsie at the farm, there was Tom Urquhart who shepherded William's sheep on the hills, and Pierce and his wife Susie, a couple who'd given up the business life in Essex in favour of early retirement, and also Leighton Watson, a single man who lived alone and kept himself to himself.

Like all groups of people who lived in close proximity there were alliances and feuds. When Fiona and Aunt Mary had their twice-weekly calls, she would be brought up to date on all the valley's goings on, but it rarely amounted to a large part of their conversation. However, Fiona knew that while Craig and

Becky were friendly with both Tom and William, they had little to do with Leighton or Susie and Pierce. Leighton lived a solitary life, but he'd never gelled with anyone, to Aunt Mary's knowledge, and his habit of parking in gateways was a constant irritant to William, Craig and Tom. Susie and Pierce were the least favoured of the valley's occupants. According to Aunt Mary, Susie was opinionated and vocal, while her husband acted as if he was nothing more than her support act.

By leaving the valley, Fiona was abandoning all these people to their fate. A killer was prowling around somewhere, or even among their number, and as the only police officer present she had a moral duty to protect them.

Fiona was a realist, though. The killer could have already completed their aim by killing George, but they could also be lying in wait ready to kill their next target. To Fiona's mind, there was little chance of anyone wanting to kill George. He was such an inoffensive and friendly man, it was unthinkable to picture him angering someone enough they'd kill him. As the blood on his cheek and the counter were still wet, he must have been murdered only minutes before she arrived at his cottage. Because the track to the Edwards' cottage ran past the farm and several other properties, it was unlikely a stranger had travelled there unseen. The odds favoured the killer being one of the valley's residents; and, with a power cut, there was no way Fiona could reasonably be expected to protect Aunt Mary plus ten people across four properties. That was working on the assumption that Isla Edwards would turn up safe. As risky as it was, a search party would be put together to find the old woman.

It would be possible to form a search party with those present in the valley, but a proper search required trained officers, and the only way Fiona could get help was to get to a place where she could call the crime in.

FIVE

With Craig heading back to his wife and kids, Fiona set off towards her destination, and a mobile signal that would allow her to summon reinforcements. There was a strong temptation to hurtle down the narrow road from the farm to the A7, but Fiona resisted the urge to drive fast.

Visibility was about as low as it could get without her car actually being underwater. Besides, the last thing she wanted to do was race ahead of Aunt Mary. A cautious driver at the best of times, there was no way her aunt would keep up with anything over twenty miles an hour in these conditions.

The road was awash with water but it was never flooded due to it being etched into the side of a hill. The left side of the road was higher than the strip of tarmac, but the right was lower which meant the road drained of water as quickly as it flooded.

A greater hazard were potholes. While they could be seen in normal conditions, when slick with rainwater they lay hidden like landmines, ready to attack the unwary driver who drove a wheel into their depths. Fiona had hit one such pothole with a Police Scotland van she'd been driving at pace. As bad as the swearing had been from her inspector, the weeks of teasing from her colleagues had stung more.

Behind Fiona, the headlights of her aunt's car sent starbursts of light through her rear window. It was reassuring to see her keeping pace. Aunt Mary was a rock, she had been a constant in Fiona's life. It was her shoulder that Fiona's heart broke on night after night, following the murder of her parents. Aunt Mary had pieced together a broken child and made her far stronger than the sum of her parts. Without the support from her aunt, Fiona would never have made it into the police. It had even been her aunt's resolute nature that had found a way to resolve the issues she had with sitting exams.

Fiona was fifteen years old when Mr Daniels had led her to the Head's office without telling her why she was being taken there. For all she'd liked and even slightly fancied Mr Daniels, even to this day, Fiona viewed his taking her to the Head's office as something akin to a Roman legionnaire leading a Christian into the Colosseum.

Aunt Mary had taken Fiona's hands, looked into her eyes and, with a voice breaking with emotion, told Fiona her parents had been murdered.

Since that dreadful day, and the ones that followed in its aftermath, Fiona had never been able to sit an exam. She'd seen psychologists about her phobia, and tried every last one of the techniques suggested to her. The coping mechanisms she'd try to employ all quit on her the moment she approached the exam room. Her breaths went shallow and her knees weak. Her heart raced as bile filled her throat and sweat pulsed from every pore on her body.

The school fought for her coursework grades to be considered by the exam board and Fiona had eked enough results for her to be allowed to apply to the police when she was old enough.

Without Aunt Mary's sage advice that she could claim

special dispensation with a psychologist's testimony and not sit the exams in the normal way, Fiona would never have made it into the police. When it came to the final exam, she was given a session where a pair of sergeants from Admissions conducted an interview-style exam on a bench outside their office. Aunt Mary had been allowed to sit off to one side, so Fiona would see her and know that the one person she had left in the world was safe and well while she was going through the interview.

It had been a concession Fiona was loathe to make. The murder of her parents touched every part of her life and, as desperate as she was to become a detective so she could hunt their killers herself, she didn't want any favours or special dispensation. What she achieved had to be on her own merit. Even now, years later, Fiona still felt like a fraud for using the equalities act to sit those exams, although she knew her feelings were more a form of imposter syndrome than anything else. For Fiona, getting into the police and making detective had to be something she did of her own agency. It was part of the healing process, and something she had to achieve through the usual channels to bolster her own confidence. She'd got into the police, but she still hadn't mustered the courage to once again sit in an exam room to earn the qualifications she needed to become a detective.

Fiona's greatest fear was that if she ever managed to bring a case against her parents' killers, her testimony and evidence would be ridiculed by a lawyer who'd throw her evidence back in her face. To get that close to a conviction and then have the killers walk free would be even worse than not knowing who they were and why they'd killed two wonderful people.

Despite making several attempts, Fiona hadn't been able to bring herself to sit those exams. She'd once managed to enter the exam room and begin, but had fled after ten minutes, just so she could call Aunt Mary and check on her wellbeing.

After joining Police Scotland, Fiona had spent two years

saving every penny she could. When she had enough saved, she hired a retired DS who now worked as a private investigator to look into her parents' murders. He'd done what he could but, when he'd delivered his final report to her, his voice was tinged with sadness and realism. He'd described the case as 'one of those that has such a lack of evidence it keeps detectives awake at night wondering how the killer had achieved it.' He'd gone on to explain that he could find 'no hint of a motive, no real suspects, and no witnesses'. Fiona had paid his bill, thanked the man, and resolved to earn detective status so she could run her own investigation.

The jolt of a wheel slamming into a pothole brought Fiona back from her reverie. Ahead of her, the road crooked to the right and started to climb. The bridge was perhaps a hundred yards ahead. As a rule the underside of the bridge would be at least ten feet above the river.

It was under this bridge that the timber heck was located. Its gate-like shape a barrier to cattle or sheep wandering under the bridge to and from the fields of the neighbouring farmer.

Fiona knew the bridge and heck well. In her teenage years she'd used it to cross the river when hanging out with Craig. They'd cross by standing on the top wooden rail and sliding their hands along the wire rope suspending the gate-like structure as they passed six feet above the water. It was under the bridge they'd shared their first kiss. Their romance had never blossomed further; Craig's father had been dairyman at Scales Valley Farm before him, and he'd been the only boy close to her age for miles around. She'd kissed him out of a desire for intimacy rather than a desire for him, the kiss a milestone on her road back to normality after her world was devastated. Bless Craig, he'd somehow understood what she needed and had put his own needs aside. They'd kissed many more times over the following weeks, but he'd never pushed her for more. When Craig told Fiona about a new girl in his class called Becky, she'd known he was ready to move on, so she told him to ask Becky out.

Aunt Mary had called Fiona out on that first kiss within minutes of her return to the cottage. She hadn't uttered a critical word, all she'd done was surmise the reason for Fiona's smile and warn her to make sure that she hurt neither herself nor Craig. When she'd gone on to suggest there were plenty of other young lads at school, Fiona hadn't known if Aunt Mary was suggesting she play the field, or trying to warn her off Craig.

Fiona pushed the memories aside and tried to see the waters as they gathered upstream of the bridge, but her headlights didn't penetrate the darkness enough to allow her to see anything. She crossed the bridge, Aunt Mary's headlights behind her a reassuring presence. For Fiona, getting the woman who'd put her broken teenage self back together to a safe place was more important than anything.

The road veered left and climbed the side of the opposite hill once it crossed the bridge. Debris lay on the road where torrents of water had carried stones down from the hillside. Fiona had to steer round a few boulders the size of footballs as she drove onwards.

On and on Fiona crept at little more than twenty. She dodged more boulders, picking her way with care. Behind the car, Aunt Mary's headlights had dropped back a little as she too guided her car through the obstacles.

Fiona's own headlights picked out a different shape in the torrents of water as she passed what she knew to be a pine wood. The shape was one she'd worried about seeing: it was a landslide. Not a major one that saw earth and boulders blocking the road, but a minor one that crept halfway across it. She veered as far to the left as she dared without risking the wheels digging into the sodden roadside, and let the car pull itself forward in second gear without any touch on the throttle.

The car's right wheels trundled over the mound of earth,

causing it to tilt a little. As soon as she judged she was past the landslide, Fiona steered back to the centre of the road and pulled to a stop ten metres away.

There were too many boxes and bags on the back seat for Fiona to see much through the rear window, so she had to track Aunt Mary's trip around the landslide using only her wing mirrors. Her hand was on the door catch, her breath held, as she peered at the mirrors.

Aunt Mary's headlights were her only guide, but she had faith in her aunt. Always good behind the wheel, Aunt Mary had years of experience driving this road.

Fiona's breath came out in a relieved gasp when her aunt's car lights tucked in behind her own vehicle and flashed a victorious beam her way. Bless Aunt Mary for having the mindfulness to indicate she was okay.

Fiona set off again, keeping it slow and steady. Alongside her the wood stretch parallel to the road; water from a forestry track cut into the centre of the wood was streaming a turbulent river across the road before swirling down the bank on its way into the Scales Burn.

There was a definite pull on her car from the torrent, so Fiona gunned her engine. The added speed would get her through okay and would also cause Aunt Mary to speed up and aid her passage through.

As the road curled around the hill, Fiona kept going until the car's headlights picked out the next obstacle. Another landslide had covered the road, this time from one side to the other. If that wasn't bad enough, the landslide had carried with it a sizable pine tree, its trunk a foot thick.

There was no way they were going to get any further along this road until someone had cleared the landslide, and that would require chainsaws and a digger.

Fiona cut her engine, climbed out, and trotted back to Aunt Mary's car.

'The road's blocked with a landslide. We're going to have to back up until we can turn round.'

'I see.' Aunt Mary's face was tight. As good a driver as she was, reversing was her weak spot. Backing along this road in the dark with next to zero visibility would test her skills to the max.

Aunt Mary put her hand on the gearstick and moved to put the car into reverse. 'Go on then. Go back to your car.'

There was determination in Aunt Mary's voice, but Fiona knew her well enough to detect the underlying fear and an uncharacteristic lack of confidence, emotions she saw in her aunt on the rarest of occasions.

'Do you want me to take over?' It was an offer borne of kindness, but Fiona was aware of what it really represented: a changing of the guard, a ceding of power.

'I can do it.'

'I know you can.'

'But... you'll probably be quicker at it than me.' And with that said, Aunt Mary exited the car so they could swap positions.

Fiona fired the engine and set off. As with her own car, her aunt's was filled with items rescued from the cottage, so the trip back was a torturously slow process. When they got to where the forestry track streamed water across the road, Fiona made a decision.

The engine roared as Fiona sped up and swung the wheel, directing the rear of the car towards the track. It bumped and scraped its way into the forestry track, until Fiona slammed the gearstick into first and hauled the wheel left. The car spun its wheels on the slick road as Fiona directed its bonnet back towards Scales Valley Farm and drew to a halt.

'Well done. Now tell me, because I've been wondering, did you find George and Isla? Are they okay?'

How much to tell Aunt Mary? The answer to that was a no-brainer for Fiona. She never held anything back from her aunt.

'I'm sorry, I found George. But... Aunt Mary, he was dead. I hate to say it, but... he'd been beaten then strangled.'

'Killed? But who would want to harm dear sweet George?' In the light from the dashboard Aunt Mary's face was pale. 'And what about Isla? Was she there? My God... do you think she killed him?'

'I don't know what to think. I didn't see her there and I shouted for her and had a pretty good look, but I don't know if she killed him and then took off, or was killed as well and her body cast into the river. All I know for certain is that George was murdered. I can't see her being able to kill George, not if half of what he said about her arthritis is true.' There was a more unpalatable truth to share, but Fiona hesitated before she dropped that bombshell.

Aunt Mary peered through the windscreen as her face blanched even further. 'Lord help us, do you think George's killer is still around?'

Trust Aunt Mary to have worked out what Fiona was hesitant to give voice to.

'I think it's a strong possibility. We know the road is blocked but we don't know how long it's been like that. Maybe the killer got away and maybe they didn't. We're going to have to go back to the farm and wait out the flood with the others.'

'Who will be up there now, do you think?' The tremble in Aunt Mary's voice cut at Fiona like a chainsaw.

'Everyone who lives in the valley. When I started loading the cars, I saw lights at every house except Tom's.'

'He'll have been in the valley somewhere. He only ever leaves once a week and that's to go to the shop.'

'You know him better than I do. Now, come on, let's get back to the farm. There's safety in numbers.'

'I agree. But do you think we should tell them about poor George? Although... what if one of them is the person who killed George? Surely that's not possible though. I don't have much to do with anyone these days, but people up here are decent folk.'

It was a good question and one Fiona knew she must consider. It made sense to let everyone know there was a killer among them, but it might also make the killer strike again. From what little she'd gleaned from Isla's diary, Fiona knew Isla and George felt threatened enough by someone to leave the valley, but there was no clue as to the person's identity. That person could be any of the valley's residents. The last line she'd read of the diary suggested that whoever was intimidating George and Isla was also a threat to all the valley's inhabitants, so if George's murder became public knowledge the killer may turn desperate and kill more people, to cover their tracks.

It made more sense to keep the murder quiet.

'We shouldn't say anything. If one of them did kill George, we'll only make ourselves targets by letting it be known we're aware of George's murder. Tell me, Aunt Mary, have you told any of your neighbours I'm a police officer?'

'No. Definitely not. If anyone asks about you, it tends to be about whether or not you've found a husband yet.'

How typical of the valley's inhabitants to only care if she'd found a man. It was a typical farming mentality. A young woman of breeding age was viewed as a wife and mother in waiting. As for the newcomers to the valley, Tom, Leighton, Susie and Pierce, they didn't know her well enough to care about her chosen career.

'Good. I don't think we should tell anyone because A, it'll give me a chance to try and work out who the killer is, and B...' Fiona changed her mind. There was no point worrying Aunt Mary for no reason. 'Actually there is no B. At least not one I can think of yet.'

'B is it'll keep you safe.'

Trust Aunt Mary to read between the lines.

'It is, yeah.' Fiona hooked her fingers through the door

handle. 'I'm going back for my car. You get yourself back into this seat and then lock the doors. When I get close you lead us back to the farm.'

'Take care, Fiona. Remember, it's only a car.'

Fiona waited until Aunt Mary was back in the driver's seat and her indicators had flashed with the central locking. With a wave that was far cheerier than she felt, she set off to retrieve her own car. Now that they were trapped in the valley, she planned to scour through Isla's diary at the first opportunity in the hope its pages would name the killer.

SIX

The rain battered against Fiona. It sluiced off her jacket and soaked her jeans. The thin hood of her jacket kept her head dry, but she could feel the impact of the raindrops on her scalp. The hood's brim dripped water onto her nose and rivers of water traced down her arms and trickled extra cold onto her hands.

Water splashed up Fiona's wellies and she felt a sideways pressure on her feet and ankles as the stream pouring out from the forestry trail clawed at her. Small stones dislodged from the hills and carried onto the road by the torrents of water, acted like marbles, making every step a treacherous balancing act.

Fiona did all she could to remove the various threats from her mind. She'd made the mistake of leaving her police torch in the car, so the only light she had was the torch app on her mobile, but it was little better than a candle.

By the time Fiona reached her car she was soaked and frozen from the cold December rain. Worse than the discomfort was the sight of her car. In the short time she'd been away, there had been another landslide.

The second landslide wasn't as dramatic as the first, but it had slumped mud and rocks against the driver's side of the car.

Fiona didn't waste time assessing the situation, she just set her jaw and strode onto the landslide. The mud oozed beneath her feet, which worked in her favour, as her weight squeezed the soil of the landslide down below the sill of the car, thereby allowing her to open the door enough to wriggle in.

Her wellies deposited great gloops of mud into the footwell. She selected first and gunned the engine.

The wheels slid and spun on the slick road, but they found enough traction to haul the car forward until the bonnet was close to the branches of the tree blocking the road.

With the gearstick in reverse, Fiona built up the revs before releasing the clutch in a hurry. The car shot backwards and whumped into the new landslide that now blocked its path. The additional momentum created by taking a run at the obstacle was enough to see the car bulldoze its way free.

When she saw the taillights of Aunt Mary's car she knew she was close to the entrance of the forestry track. To get her distances right, she opened her window and shone the police torch out to identify the exact location of the track. Deeper water streamed across the road, so she angled her car as best she could before powering her window up and sliding the torch into a pocket. As a precaution, she unclipped her seatbelt and let it spool back into its housing. The sensor could beep all it wanted, she needed to be free of the belt's restrictive embrace.

Once again, Fiona built the revs up before releasing the clutch so the car thundered at the track's entrance.

She'd got it wrong. The entrance of the track had been widened by the increased water pouring through it, and by the time she was spinning the wheel over it was too late: the current had gripped the car and was pushing it towards the drop into the Scales Burn.

'Come on, damn you. Go, go, go.'

Fiona threw the gearstick into first and tried to drive out before the rear left side of the car slipped from the road onto the steep verge. Just as the car started to move forward, she felt it tilt, the driver's seat rising as the car balanced on two wheels.

Due to the car's new angle, the door was heavier than usual to open, but Fiona used all her strength and flung the door wide. Her plan was to shift her weight onto the door in the hope it would rebalance the car enough for the front right wheel to touch the road and she could haul it free.

All that happened was the engine continued to race as the front wheel that was suspended over the bank spun a furious whirr now it was freed of resistance.

The car tilted further as the water pouring across the road fought to finish the job it had started. Fiona didn't hang around. She was no captain prepared to go down with her ship, so she leapt from the car as it teetered on the brink of rolling down the bank into the Scales Burn.

Fiona's feet thwacked into the water pouring across the road with a splash, but she was unbalanced. Her body pitched forward and, although she tried to stand, the sucking water prevented her from bringing her feet under her torso in time.

She fell onto the road. The small stones littering the tarmac scraped her hands and preventing her from properly breaking her fall. Fiona's left hand skittered out from underneath her, and then her shoulder thudded into the road.

As soon as Fiona's body connected with the tarmac, the water coursing across the road rebelled at the barrier she created. Right from the first second, Fiona could feel its pressure forcing her sideways towards the Scales Burn.

SEVEN

Fiona fought to get her face above the water's surface to draw some precious air into her lungs. It was only the hard surface of the road that gave her a reference point so she knew which way was up. Other than the dim red lights sparking out from the rear of her aunt's car there was no illumination to help Fiona orient herself.

She tried rolling her body into the current but its grip was too strong. When that didn't work she flung an arm out and made sure that when she let the water roll her onto her front it didn't keep her tumbling towards the edge of the road.

Squirming against the water's force, Fiona managed to draw her knees under her body, the rough stone-covered tarmac scraping at her jeans. As soon as she lifted her body she felt the weight of water pressing against her decrease as it found a way under her. She was still being pressed sideways though.

Fiona was on her hands and knees; she pressed down with her toes, ready to start crawling forward to a position where she could crab sideways out of the current. Her toes found no purchase. She pressed down some more and the top of her shins encountered a rough hard surface. That would be the edge of the road.

There was no time for Fiona to waste taking a calming breath. She inched her right leg forward, and then her left. The water sucked at her, trying to pull her over the edge, but the tactic of diminishing the areas of contact worked and she was able to crawl her way forward.

As soon as Fiona's toes regained contact with the road, she changed the direction of her travel from straight forward to a forty-five-degree angle that drove her through the torrent and towards the safety of Aunt Mary's car.

Raging waters plucked and pulled at her, but Fiona kept pushing forward. Eventually the sucking grip around her submerged limbs began to lessen as she neared her goal. When the water was forearm deep she drew her feet under her, rose to a standing position and squelched her way through the last of the torrent.

Rather than climb into the passenger seat, Fiona approached the driver's door.

Aunt Mary was out of the car. 'Oh my goodness, Fiona. Are you all right?'

'Yeah, I'm soaked through and cold, but I'm okay.' There was no point mentioning the various bumps and scrapes she'd picked up. 'Get back in the car and stay dry.'

'You get in too. Get yourself warmed up.'

'No. There's no point ruining the seat of your car. I'm so sorry, but it's bad enough mine has been swept away, and every-thing we saved from your house with it, without me messing up your car. I'll walk back to the farm, it's only a half mile, and the exercise will warm me up. Now let's get out of here before there's another landslide.'

A wave of guilt washed over Fiona as she thought about all of Aunt Mary's precious belongings that were now lost along with her car. Every new drop of rain that collided with her added to her miserable discomfort. The soaking she could handle. The myriad of minor injuries too. What really snarked at her was the loss of her car. It was insured, but it would take time to source another and there would be endless forms to fill in as the insurers questioned why she'd taken the risk of driving in such treacherous conditions. Plus there were the bags of Aunt Mary's clothes, the other bits and pieces she'd rescued from the cottage, and the precious Lladro figurines. With luck the figurines may be recovered when the raging waters dissipated, but there was no telling if they'd survive being in a car that had tumbled into a flooding river. The almost certain loss of the figurines stung far more than the certainty she'd lose her no-claims bonus.

As for losing Isla's diary and the clues it would hold about the killer, it burned at Fiona's sense of professionalism like a branding iron.

Even as Aunt Mary was climbing back into her car, Fiona was pulling her left welly off and tipping the water out of it.

A minute later she was striding her way back to the farm, plucking at her pockets as she went. When she tried the police torch she was pleased to find it had survived its ducking. Her mobile hadn't, but she hadn't expected it would. At least she could scan the road ahead of her as Aunt Mary's headlights covered the road beneath her feet.

The first landslide they'd encountered had moved further across the road, but it wasn't that much worse and, with a few directions from Fiona, after she'd rolled the biggest boulders out of the way, Aunt Mary's car was through and they were clear.

When Fiona got to the bridge she couldn't resist the urge to stand at the upstream parapet and take a look at the obstruction causing the Scales Valley to flood. On either side of the river stood large trees. Oak or ash or elm, she wasn't sure which, but it didn't matter. What mattered was they were both mighty hardwoods, and it was between them the gate-like feature they called a heck was strung to stop sheep and cattle escaping.

But there was no sign of the heck now. Instead there was a collection of trees and branches that had been swept here by the raging waters until they'd snagged on the heck and formed a dam.

Water coursed through and over the dam, but even in the few seconds Fiona gave to examine the blockage, she saw fresh debris adding to the dam's bulk. Fiona was no expert on such things, but she couldn't see a way the waters pooling against the dam could be released without the heck breaking or being removed.

A part of Fiona knew she ought to be happy she'd survived when the car hadn't, but she couldn't square that in her mind. A sense of euphoria at having cheated death may come later. Fiona doubted it would. All she could think of was what lay ahead. It was as if crossing the bridge had flicked a switch: instead of her thoughts being on the loss of her car and its contents, she was now focused on keeping both Aunt Mary and herself safe. She'd also have to work out if the killer was one of the other people trapped in the valley with them.

When they reached the farm, Aunt Mary parked on high ground and joined Fiona as she strode to the farmhouse and banged on the door. As her aunt's knuckles collided with the wooden door, Fiona was wondering why the farmhouse had electricity.

EIGHT

William Green opened the farmhouse door and let them in. His family had farmed this land since the days of the Border Reivers. William was as tough as the land he owned, and while he'd always treated her well enough, Fiona was well aware the ruddy-faced farmer deserved his reputation for being tight.

'How come you have electric? Ours went out an hour ago.'

'I've a generator for the milking parlour. I got it connected to the house last year. Cost a bloody fortune, but it keeps Elsie from nipping my lug.'

That made sense. Back when she'd moved in with Aunt Mary, the valley's electric supply had been unpredictable, so William had made sure the farm was equipped with a generator. Cows needed to be milked whether the electric was on or off, and once they had been, the milk had to be chilled to prevent it from spoiling.

William's description of Elsie's nagging was typical of his brusque nature. Elsie was a meek woman who tended to twitter around in a permanent flap, and while William's nature wouldn't make him easy to live with, there was no doubting how much he cared for his wife.

Inside the farmhouse all of the upper valley's occupants were gathered around the long kitchen table, with the exception of Tom the shepherd, and of course George and Isla.

All the faces that looked Fiona's way were grim, and no wonder. Everyone around the table would be coming to terms with the destruction of their homes. The way the waters were rising, it would probably only be the farmhouse that escaped being flooded.

William's wife Elsie stood by the Aga that radiated warmth into the kitchen. There was a wooden spoon in her hand and she was using it to stir at the huge pot on the Aga's left ring. As always she wore a long skirt topped by a jumper. Her grey hair hung in a shapeless mess to her shoulders. Elsie might be shaped like a barrel, but there was no mistaking the kindness that radiated from her every pore. She was one of life's carers. If someone was ill or hurt, she'd be the first to help and would provide them with enough food to feed a small army. Elsie was the epitome of a homely grandmother and her baking skills were legendary in the valley.

'Jesus wept, lass, you're drookit.' William gestured at Fiona and then spoke to Elsie. 'Have you any dry clothes for her?'

'I'll get some dry clothes.'

Fiona nodded her thanks and stepped towards the Aga. Elsie rarely said anything that wasn't an echo of what William had just said. As a teen Fiona had thought Elsie was of limited intelligence and had nothing of her own to contribute, but as she'd aged and learned more about relationships, she came to realise William's dominant personality had eroded Elsie's self-confidence, to the point where she only felt comfortable parroting her husband's words.

As Elsie wandered off in search of dry clothes, Fiona was at a loss at what she was supposed to do now. There was no invitation to follow Elsie and she realised, in all the years living in the valley and visiting here, she'd never been in any other part of the farmhouse bar the kitchen. Although there was no way she was going to change in the kitchen, not with so many people watching her.

'How did you get so wet?'

The question came from Jamie, Craig and Becky's five-year-old son. He sat holding his mother's hand dressed in SpongeBob SquarePants pyjamas. Becky wore her usual attire, a denim mini atop black leggings and UGG boots, with an off the shoulder T-shirt. A part of Fiona admired Becky for always trying to look good, while another part wondered why she bothered when cooped up at home with two young kids all day. In Becky's position she'd have dressed for comfort and nothing else.

Becky was someone Fiona had never been able to gel with. She'd always been polite to Fiona, but there was no way she'd got close to extending a hand of friendship.

Fiona had always supposed Becky feared she'd make a move to reconcile with Craig, but that hadn't ever been her intention. As much as she'd always liked Craig, Fiona was happy that he'd found a wife who adored him, as she didn't ever see him as her soulmate.

'I fell in a puddle when we were trying to go to Hawick.' Fiona saw no point scaring Jamie with details of her ordeal.

'Oh.' Jamie's eyes widened. 'Why did you come back?'

'The road was blocked.'

Fiona watched the adults as she answered Jamie. Every set of eyes she connected with held dismay. A harrumph came from Susie as she glared at Pierce, as if it was his fault the road was blocked. Susie and Pierce were from Essex, and from what little Aunt Mary had told her about them, Fiona knew they'd owned a building firm and had sold up and moved into the valley around three years ago. Both were well-dressed and well-groomed. The clothes they wore were better suited to a business meeting than sheltering from a storm, but, according to Aunt

Mary, they were always clad in designer clothes. Pierce was a tall handsome man with salt-and-pepper hair, while the slight Susie would be pretty if she could ever chisel the disapproving expression from her face. As always, Susie's hair and make-up were so well done as to give the impression she'd just walked out of a salon after a makeover.

'How bad is the blockage?' William's face was serious as he picked up the wooden spoon Elsie had laid on a plate by the Aga. 'The tanker's due tomorrow morning and our tank will be full by then.'

Fiona understood his concern. If the tanker couldn't get in to remove the milk, any milk they couldn't store in the tank would have to be disposed of. She had no idea how much money he might lose, but knowing William as she did, she was sure every penny would be grieved.

'It's bad. There's been a couple of landslides and one has brought down a big pine with it. I don't know what the road's like beyond that, as I had to turn back. It could be clear, or there could be several other blockages.'

'I'll have to go and see if I can get it cleared.'

Fiona stepped across the kitchen until she was between William and the door. She kept her voice low so as not to scare the children. 'Forget it. There's every chance you'll be killed. My car was swept over the side and I was only just able to jump out in time. There's no way of knowing how much more of the hill will slip onto the road.'

William hesitated. It was clear to Fiona he was assessing the accuracy of her warning. He cast a look towards Aunt Mary.

Aunt Mary straightened her back as she returned his gaze. 'William Green, listen to Fiona. I was there with her. You go out to clear that now, you might as well shoot yourself.'

Elsie's return with a bundle of clothes and two fluffy towels cut the tension, although she wore a confused expression as she'd only caught part of the conversation. 'Why would William shoot himself?'

Fiona took the clothes with a grateful nod. 'He wouldn't. The road is blocked and he wants to go try and clear it when there's landslides still happening.'

'No, William. It's too dangerous.'

William retreated back to the Aga, a hand pointing at the door Elsie had just come through. 'You can change in there.'

Fiona stepped towards the door, unsure as to whether or not William would take the opportunity of her absence to go and try to clear the road. In the end she left him to make up his own mind. It was his call and she was desperate to get out of the sodden clothes.

In the lounge, Fiona drew the curtains across and began to peel her wet clothes from her body. When she'd removed her jumper, T-shirt and bra she used a towel to scrub at her hair and upper body.

Elsie had provided outer clothes but no underwear beyond a thick pair of socks. It wasn't too much of an issue, as the jumper she'd given Fiona had a cable knit design and was more than bulky enough to protect her modesty.

She replaced her jeans with a dry pair. They were clearly William's, as the buttons were on the wrong side, and his narrower hips meant the waistband cut into her flesh, but so far as Fiona was concerned that was a big improvement on trying to wear any of Elsie's clothes and their being too big. That way she'd end up having to wear damp underwear in case they slipped down.

As Fiona was gathering her wet clothes together, her eyes landed on the most precious of items. A telephone. An old-fashioned landline and, with the generator up and running, it would surely have power.

The damp clothes hadn't hit the floor by the time Fiona had lifted the handset and jabbed at the number nine three times.

Fiona's thumb pressed down on the green button and she put the phone to her ear again.

Still nothing.

Fiona tried a second time with the same absence of success, and when that didn't work she gave up trying to dial out and just listened for a dial tone. No matter what she pressed, no sounds came from the phone's handset. Rather than throw it at a wall, as she wanted to, Fiona replaced the handset in its cradle.

It didn't take long to figure out why it wasn't working. While the electricity supply came directly up the valley with its poles in the fields, the phone lines followed the road. The tree brought down by the landslide was more than tall enough to have landed on the phone lines.

As Fiona again picked up the damp clothes, the slamming of a door reverberated through the house. She hurried back to the kitchen and found Tom had arrived and was peeling off his waterproof clothes as William fired questions at him.

'They're all hunkered down the back of the wall. One had got itself tangled in a fence. I freed it and it buggered off with the rest.'

William's nod suggested that he was happy with the condition of his sheep.

Tom bent down and lowered his waterproof leggings, wrapping them around the wellies he stepped out of. The shepherd was a squat man, his shoulders broad and his face so rugged it looked like it had been danced on rather than lived in.

When he turned to Fiona she could see dark red stains on his jeans. Each stain the exact colour of dried blood. It raised her suspicions at once, but she was beaten to the obvious question.

Craig pointed at Tom's jeans. 'Have you hurt yourself?'

'It's nowt. Skinned my knuckles freeing the ewe.' Tom

showed his knuckles, and sure enough there were healing scabs on them, and looked around. 'Where's George and his wife?'

'I don't know.' William shrugged, his face a picture of indifference. 'Don't care either. He's all right, but she's nowt but a two-faced bitch.'

While a part of Fiona agreed with the negative assessment of Isla, she couldn't help but notice that nobody else had seemed to wonder about their whereabouts. It was time to find out what the others knew. As one of the last to arrive at the farmhouse, it was entirely possible the conversation had already taken place. 'Their cottage would have been flooded first. Has anyone been to see if they are okay?'

'Sod them. It's bad enough all of us being stuck here and that old cow wouldn't make it any more pleasant.' The Essex accent spilling from the mouth of Susie sounded even more harsh when compared to the soft burr of the Borders natives. As they always were, Susie and Pierce were dressed to impress. Both were what Fiona thought of as Label Mabels. It was a trait that made her distrust people as a reflex action. There was nothing wrong with having nice clothes and dressing well, but the way Susie and Pierce went about it gave the impression they felt superior to everyone else. Susie and Pierce had that air about them; besides, they were dealing with a power cut and their home being flooded, not attending a swanky restaurant. If Fiona hadn't seen them lounging in their garden, or Pierce washing his car in such clothes she would have given them the benefit of the doubt, but to wear such expensive gear when lounging about the house reeked of show for show's sake. She guessed Susie was the type of person who checked her hair before answering the phone.

'Susie.' There was warning in Pierce's tone but his glare was met with one of equal intensity. 'It was very good of William and Elsie to give us shelter considering everything that's happened between us. Maybe show a little gratitude, huh? We'd be sitting in our car if it wasn't for their kindness.'

'Sorry, I didn't mean it like that.' There was ten times the contrition in Susie's words than her tone.

'Aye, whatever.' William gestured at the soup and looked at his wife. 'Do you want to get some bowls? It looks ready and I'm starving. I bet the lass could do with it too after her soaking.'

'I'll get some bowls.'

'I don't want soup.' Jamie looked at his mother. 'Can we phone a pizza?'

'No, sweetie. The road's blocked, remember?' Becky's attempt at a smile did little to help.

'Boo.' Jamie's bottom lip stuck out as he eyed the pan of soup with suspicion.

'Nobody's answered Fiona's question. Does anyone know how George and his wife are?'

Bless Aunt Mary. She'd picked up on Fiona's intent and hadn't let the subject go.

There was no answer. Just a collection of glances back and forth as each person asked the question of the others without speaking.

'We made our own way here, as did everyone else. I just assumed they would have done the same, or maybe they saw the writing on the wall and got out a few hours ago.' Pierce directed his gaze at Aunt Mary. 'You don't think they've got caught in a landslide, do you?'

'I don't know. I'm just wondering if they're okay. I hate to think of them being trapped down there by the rising water. George is a lovely man and you can be sure he'd help us if we needed it.'

Fiona didn't like the direction the conversation was taking. As much as she wanted to search for Isla who was still missing, she didn't want George's murder to become public knowledge. Not when his killer could be in the kitchen. She'd also have to fess up to being a cop and that was fraught with danger. She needed to steer the conversation elsewhere before someone decided to go and check on George and Isla. The more people entered that house, the greater risk there'd be of any evidence that hadn't been destroyed by the floods being contaminated. George had two children who'd want answers about his death. They'd want to know who'd killed their father. If she were still alive, Isla would want those answers too.

Fiona had never been given those answers. Her parents' deaths were still unsolved.

Dad was the fun parent, while Mum was the strict one. Mum was still fun, but it was Dad who'd taught her how to ride a bike. Dad who'd slipped her some money and waited in the car while she went shopping with Olivia.

There was more to Fiona's long-term plan than selfishness. If during her police career she could bring closure to just one person, all the anti-social hours, the being abused and spat at, the lack of gratitude from a public that had no idea how challenging policing could be, would be worth it.

'I can't see them staying put. As much as he loved his home and garden, George would have had the sense to evacuate before it was too late. With luck they'll have made it out before the landslides and will be in a hotel in Hawick.' Fiona pointed at Aunt Mary. 'That was our plan after all.'

'You're likely right, lass.' William slipped his feet into a pair of wellies. 'I don't trust the way that water is rising. I've got what I can to higher ground, but I'm not risking the tractor that's running the genny. Elsie, dig out the candles so they're ready. I'm going to see where the water's up to, and if it's close to the tractor, I'll be moving it to higher ground.'

'I'll dig out the candles.'

NINE

Craig was the first to rise to his feet. 'I'll come with you. Those calves in the bottom shed will be at much the same level as the genny.'

Tom didn't say a thing, he just walked towards his wellies.

'Never mind the calves, there's three of them. The dairy herd are worth far more, we should move them first.'

Craig shook his head. 'The water will get to the calves first. They should be our priority.'

'No. The milkers are. End of.'

'I'll come and help too.' Leighton rose from his seat beside Jamie. Fiona didn't know much about him, but he seemed to be the same age as her and, while he wasn't the most handsome, he was as well-groomed a man as she'd ever met. Although in the present company, Pierce excepted, that wouldn't be hard. Aunt Mary didn't have much to say about the man who'd taken over the Andersons' cottage; and the little interaction she'd had with Leighton had been limited to polite small talk on the rare occasions their paths had crossed.

'Craig, you make sure you stay safe. Don't you be going near the water.' Becky smoothed the very pregnant bump of her stomach and nodded at her children to emphasise her point.

'You too, William. Don't be going near the water.'

Neither man answered their wife, but Fiona could see Craig was the most likely to heed the warning. He had a young wife and two kids, with a third expected to arrive within a week. Craig had told her Becky wanted to call the kid Holly if it was a girl and Noel if it was a boy, but from his tone Fiona could tell he wasn't convinced about saddling the child with a festive name.

'Pierce will come help too.' Susie's elbow dug into her husband's ribs. 'Don't just sit there, go and help.'

'And me.' Fiona stood up. 'Elsie, do you have a dry pair of wellies I can borrow, please?'

Tom shook his head. 'We'll be fine, lass. Leave this to the men.'

'Nonsense. You may need help and I'm willing to provide it.' Tom's misogynistic comment flew like an arrow and embedded its barb at the heart of her psyche. No way was she going to let him patronise her like that.

William caught Tom's arm. 'She's a good hand. Many's the time she helped us when she lived with Mary. She'll be right.'

Fiona joined the men as they drew waterproofs over their jeans and jumpers. Both Craig and William had chest-high waders to keep them dry.

Most of all she wanted to be with the group of men. Of the women in the Scales Valley, Fiona had been with Aunt Mary all afternoon, Becky was due to have her baby any day now and, while she'd never warmed to Fiona, she was a good and kind person. That left Elsie and Susie. Elsie was too much of a carer to ever cause harm to anyone, and while Fiona could picture her as a vindictive person, Susie didn't seem the type to dirty her own hands with someone else's blood. There was also the fact that Susie's slight frame meant she'd struggle to overpower

George without using a weapon, and from what Fiona had observed of George's injuries, there had been none of the grievous wounds that a weapon of any kind would leave.

That left the men as Fiona's suspects; all of them had the physical strength to best George with a couple of punches and then wrap a string around his throat. If her suspicions were right and one of them was the killer, she could make sure they stayed in groups of three rather than a three and a two, should they split up. That way there would be two pairs of eyes on the killer to prevent him striking again. She'd paid close attention to each man's reactions during the conversation about George and Isla. While she hadn't noticed any significant tells, she'd also picked up on the fact none of them had volunteered to go and check on George and Isla. If one had suggested they go alone, she'd have been tempted to let them, as what they said upon their return would be very informative. However, the flip side to that was, if someone did check on them and came back to inform the others George was lying dead on his bed, Fiona would have no choice but to reveal she was a police officer and had been the one to put George's corpse where they'd found it.

TEN

'You're not coming, lass. You're lucky to be alive after your car was swept away. Leave this to us men.' Tom turned his back on Fiona as if the matter was closed.

'No way.' Aunt Mary was on her feet and standing in front of Tom before he could say another word. 'We went through it all a minute ago. Fiona's here and willing to help. Are you daft enough to refuse her help just because she's a woman? I thought you were better than that, Tom. I really did.'

William ran a hand over his face. 'I know how good a help you are, Fiona, but Tom has a point. It'll be tough enough getting the herd out into the night without having to look after you.'

Fiona drew in a slow, calming breath before speaking. 'I don't need looking after. Come the hell on, William, you said yourself I've helped you many a time in the past.'

'Aye, in daylight with a calm herd. They'll be spooked tonight and the way the rain's coming down, visibility is rubbish. I've enough to worry about with worrying about you too.'

'You've no need to worry about me. I can take care of

myself.' Fiona cast her gaze towards Craig. He was an ally she could count on, and one of the few people in the room William might listen to.

Craig made a point of not looking at Fiona as he opened his mouth. 'William's right. The cows will be spooked. They'll not want to go out into the field. Not in this weather when they're used to being sheltered and dry.'

'All the more reason you should let me help.' Fiona had to fight to keep the anger out of her voice. Screw Craig and his betrayal. She was going to go out and help regardless of what William and Craig said.

'Maybe she can help.' Tom dropped the hint of a nod towards Fiona, but his eyes were on Aunt Mary as he reversed his stance.

The men's insistence she stay in the house puzzled Fiona, and she couldn't help but think about their reasoning. The more she chewed at the question 'why', the more she suspected that one of them knew she was a cop and, as they were the person who'd killed George, they wanted to keep her out of the way while they disposed of evidence.

'Never mind about the cows. What about one of you going to get help.' Susie pointed at Becky's stomach. 'We've got a pregnant woman and she's sure to need better care than sitting here. Surely one of you big tough men could get across the hill to civilisation.'

Fiona agreed with the idea of someone fetching help, but not for the reasons Susie was giving. Becky was a week from her due date and, even if someone could summon help, unless that help could be helicoptered in, there was no easy way to get into the valley while the rain kept pouring. Susie's use of the word 'civilisation' made Fiona suspect the woman was more concerned with her own comfort than Becky's wellbeing and that of her unborn baby.

Craig shook his head. 'It's too dangerous to go over the hills.

Fiona said there were landslides by the road. There's probably a few other areas of the hill at risk of slipping too. Plus there's heather in a lot of places. In the dark with only a torch, there's every chance that whoever hiked out would end up lost, and if they tried to cross the heather moors in this weather, there's a very good chance they'd end up doing their ankle in.'

'Who said about going over the hills? What's wrong with following the river downstream until you get to the next farm or the road? You could even take that bloody noisy quad bike thing Tom's always riding around on.' Susie flashed defiance at the men as if they were too dumb to realise how to find a way out.

As much as Fiona liked the suggestions Susie was making, she'd already had the same thoughts and discounted them. Susie may have lived in her cottage for the best part of three years, but she didn't know the valley.

Hawick was two and a half miles away as the crow flies, but with the undulations of the Southern Uplands taken into account, a straight route would be more like four miles. What made matters worse was that to get to Hawick, anyone going over the hills would have to cross the Scales Burn. Yes, the bridge was intact, but the hill on that side of the river was as steep as any around. No way could the quad go up it, and to attempt it by torchlight in the middle of one of the most severe storms ever would be suicidal. To go the other way would mean a hike of at least five miles to the nearest house or farm, and there was no saying that place would be in a position to help or have power and a phone signal so professional help could be summoned. Plus, and this was a big part of Fiona's thinking, there would be two other valleys to cross and, like the Scales Valley, each of them would have an overflowing burn or river at its base.

William's expression was half sneer and half exasperation at a townie thinking they knew better than him. 'That'll no' work. Half a mile down from the bridge, the river sweeps across to this side of the valley. It's been eating away at the hill for years. There's a forty-foot bank of exposed soil and on top of that is a steep hill. I wouldn't walk at the top of that bank on a summer's day. As for the quad, it can only go up slopes of a certain gradient. The way the water's running off those hills, you'd be lucky if it got a hundred yards from here. Right, Tom?'

It was a smart move by William to involve Tom's knowledge. Even though he'd only worked for William for a couple of years, it was no secret the shepherd was as familiar with the surrounding hills as he was his own face.

'Aye.' Tom never used two words when one would suffice, but from the brief chats she'd had with him, Fiona had learned that when he did speak, he was worth listening to. 'Safer walking.'

'So we can't go for help. How about we get those cows of yours moved?' Leighton's Scouse accent was thick enough that Fiona had to reconsider his words in case she'd misheard them. 'And for what it's worth, I think Fiona should be allowed to help if she's offering. Many hands make light work and all that.'

'Agreed.' Tom pulled his waterproof jacket on and brushed past William to open the door.

'She's not coming. End of.'

'William Green, will you stop being a stubborn fool and recognise Fiona wants to help you save your cows and anything else that you can get out of reach of the flood?' Aunt Mary's lips were thin as she glowered at William. 'You do realise that every minute you're wasting on ridiculous arguments is another minute the water is rising out there?'

'Come on, let's just get the cows moved before you have to shut off the genny.' Fiona ended the argument by following Tom out the door.

ELEVEN

William led everyone to the cow shed, where he laid out his plan, his voice a near shout as he battled to be heard over the raindrops scudding onto the shed's tin roof. He and Craig would usher the cows out, the others were to make sure they kept on track until they reached the field at the other side of the road. Fiona knew the field, it was bordered by a stone dyke, and it curled up the slopes of the hill. In there the cows would be able to get as high as they needed to escape the floodwaters.

The field was the best place for the cows, and she knew that it had already been chosen as a safe place to park the implements and tractors William and Craig had removed from the farm sheds.

'OK then. Tom, you go with Fiona to man the track, make sure all the gates and shed doors are shut. Leighton, Pierce, you stand in the gaps where there's no gates.' William cast a look at Craig. 'Once we get them out the shed and into the field, you lot can get yourselves back in the dry while me, Tom and Craig go to check the calves.'

'I'll come with you in case you need help with that too.'

Pierce's offer of further assistance sat at odds with what little Fiona knew about him. Aunt Mary had often mentioned the ongoing dispute between William and the couple who'd bought a portion of his land on which to build their dream home. It may be that Pierce was being helpful because, even with their enmity, William had been decent enough to offer Pierce and his wife somewhere to shelter when their home was flooded, or it may be something else. If Pierce killed George, the running dispute he had with William was sure to put the farmer's name at the top of any list he had of future victims. She had to make sure she kept him where she could see him. If only she'd had the time to grab Isla's diary as she abandoned her car, she'd have had a chance of learning who the killer was without having to rely on deduction and snippets of information.

Fiona helped Tom with the gates and shed doors, but there weren't many. Scales Valley Farm wasn't a sprawling complex – there was no room for it to be, as every square yard of flat land was precious – and the cow shed sat near the track.

With the gates shut, Fiona took up her position, her torch gripped tight by numbing fingers as she scanned around herself every few seconds.

When Fiona wasn't scanning her surroundings, she was checking out the location of the others. Tom was further along the track, while Leighton and Pierce were still within the confines of the farmyard.

Inside the cow shed a row of hanging bulbs gave off enough light for her to see the struggle William and Craig were having. Instead of taking the cows out the door to the milking parlour, they were bringing them out where they usually entered to replenish food or bedding.

Dairy cattle grow used to routine. Twice or thrice a day – depending on the farm – they'd be taken from their shed to the milking parlour. When the doors to that route opened, they walked without urging, each one trained by familiarity into blind obedience. That same obedience had them remain in the shed when the feed and bedding door was opened. They didn't know what was out of this door, but they knew good things came in that way.

The torrential rain was another deterrent to them exiting the shed. Cows might not be as intelligent as dogs or dolphins, but they had enough sense to resist being moved from a dry shed to an exposed field.

Both Craig and William held yard-long pieces of blue water pipe. They used these as sticks to direct the cows where they wanted them to go. Every now and again one of them would tap a cow's hind quarters to get them moving, or slap the tip of the pipe into the ground. Fiona knew the pipes could generate a whip crack sound when slapped against concrete, but all she could hear tonight was the patter of rain on her hood.

All five of the men were visible to Fiona and that gave her comfort. If she could see where they were, none of them could sneak up behind her. Everyone was accounted for except Isla, and as vicious as the woman's tongue may be, Fiona just couldn't see her being the person who'd strangled George.

It could be that there was a stranger in the valley who was George's killer, and they were hiding out, but she'd seen no signs of other vehicles having tried to pass the landslide, and unless the person had hiked into the valley, there were no strange vehicles parked anywhere obvious.

The more she thought the killer might be a stranger, the more Fiona doubted the theories she formed. Isla's diary had intimated the threat came from within the valley, because she and George were in the process of selling up to escape the threat. Therefore the killer had to be one of the valley's occupants. She'd already discounted the women as killers, although she'd be the first to admit she wasn't a hundred per cent sure about Susie.

The first cows began to edge their way out of the shed. It wasn't so much they were leaving of their own volition, more that they were being pushed out by the cows behind them.

One of the first cows lowed a protest, its head lowered and stretched forward to give voice to its reluctance to be out in the rain. Others joined in with the lowing, but still they kept coming, every step forward grudged and hesitant. Fiona couldn't blame them.

Someone's torch flashed over the backs of the cows and illuminated William's face. He looked distraught. Fiona got it. The cows were his best source of income. By rights Craig should be milking them now, but the dairy parlour was too close to the rising waters for them to start something they couldn't finish. The milk in the cow's udders would go off if they weren't milked soon. Their production would drop in the harsh conditions they were being forced to endure.

The cows weren't pets. They were a business tool, like a gardener's spade, but they were also William's herd. The majority of them would have been sired, born and then reared at Scales Valley Farm, and William would feel a connection with them no gardener would for his spade.

The cows kept on coming. Docile and hesitant, but they were moving. And then they were moving a lot faster. The lead cows had ideas, or they were spooked by something as they set off at a charge. Right towards Fiona.

Despite her heart racing as the half tonne beasts bore down on her, Fiona stood firm. She flapped her arms and yelled at the cows. Not words, just a loud, rolling 'hah' sound that she'd heard Craig and William using in the past.

The cows slowed, plumes of steam coming from their noses as they ground to a halt and huffed their contempt at her.

Fiona stepped forward, still yelling, still flapping her arms. The cows turned. Not fast, but quick enough to redirect those bringing up the rear.

Over the years, Fiona had often helped out herding sheep or cows and she knew what needed to happen now. As she stepped forward, the others would too. Yard by yard, they'd close in on the dairy herd until the only flaw in their encircling ring was the gate to the field.

A cow at the front of the gathered herd saw the opening and looked over its shoulder at the other cows. Something must have been communicated as the lead cow stepped through the gate and was swiftly followed by the others.

Four of the men strode back to the farmyard, William's arm pointing at Fiona, Leighton and the gate. She got his message and, with Leighton's help, half carried and half swung the cast iron gate closed so she could wrap the fastening chain around it and hem the cows into the field.

'Thank goodness that's done.' Leighton's face echoed his words. 'Also, hello. Fiona, isn't it? I can't believe I haven't actually introduced myself. I know everyone else in the valley, but other than knowing you're Mary's niece, I don't know anything about you. I'm Leighton.'

'What do you need to know to get through tonight?' Fiona gestured at the valley. 'We're stuck here and we have to make the best of it.'

Even to Fiona's ears she sounded brusque and, while her sense of decency compelled her to apologise, she had no time for idle chit chat. Fiona had always prided herself on her people-reading skills and this inane chatter from Leighton set her antenna jangling. A further irritant was the way his head torch dazzled her every time he looked her way.

'Whoa, easy there. I'm just making conversation. Call me old-fashioned, but in situations like this, I think it's wise to know whose company you're keeping. I'm sorry if that offends you.'

There was a hint of censure in his voice that set Fiona's teeth on edge. Not only was he telling her off, but there was enough in his words to suggest he knew more than he was letting on. At the first chance she got, she'd speak to Aunt Mary about him again. She'd know all the little secrets and petty feuds. Aunt Mary was the kind of listener people opened up to, as she never gossiped about the things she heard.

Fiona chose her words with care; she didn't want to alienate Leighton in case he was the killer and he made a mistake and said the wrong thing to her. Plus this would be a good chance to learn more about him. Provided he told the truth, of course. 'If it makes you happy, I'm mid-thirties and I do boring work for the Scottish Government.' That last line was a lie. Being a police officer was a lot of things, but boring wasn't one of them. To help her learn about Leighton, she turned his question back at him. 'What about you? What's your story?'

'I'm thirty, from Liverpool originally, and I design apps.'

Leighton was obviously a computer geek, but he hadn't named any of the apps he claimed to have developed. That rang alarm bells for Fiona, as most people liked to boast of their creations.

Fiona didn't know much about the tech world, but what she couldn't work out was why Leighton had moved from a city to such a rural location. According to what she did know about him, he worked from home. Something that was way more prevalent after the pandemic, but to her way of thinking, an app designer would have to meet clients, brainstorm ideas and designs. Cities were where such things happened. Not the arse end of a valley in the middle of the Southern Uplands. With modern apps such as Zoom and screen-sharers, developers could easily work from home, but Fiona reckoned there would still need to be old-fashioned face-to-face meetings, and as tranquil and beautiful as it was, the Scales Valley was over an hour in any direction from a motorway, let alone a city. If Leighton did have to have in-person meetings, he'd waste hours in travelling back and forth. Because this didn't make sense to her, Fiona had to think Leighton's supposed occupation was a lie. She'd ask him about the apps and how he managed to work in such a remote area later to try and prove the lie, but for now she had to focus on the task at hand.

If Leighton was lying about this, what else was there about him to mistrust?

TWELVE

Now she was suspicious of Leighton, Fiona made sure he was kept in her sight as she trudged after the others. The calf shed had always been at the lower edge of the farmyard. From Craig's earlier concerns about the calves being under a more immediate threat than the cows, it stood to reason it was still in the same place.

There was no let-up in the downpour; the rain was falling as heavily as it had all afternoon. This had to be one of those freak weather fronts that deposited a month's rain in a day. Worst of all was the way the wind was now picking up. Where the rain had earlier been falling pretty much straight down, now it was slanted off the vertical.

The waterproofs she'd been given by Elsie kept the rain from soaking Fiona, but her exposed hands and face were numbed by the stinging cold. She didn't complain, though. To do that would be to fuel Tom's and William's misogyny. Fiona had to be as tough as at least the weakest two men. Considering William, his dairyman Craig and shepherd Tom all worked the farm, they'd be used to foul weather, to being chilled to the bone. Leighton and Pierce, her chief suspects, were the ones whose stoicism she must trump. William and Craig were at the bottom of her suspect list, as she'd known them for years. The two men had a friendly relationship due to working together for so long, but to Fiona's knowledge, they never socialised together beyond a pre-Christmas piss-up in Hawick. She guessed it was the way they both preferred it, as it maintained certain boundaries established by William's position as Craig's employer and landlord.

A massive blue tractor was running a steady beat from its position – reversed up to a stone shed next to the milking parlour, the power drive at the back powering the generator. Someone had had the sense to switch all the tractor's many lights on, which added an ethereal glow throughout the downpour. There was a two-foot gap between the tractor's front wheels and the water. They found the others in a knot ten yards upstream from the tractor. William's and Craig's torches were aimed into the blackness untouched by the tractor's lights.

From her days exploring the area with a youthful Craig, Fiona knew they'd be trying to pick out a small block-built shed. The shed had those stable doors that have two parts, a top and bottom, so horses could look out. Fiona knew from experience there was a door at either end of the shed, each leading to a separate space where calves were kept.

The bottom part of the closest door only showed its top third. Its lower portion was submerged by swirling brown murk that pushed the open door back and forth. She cast her torch along the shed looking for the other door, but there was too much rain coming down for the torch's beam to extend that far.

As they joined the knot of men, Fiona could hear them arguing. William was standing in front of Craig and telling him they were too late. That it was too dangerous for him to wade out and try to rescue the calves.

'Give over, will you?' Craig pointed towards the shed door. 'The water's not that deep. It'll not even come up to my balls.'

'Aye, and what if you trip and fall in? Those calves will be going nuts in there. As soon as you open the door, they'll knock you flying.'

Fiona noticed Tom slipping away. That could mean anything, but knowing what she knew about George, she didn't think it meant anything good.

'I can't believe you're going to let them die. They're your calves. I reared them for you myself. We should have saved them first.'

'I don't want to let them die, of course I bloody don't. But better them than you. You've a pregnant wife and two kids to think of. Calves we can breed, husbands and fathers we can't.'

Fiona could picture the calves inside the shed. They'd be terrified as water crept in and up their legs. The higher it got the greater their panic. They'd fight to keep their heads above water for as long as they could, but there was no way of knowing how high the waters would rise.

So far as Fiona was concerned, William was the one talking sense. He was thinking with his logical brain, whereas Craig's emotional attachment to the calves was compelling him to take dangerous risks.

Tom reappeared, a length of blue nylon rope in his hands. 'Tie this round me.'

Nothing needed to be explained. Tom was launching his own rescue mission.

William looked at Craig then Tom, and gave a brief nod.

Craig took the rope from Tom, and fashioned a knot that would encase Tom, but wouldn't constrict him if they had to drag him back. Once the knot was tied, he laid one of his hands on Tom's shoulder. 'Thanks for this, and look after yourself out there. If owt happens, don't worry, I'll be on this end of the rope.'

William took a hold of the rope a foot from where Craig's massive paws encircled it. 'Give two sharp pulls on the rope if you want to be hauled back and three if you need more rope. Pierce, Leighton, grab the rope. Fiona, take my torch and shine it and yours in front of Tom.'

'Here.' Leighton stripped off his head torch and offered it to Tom, who slipped it over his bald head.

Without a word, Tom waded out towards the calf shed. A memory of his wader-style leggings and boots came to Fiona and she realised that while they'd offer little insulation against the cold, they'd at least keep Tom dry.

Fiona's entire focus was on her task of trying to give Tom as much illumination from the torches as she could. Even as Tom was taking his first steps into the water, she was on his heel until the water was no more than an inch from filling the borrowed wellies.

Tom was slight in build compared to Craig, but he possessed a wiry strength that saw him make steady progress towards the calf shed. He went past the first door without any problem.

A good start. As good as they dared hope for.

Tom's back disappeared into the falling rain, the twin beams of the torches underpowered against Mother Nature. There was the occasional pinprick of light that chinked through the downpour and showed the yellow of Tom's waterproof jacket. It was these moments that kept Fiona rooted where she was. They gave her hope that some light would filter through to aid Tom.

From behind her, Fiona heard shouts from all of the men. She spun round not daring to guess what she might see. They were all wrestling with Tom's safety line. At the front of their tug of war, Craig and William were being dragged towards the murky water as the rope they held swung downstream.

THIRTEEN

Fiona ran back to grab the rope; her bobbing torches picked out Leighton and Pierce snatching at the rope as they added their strength to that of Craig and William.

As soon as she neared the others, Fiona tossed both torches so they'd land away from the teeming water and wrapped both hands around the rope. She was in front of Craig, but behind the other three men.

In Fiona's cold-numbed hands the rope felt puny, and she had to summon every part of her strength to grip it hard enough that her hands didn't slide along it.

Like everyone else, Fiona's feet skittered over the damp farmyard as she tried to arrest Tom's journey downstream. Each man was grunting at the effort they were expending, and William was swearing more than a drunken trooper.

Fiona's feet stopped sliding and found real purchase. She didn't know if it was from her own efforts, or the combined strength of the group that had made this breakthrough, she was just thankful for it.

'Heave.' William's voice rang out loud.

Fiona heaved at the command, and obeyed each repetition,

until they were making steady progress as they dragged Tom back to land. How he'd fared during his ducking was unknown, but as much as she wanted to grab the torches so she could pinpoint Tom and check his condition, she knew that until they had dragged him to the calmer, shallower waters, she was needed on the rope.

'Stop pulling, it's gone slack. Fiona. Grab a torch.'

Fiona didn't need the instruction. She'd felt the rope's tension fade before William's shout and had freed her hands ready to grasp the torches.

William's heavy torch was dimming as its battery failed, but hers was fine. When Fiona picked it up her fingers squeezed a clump of sodden soil with it. As she was in a farmyard, she had to hope it was soil.

Fiona swung the beam of her torch at the river and picked out the rope. A second later it was travelling along the rope's length and was illuminating the hood of Tom's jacket.

Tom was on his hands and knees, his progress forward a slow crawl that inched him gradually out of the water.

When the water around Tom was no more than a foot deep, he rose to his feet, his face a mask of exhausted determination. 'Thanks.'

Without another word, Tom set off for the calf shed again.

William got in front of Tom, placed a hand on his chest. 'No way. You nearly got swept away. You're not going back.'

'I am.' Tom went to brush the hand away from his chest, but one of Craig's massive paws fastened around his wrist.

'Wait. What made you fall into the water?'

'Lost my grip on the door. Fell back.'

Tom didn't need to say anything more. Fiona could picture what had happened. The far door of the calf shed was hinged on its left side, and opened outwards. It would be nigh on impossible to hold the door open against the force of the water flowing downstream.

'I'll come help you. Wait a second though.'

Fiona watched as Craig dashed off. It had been a close thing for Tom, and as much as she admired his bravery and dedication to saving the calves, she knew making another attempt was foolish.

Craig returned with a heavy bar she recognised as a pinch bar. Used for making post holes, it was five feet long and an inch and a half thick. In Craig's hands it looked like a pencil. 'I can use this to pop the door off its hinges.'

'I'll never see that door again.'

Typical of William to think of the cost.

'Three calves are worth far more than one door.'

William tied a rope around Craig's chest, his head shaking as he did so.

'You pair are mad. They're only dumb animals. Why are you risking your lives for them?'

Pierce's words earned him stern glares from each of the three farmers, and Fiona saw Craig's knuckles tighten around the pinch bar in his hand.

'Fiona, you and Pierce take Craig's line.' William still held Tom's, and Leighton filed in behind him. 'If either of you goes down, the other has to stay put. We'll tie off the end of your rope until we get the other out. Everyone understand?'

They all nodded and took their positions as Craig and Tom waded out into the darkness.

As Fiona was paying the rope out, she could hear Pierce grumbling away behind her. Only snatches of words came her way, but there was no doubt he was questioning the wisdom involved in rescuing the calves.

Fiona had spent the latter part of her formative years hanging around the farm, and she'd soon learned how good farmers felt about their stock. There was never the unbridled love for farm animals that pets got, but the cows and sheep were cared for. They were fed, housed where appropriate, and if they got ill their ailments were treated. Yes, the sheep may be reared only for the meat and wool they provided, but they were looked after until the day they were sold to the abattoir.

As a townie, Pierce probably wouldn't know this. He might be one of those people who had no time for animals. Whatever he was, he'd be wise to keep his opinions to himself, as even William, the most pragmatic of the three, had been obviously livid with Pierce's comment.

The more she thought about it, the more Fiona believed one of the five men with her had to have killed George. If Pierce wasn't the killer, then surely his condemnation of the others put him at high risk? She shook her head. Something in her was instinctively telling her they weren't safe. Maybe it was the storm. She truly wanted to believe that the killer wouldn't strike again. But if they did, had Pierce just put a target on his back?

FOURTEEN

There was a triple jerk on the rope in Fiona's hands so she loosened her grip and kept paying out more rope. Try as Fiona might, there was no way she could track Craig's progress beyond following the dim light oozing from his head torch. The further Craig travelled into the streaming darkness, the harder it was to see the faint glow.

Torrents of rain plummeted to earth in a series of relentless waves, their angle of descent shallowing as the wind increased.

Fiona was facing into the wind, her exposed face numbed by icy tentacles of rain that sought ways past waterproof clothing. She stood resolute, her eyes seeing little of use and her ears hearing nothing but the strum of rain on waterproof.

It was Fiona's hands that fed her the most information. As Craig moved forward she could feel a steady pull. From time to time he'd grow impatient at the way she was keeping a good amount of tension on the rope and give a trio of savage yanks. Without a viable sightline, and no other way of communicating with Craig and Tom, the tension on the rope was her library, her font of all knowledge.

The rope went taut, pulling Fiona forward. She dug in, her

feet sliding into the water as she tried to both keep her balance and halt whatever force was dragging at the rope.

Fiona felt the rope slither between her fingers as her numb hands struggled to grasp the wet nylon. She gritted her teeth and clamped down on the rope in time for there to be a sudden jerk that pulled her forward until she was knee deep in the murky water. For the second time that night, icy water flooded her wellies.

Three hard yanks on the rope were followed by another three a second later. Fiona paid the rope out until there was only a slight amount of tension on it.

The rope went slack. Not a lessening of tension, a complete absence of it.

'Help!' There was no need for more words.

Fiona's hands moved in a blur as she hauled the rope back to her. Instead of leading towards the calf shed, the rope was now being carried downstream by the current. After several arm lengths of rope had passed by her, Fiona felt it begin to tighten as her efforts bore fruit.

Just as Fiona built an amount of tension on the rope, it yanked her forward. She dug in, clung on to the rope for all she was worth. Craig's life was in her hands. The waters rose up her thighs, yet still she held the nylon strand tight.

Where the hell are William, Pierce and Leighton?

As soon as the thought entered her head she knew the answer. There would have been no more than two or three seconds between the rope going slack and her being hauled to her current position. That was nowhere near enough time for William and Leighton to tie off Tom's rope and rush to help her and Pierce. She'd felt no assistance from Pierce, but that was a matter for later. Right now she had to save Craig.

Fiona looked ahead of her, the limited night vision she'd built up not even close to being powerful enough to penetrate the blackout. All she could see was a taut rope disappearing into darkness.

The brown waters reached Fiona's waist. She could now feel the pull of the current on her body adding to the steady drag of the rope.

Still she hung on as she leaned into the current.

Fiona's sense of despair eased when she felt the rope behind grow tight. William and Leighton and Pierce must all be digging in to help now. The rope stopped moving as the opposing forces matched each other and created a stalemate.

Two shapes emerged out of the gloom. They came from upstream and they came fast, gripped by the current as they were. The shapes were bulbous and alive. As they closed in on her, Fiona recognised what they were: the calves. Tom must have freed them from the shed.

The first calf's head snagged on the rope with enough force to knock Fiona sideways. Fiona fought a desperate fight to regain her footing as the calf wriggled itself free of the rope, found some traction and scrambled its way out of the waters, braying a teenage whoop as it went.

Fiona wasn't swift enough in getting her balance back. The second calf was side on to the current, its body a three-foot wrecking ball that bowled Fiona off her feet and sent her under the raging brown waters.

FIFTEEN

Fiona had just enough time to gulp in a lungful of air before her face slapped into the water. Her eyes screwed tight and her mouth clamped shut lest she gasp at the sudden assault of cold from the icy waters swirling their chilly tentacles around every part of her body.

Most of all, her fingers curled ever tighter around the rope. If she was to survive, it would only happen if she kept hold of it.

The calf that had flattened Fiona writhed to be free of her. Its feet scrabbling for purchase scored at Fiona's body and stomped into her stomach, until a combination of its struggles and the current separated it from Fiona.

Instinct made Fiona want to thrash with wild abandon, to release the rope so she could swim for the surface. The cinematographer of Fiona's mind was playing images of her being swept away by the current. Of people in the days to come searching the river for her body. She saw faceless men and women looking down at her half-submerged corpse. Aunt Mary, Sergeant Dave Lennox and a few of her other closer colleagues like Heather Andrews and Peter Granton were standing by a grave as a coffin was lowered.

Before she did anything, Fiona had to defeat the panic constricting her chest; she had to sack the cinematographer, and replace them with a Disney one, who depicted her emerging from the water; one who showed her swaddled in warming blankets as she sipped at a cup of Elsie's soup.

If Fiona hadn't been underwater, she'd have taken deep calming breaths. That wasn't an option so she dug into the depths of her psyche and took control of herself. She wasn't going to allow the Scales Burn to claim her as its victim. She wasn't going to die. She couldn't die. There was unfinished business to attend to.

At the thought of the most important thing in her life, Fiona calmed her panic enough that she could function as a logical human being once more.

Hard objects bumped into Fiona as she flailed her legs in an attempt to find the ground beneath her. The current objected to her efforts like a lawyer defending a losing case. Whenever Fiona's feet or knees touched the ground beneath her, either the current washed them aside, or they were bumped sideways by some unidentifiable object in the current's grip.

Fiona's hands ached as she gripped the rope. Her arms curled as she used the tension on the rope to haul herself towards the surface. When Fiona's head breached the surface she didn't bother trying to open her eyes, instead she concentrated on sucking air into her burning lungs.

Beneath the water, Fiona's leg bumped into something hard and unyielding. The obstacle enough to unbalance her again.

Thanks to the rope, Fiona didn't get a second ducking, but it was a close thing. The solid object gave her enough purchase to plant a foot on the ground. Her other foot joined it and she felt for the first time since being plunged underwater that she might survive.

The tension on the rope changed. Instead of being taut between two matched forces, one side went loose. The sudden imbalance caused Fiona to be dragged towards the men hauling on the rope.

Fiona squirmed as she was pulled against the current. Thanks to the slow steady pull of William and the others, there was no chance of her getting her feet back under her. Fiona had to fight to keep her head high enough that she could snatch occasional breaths as the undulations of the brown waters crashed into her.

An attempt to open her eyes and see was greeted with eyefuls of the grit colouring the waters from clear to murky brown. Fiona screwed her eyes back shut and ignored the grains of earth that scratched at her eyeballs.

It was when Fiona snuck her third breath that she realised the significance of Craig's end of the rope going slack. His huge frame would have caught a lot of water and created the pull they'd battled against. The removal of that pull could only mean Craig hadn't tied the rope around himself well enough.

Fiona tried to imagine Craig's strength had aided his rescue and that he'd untied the rope himself as he'd found a place of safety, instead of being tumbled from the rope's embrace. It was a forlorn hope, but she clung to it as tightly as she clung to the nylon rope pulling her to the edge of the water.

The pull of the waters eased and Fiona risked opening her eyes again. Dirty water streamed over her lids, but she was able to see the edge of the water. It was some fifteen feet away, but the men on the bank were hauling for all they were worth and she covered the distance in a few seconds.

Fiona got herself onto her hands and knees where she alternated between wet hacking splutters and crisp inhalations of wonderful air. Hands fastened themselves around both her biceps and she felt an upwards pressure as two of the men went to lift her to her feet. She squirmed against it, shaking her head to emphasise her wishes.

As much as she wanted to stand. To pick up her feet and

sprint away from the river at her best speed, Fiona resisted the urge. She had to know how Craig was, and she had to ask Pierce why he'd not been holding the rope properly. The lack of help from him was a huge part of the reason she'd been dragged into the water.

First though, she had to get her breathing back under proper control and finish hacking up the water that had seeped into her stomach.

By the time Fiona had recovered enough to stand the three men had peppered her with a barrage of questions. Most were about her wellbeing and whether she'd seen anything of Craig. Fiona answered none of them.

As Leighton helped Fiona to her feet, William and Pierce returned to Tom's rope. Fiona paid attention to Pierce's input as she ignored Leighton's attempts to check she was okay.

Pierce was doing the bare minimum. Like one of those people who are good at looking busy, Pierce's hands never left the rope, but there was a profound dip in the rope between him and William. That extra hanging foot of rope was the difference between being supportive to the front man and not being ready to assist at a moment's notice.

Tom's shape came back into the light, his face grave as he waded through the water.

'Where's Craig?'

William laid a hand on the shepherd's shoulder. 'I'm sorry, but he got washed away. Fiona was bloody lucky she wasn't washed away too as she tried to pull him back.'

Tom's eyes closed as he digested the news. A liver-spotted hand ground against the stubble decorating his chin. He gave three hefty swallows before speaking. 'That wasn't Craig on the rope.'

'You what?'

Even as Fiona waited for an answer, her mind was whirring. Tom looked to be upset about Craig being swept away, but was his show of grief a genuine reaction to the probable death of a colleague? Or was it all an act?

'He put his rope round a calf. Last I saw, he was by the door. T'other calves went mad and bolted, knocked the big bugger flying.'

Fiona could picture the scene in the shed from Tom's sparse telling. Craig had been confident enough in his own strength that he'd used his safety line on a calf. It had been the calf on the end of the line. As he'd replaced the shed door by positioning his bulk in the doorway, one of the other panicked calves must have barged him hard enough for him to lose his balance. After that, with no safety line, the waters had done the rest.

It was a tragic situation that spoke more highly of Craig's love for the animals in his care than of his common sense. Or it would if it was to be believed.

Fiona didn't dare trust any of the men, and if Tom was the person who strangled George, then it was possible everything he'd just said was a lie, and that he'd pushed an untethered Craig into the swirling waters.

SIXTEEN

Everyone swapped glances with each other. Fiona saw all their faces were grim as they contemplated Craig's fate, but she wasn't done. If, by some miracle, Craig had managed to cling on to a tree or something, they had to try and find him.

To Fiona's way of thinking, Craig might need their help right away so there could be no delay. She pointed at William. 'Quick, get your tractor. Its lights are far better than any of our torches. We have to look for Craig. Tom, go and look in the tool shed, see if you can find anything that would work as a grappling hook. Leighton, Pierce, grab your torches and start looking downstream. Concentrate on the areas the tractor won't be able to get near.'

As the men set to their various tasks, Fiona bent down and lifted the rope that had been around Craig. She drew it through her hands, gathering it between outstretched arms until her left hand held a thick coil. As she neared the end of the rope her eyes were searching for the knot that had been tied to Craig.

Fiona found the knot, but its loop was far too small to encompass Craig. Where it should have a three-foot-plus diameter, it had one closer to eighteen inches. She pressed her fingers against the knot and tried to slide it tighter. It didn't budge. So far Tom's story was backed up by the evidence. While she'd never sat the detective's exam, Fiona had studied hard for it, and while study would never be as good as practical experience, she'd befriended a DC whose brains she picked at every opportunity. Heather Andrews had shared a lot with her and, as most cops did, enjoyed telling the stories of the cases she'd solved. It was those stories and all the little tricks Heather had passed on that were pinballing around Fiona's head now.

Underneath the waterproofs Fiona's borrowed clothes clung to her body. They were damp and clammy, and the constant restrictions provided by the soaked waterproofs had Fiona wanting to remove them. She couldn't get any wetter, after all.

But Fiona knew better than to discard the waterproofs. As uncomfortable as they might be, they provided a layer of insulation. Her exposed hands and face stung from the wind and rain, but the rest of her body was nothing like as cold.

The tractor's horn sounded and, when Fiona turned to look at William, she saw him use a leapfrog gesture to say he was going to the field downstream.

Fiona followed the tractor, with Leighton on one side of her and Pierce on the other. As they passed the tool shed, Tom emerged with a makeshift grappling hook that was nothing more than a collection of metal strips bolted together in an X shape. The ends of the four parts had been bent into hooks of varying angles, but in the few minutes he'd had, Tom had worked wonders.

Tom's rapid improvisation counted for a lot in Fiona's book. Had the shepherd returned with empty hands, saying he couldn't find anything, she'd have had to take the statement at face value. The way he'd solved the problem suggested he wanted to help rescue Craig. That he was mucking in to help and had not just found a solution, but engineered it.

As she walked after the tractor, Fiona handed him an end of the rope she was carrying, so he could attach the homemade hook to it.

Tom fished under his waterproofs until he produced a knife from a pocket and cut a fresh end on the rope, to better feed it through the narrow hole of his makeshift hook.

Fiona didn't miss that he carried a knife, but, then again, farmers tended to always have a knife on them and often a length of baler twine in their pockets. When she thought about it, she would have been more surprised had Tom not had a folding knife in his pocket.

As she moved beside the tractor, Fiona's eyes were scanning for Craig. She had no success. A look at the men with her saw their eyes reflecting her disappointment.

Ten times William moved the tractor along forty or so yards before pointing its lights across the brown torrent.

Not once did Fiona spot Craig. Neither alive, nor dead.

When they reached the stone wall that divided the field from the next, William shook his head and pointed back at the farm.

Nobody spoke as they trudged their way back. Everyone's head was bent against the weather, and Fiona expected they'd all be having the same terrible thoughts about Craig that she was.

Upon returning to the farm William swung the tractor down the yard and used its powerful headlights to sweep the swirling brown waters once again.

There was a shape in the water. It was thirty yards away and was being carried downstream by the current. Fiona's arm pointed at the shape just as William leaned on the tractor's horn.

It was a shape Fiona recognised. Not from a real-life experience, but from her training. When a body was immersed in water it invariably ended in the same position. That of someone touching their toes as the arms and legs hung down from the more buoyant torso.

It was a back she could see. The dirty water had discoloured the clothing on the body, yet there were isolated flashes of colour poking through.

'Here?' Tom held out a hand for the rope and grappling hook Fiona held.

Fiona shook her head. 'I've got it.' To shorten the throw, Fiona waded forward until she was knee deep in the water.

With the rest of the rope in a neat coil on the bank, Fiona took the end with the grappling hook and started to whirl it in a vertical circle. When she'd built up as much momentum as she could without the hook splashing into the water, she let fly.

Fiona held her breath as the hook arced towards the body; she was already bending down ready to grab the rope and haul the hook and body back. For a moment she thought it was going to fall short, but her aim was true, and it passed over the floating corpse with a foot to spare.

As soon as the hook dropped Fiona started to reel the rope back in. Steady at first, then when she saw the body roll a little as the hook caught, she increased her efforts in hauling the body back to her.

It was a heavy pull. She was fighting not just the current, but the body's un-aerodynamic position.

Behind her Fiona could feel others joining in with the pull. Then she felt a tap on her shoulder. When Fiona looked round Leighton was pointing at the front of the tractor, where Tom was lashing the rope to part of the linkage. She stepped aside as William inched backwards. He was taking care to not use too much of the tractor's mighty power. Something Fiona approved of.

SEVENTEEN

As the body drew closer to the edge of the water, Fiona stayed where she was. She wanted to be the first to see who had been found. The closer the body got, the more Fiona was sure she was not looking at Craig. She was looking at Isla Edwards, George's wife. The flashes of colour she'd seen earlier would be one of Isla's trademark floral dresses or tops.

When the body got to Fiona, she took a handful of the dress and waved to William. He got the message and stopped the tractor.

Fiona eased the homemade grappling hook free and guided the body towards the shore, rolling it over onto its back as she did so. Her eyes were scanning the body, looking for two things: a sign of life, and a source of injury.

Isla's eyes were lifeless, but they showed none of the haemorrhaging George's had. Nor were there any signs of strangulation marks around her throat.

Fiona's eyes travelled downwards, looking for evidence of foul play. Just off centre of Isla's chest there was a rent in her dress. Fiona's first thought was that it had been caused by the makeshift grappling hook, but there was a straightness to the tear that made a fool of that theory. The grappling hook would have caused a triangular tear or none at all. This looked more like the cut a narrow-bladed knife would make when plunged into her heart. There was no blood on the torn fabric, but the waters of the river would have seen to that.

As Leighton and Pierce helped her hoist the body out of the water and lay it on the bank, Fiona made sure to put Isla's arms across her chest, to hide the wound she suspected had ended the woman's life.

In death, Isla's face had shed its usual pinch. There was a calmness about her, as Leighton's hand felt at her throat for a pulse.

Fiona knew Leighton wouldn't find what he was looking for. She peeled off her waterproof jacket and used it as a sheet to cover Isla's body, the hood covering her face, and affording her the tiniest shred of dignity as she lay on a muddy farmyard in the pouring rain.

Tom appeared, carrying one of the pieces of decking from William's cattle trailer. He laid it down beside Isla, and Fiona saw the wisdom of what he'd done. The light aluminium decking would make an ideal stretcher.

Together with Tom, Leighton and Pierce, Fiona lifted Isla's corpse onto the decking, then carried it up the farmyard to a barn beside the track. The barn was stacked with hay bales and it was on these they laid Isla's body.

Fiona reached for Pierce's torch. 'Craig must have been swept away downstream. There's no telling where he's at now.' What Fiona didn't say, couldn't begin to say about a friend of twenty years, were that the chances of Craig still being alive were minuscule. 'You guys go back to the house. I'm going to say a quick prayer for Isla and then I'll join you.'

Leighton touched her shoulder. 'I'll stay if you want. Keep you company.'

'I'm fine.' Fiona didn't want any company. Nor did she want to be left alone with just one person. Especially not a stranger, not when she knew there was a murderer loose in the valley.

'Fine my foot. Your teeth have been chattering since we pulled you out of the river. You need to get in the warm before you catch hypothermia.'

'I'm just going to say a private prayer for her and then I'll be in.' Fiona added as much of a sliver of steel to her tone as her chattering teeth allowed. 'Okay?'

The men filed away, and Fiona set to work by the light of the torch. Now Leighton had pointed it out to her, she realised how cold she was. There was no feeling in her hands or feet, and the warning about hypothermia sounded accurate.

Fiona dropped to a knee and directed the torch at Isla's chest. As sure as she was the elderly woman had been stabbed, Fiona needed proof before she could count her as a murder victim. Under the beam of the torch Fiona examined the tear in Isla's dress.

It was just as she'd glimpsed in the shadowed light from the tractor. The tear was one inch long and was situated in the exact place it should be for a stab wound to the heart.

Fiona teased a finger into the rent and followed it with both her eyes and the torch beam. The rent went on through Isla's slip and into her flesh. There were tiny dark blotches on Isla's skin beside the wound that, when tested, Fiona expected would prove to be Isla's blood.

She was now certain. There had been two murders in the valley that night.

Lots of scenarios went through Fiona's mind. A mystery killer slinking into and then back out of the valley unbeknownst to the valley's occupants. Isla strangling George, and then fuelled with regret, stabbing herself by the river, to make sure her children never found out what she'd done. These and other ideas played out in Fiona's mind, but the one she kept coming back to was the one she believed to be the most likely: one of the people in the farmhouse had killed George and Isla Edwards.

EIGHTEEN

Fiona entered the farmhouse kitchen and found herself entering the middle of a candlelit argument. Becky was on her feet, her face purple as she yelled at William and Tom. 'Where is he? Where's my Craig?'

Neither man answered her. They were looking everywhere but at Becky. Pierce and Leighton shuffled their feet until they could get past Becky and reach the safety of the kitchen table.

Fiona's training kicked in. She'd had to deliver death messages on two occasions and had once assumed the role of Family Liaison Officer to a couple whose daughter had suffered a savage beating after being sexually assaulted. She strode across the room, stepped in front of William and took Becky's hands in hers. By using gentle movements, Fiona steered Becky to a chair and sat her down. A glance Fiona shot towards Aunt Mary was met with a terse nod, and it was only when Aunt Mary had ushered Becky's children from the kitchen that she broke the news.

'I'm so sorry to have to tell you this, Becky. But we think Craig was washed away by the floodwaters. He was helping

Tom rescue some calves and one of them barged him over when he was in the water. I'm so sorry.'

'No.' Becky's head sawed back and forth. 'You're wrong. You're lying. My Craig is too big for some calf to knock him over. Why are you lying to me? Where is he really? He's taken the quad, hasn't he? He's gone for help, the bloody heroic fool.'

William appeared at Fiona's shoulder. 'She's not lying, Becky. He got swept away by the waters.'

Becky was on her feet in a flash, her head sawing side to side. 'No. No way. He's too big. Too strong. He'll turn up. He'll swim his way out. You'll see.'

All four of the men said nothing. Neither did Fiona – there was nothing to say. If Becky was right, and Craig could swim himself to safety, it would be fantastic. The best possible outcome of a terrible situation. Fiona didn't believe it though. She'd seen the raging waters. Felt them push and pull at her body as she was submerged beneath their murky surface. To swim free of those waters would require superhuman endurance coupled with an Olympic swimmer's technique. Craig wore chest waders that he'd have to shed lest they pull him down as they filled. The cold would leech at his strength as it had hers. Even in the cooling warmth of the kitchen her skin felt as if it was on fire.

Leighton came into the periphery of Fiona's vision. 'Becky. Becky love, we looked for him. We all looked for him before we came back in. And there's something we haven't told any of you ladies yet. While we were looking for Craig, we found someone else in the water.'

'Who?'

'Isla Edwards. There was no sign of her husband, George, but you have to believe us, that the water out there is running fast. As big and strong as Craig is, if he's been swept away, I'm sorry, but you have to prepare yourself for the worst.'

Whether it was Leighton's words, or the tone in which they

were delivered, they permeated Becky's denial. Her knees wobbled and Leighton had to grab her arm to stop her falling. With William and Tom's help Leighton sat Becky back down, while an ashen-faced Elsie put a kettle on the Aga. The oil-powered stove was no longer working, but retained more than enough heat to boil a kettle.

'Here.' Elsie passed Fiona another bundle of dry clothes and fluffy towels. Another set was handed to Tom by Aunt Mary, and Fiona caught a strange expression on her aunt's face as she turned towards the Aga. It was as if Aunt Mary was hiding something, but Fiona didn't know what or from whom. At the first opportunity she got, she planned to get to the bottom of it. There were more than enough secrets in this room without Aunt Mary keeping some.

All the others were shedding their waterproofs and huddling around the Aga.

As she left to change into dry clothes, Fiona took a look at Becky, her face a picture of defiant disbelief.

Even as Fiona was starting to peel off her sodden clothes for a second time, in the lounge, she could hear Becky raging at William and the others, demanding to know why they weren't out there searching for Craig. It was a good question that had a bad answer.

Fiona stripped with as much haste as her numb fingers allowed. The sooner she could get back to the kitchen, the sooner she could continue observing the men and how they reacted to Becky's pleas. She held suspicions about Tom, but not as many as she held about Pierce. He'd not been ready to help her with the rope. Fair enough: at the time they'd thought it was Craig on the other end; but his slowness in reacting had almost seen her swept away. And there was Leighton to consider. If it had been another setting, she might have allowed her ego the massage of thinking he'd been hitting on her, but she'd been drenched and curt, and his questions had felt like he was sounding her out rather than trying to hook up. Fiona was under no illusions that she was any great looker, or that she had the figure of a model. She was average. Average height. Average looks. Average body shape. Sure, there were times when she attracted male attention, but it wasn't going to be when she was dressed in a farmer's clothes and soaking wet.

Besides, who the hell hits on someone at a time like this?

Fiona teased the kitchen door open in time to see Becky rising from her seat, her finger jabbing at William, Leighton and Pierce. 'Why the hell are you back here? You should be out there looking for him. What if he's got himself out of the water but is injured or plain exhausted from the effort? He'll bloody well freeze in this weather, yet you're all here in the warm and dry.' Becky's finger speared into William's chest. 'If anything has happened to my Craig, I'll make sure you pay. I'll have everyone look into his death from the police to whatever health and safety body covers farms. They'll ruin you. It's your fault my Craig is out there in those waters. Nobody else's.'

'Now just you hang on a minute. I told him not to try and save those calves. He didn't listen. Nor did Tom. Don't you be blaming me. We had safety lines on him and Tom, and Craig took his off and put it round one of the calves.'

'You're lying. You're lying to save your own skin, you horrible, horrible man.'

Becky's insult to William seemed tame to Fiona considering what a foul mouth Becky used to have, but she supposed motherhood had taught her to temper her language.

'He's not.'

Fiona hadn't heard Tom return from wherever he'd gone to get changed. That was something to bear in mind, the way he could slink about.

'I don't believe any of you. My Craig wouldn't be that stupid.' Becky reached for her jacket. 'If you're not going to look for him. I'll go myself.'

William and Tom blocked the door by shifting their feet. Both the older men's faces were layered with guilt as they made a silent obstacle. Side by side they looked an odd pairing, the taller farmer towering above the squat shepherd.

William slung a jacket over his shoulders. 'Come on, Tom. We'll get the tractors out and keep looking. Pierce, Leighton, if you're game again, there's room for one of you in each tractor.' Fiona rose to join the search party. 'No way. You're lucky to be alive and have been soaked through twice. You stay where you are.'

As much as Fiona wanted to argue with William, she was still numb from the cold and knew there would only be room for two people in each tractor anyway. Better to catch a break while she could. Having all of the men out of the house would also give her a chance to pick Aunt Mary's brains and perhaps learn something from the other women.

NINETEEN

The sweater Elsie had found to replace the sodden one must have belonged to her as it swamped Fiona. She'd pulled the cuffs into a fold that stopped just short of her elbows, which left her forearms looking as big as her biceps, but it didn't bother her too much. The sweater was toasty warm and that's all she wanted it to be.

Aunt Mary scuttled between the pantry and the Aga as she made a round of cuppas. The door opened, but instead of the men, it was Elsie. Water cascaded off her jacket, but there was triumph in her face as she lifted her hands to show what she'd gone out for. Her left hand held three old Tilley lamps and her right a one gallon can.

'Great work, Elsie.'

The farmer's wife blushed at the rare praise and twittered a few words about remembering these old kerosene lamps were in the bothy.

A guttural Essex accent crashed against the backdrop of Elsie's burring tones. 'What on earth is a bothy?'

'It's a Scottish term for somewhere that offers rudimentary accommodation.' Aunt Mary gestured at Elsie. 'William and

Elsie use it as a tool shed now, but back in the day, a shepherd or dairyman might have slept in it.'

Elsie put the lamps on the kitchen table beside a candle and moved to undo their filler caps.

Fiona stepped forward, her hand forming a gentle clamp on Elsie's. 'Maybe we should fill them in the lounge by torch light. We don't want any accidents, do we?'

'Don't want any accidents.' Elsie picked up the lamps and set off for the lounge.

Fiona's heart ached for poor Elsie. She'd had the wit to remember the lamps, and the strength to go and get them, but hadn't given a second thought to the dangers of dispensing paraffin by candlelight. Fiona didn't know if paraffin vapours would ignite the same way as petrol ones, but she didn't want to take the chance.

'They should be thinking about trying to get someone to get us out of here.' Susie cast an apologetic glance Becky's way. 'After they've had a look for Craig that is. Maybe they should have split up. Those tractors are huge. You're not going to tell me they couldn't drive one of them over the hills to get some help, are you? They're all four-wheel drive, after all.'

Becky snuggled against her daughter, Adele, and shot back a contemptuous look at Susie, so Fiona made sure she answered before Becky did. Becky had yet to shed a tear, but her face was becoming ever more downcast as she faced the reality of Craig's likely fate. Fiona was surprised she'd even heard Susie, such was her vacant expression.

'The hills are too steep. All that would happen is the front end would rear up and flip the tractor, or because of the angle, they wouldn't get enough grip to pull themselves up. Think, how many times have you seen a tractor anywhere but low in the valleys? If they could go up into the hills, they'd be up them on a regular basis.'

'I still say they should be trying.'

'Why?' Where before Fiona had kept her tone level, she was now allowing her true feelings to show. 'So you can get what you want? Is it not bad enough that Mrs Edwards has been killed in the floods and Craig is missing? Maybe you want to try going out and taking a look at the conditions instead of sitting there like Lady Muck and telling those of us who've been out there what to do.' Fiona caught Aunt Mary's eye and slid her gaze to the lounge door. 'We've not been here long, but so help me, I've had enough of you and your nonsense.'

Fiona made a show of stomping off to the lounge with a Tilley lamp, but as soon as she was there she perched herself in a chair that allowed her a narrow view of the kitchen door. With the men out searching, she didn't think Becky would try looking for Craig herself, but she wanted to be ready to stop her if she did.

Aunt Mary padded into the lounge, a steaming mug in each hand and the beginnings of a wry smile on her face. 'You need to calm yourself down, Fiona.'

Fiona took a mug and ignored the comment from Aunt Mary. She wasn't anything more than ticked off and her aunt knew it. There had been a sparkle in Aunt Mary's eye when she'd put Susie in her place.

'What do you want?' Aunt Mary never was shy when it came to getting to the point.

'What's been happening in here while I was away?'

Aunt Mary gave a defeated shrug. 'Pretty much what you'd expect. The kids were grumbling about pizza and electronic games. Susie spent the whole time banging on about someone going to get help, and Elsie was twittering about as she does. Poor Becky has been beside herself worrying about Craig. I tried to reassure Becky, but it seems that she was right to worry and I was wrong to tell her he'd be okay.'

'Don't blame yourself. It's not your fault. It was as hairy as anything out there, and Craig should never have risked his life trying to save those calves.'

'That's a big statement for you to make considering how much you like animals.'

'It's the truth.' Fiona cast a look towards the kitchen and lowered her voice. 'I hate to think of those calves drowning, but when it's a choice between a human life and an animal, I'll always choose the human. Besides, I'm not convinced it was an accident.'

'What do you mean, not an accident?'

'Remember how I supposedly stayed to pray for Mrs Edwards? Well, that was just an excuse for me to have some peace so I could examine her. She'd been stabbed.'

Fiona paused to let her words sink in. She wasn't going to share any of her theories with Aunt Mary and she wished she didn't have to tell her this much. In an ideal world she'd have saved her aunt the worry until they were safe, but she needed something from Aunt Mary and the only way to get that was to level with her. It was her aim to spend an hour, two, if necessary, mining the information Aunt Mary had about the valley's inhabitants, so she could identify the killer in their midst.

'I did wonder if anything had happened to her after you told me about poor George. I could never bring myself to like Isla, but I hate to think that she's been murdered.' It was Aunt Mary's turn to slide a glance in the direction of the kitchen. 'Maybe that infernal Susie is right, maybe we should get someone to go for help.'

'You know as well as I do that going for help is not an option. I'm a police officer, and it's up to me to keep everyone safe. All I need to do is identify the killer. And for that, I need to know more about the people who live in this valley, and that's where you come in. I know you never talk about your work at the solicitors, but I need answers, and I suspect you have them, so you have to put your professional discretion to one side and tell me everything.'

Aunt Mary's mouth twisted, but that was no surprise to Fiona. She knew fine well her aunt took her role as office manager at Cummings and Co seriously. Never in all the years Fiona had known Aunt Mary had she heard anything about her working day other than banalities about it being really busy or fairly quiet.

Cummings and Co was one of two solicitors in Hawick, and as most of the town's legal business was conducted by one firm or the other, almost every legal document in the town would pass across Aunt Mary's desk at some point, as the two firms almost always represented both sides of every transaction.

'I suppose you're right, but I have to say, I don't like it. Not once in all the years I've worked there have I spoken about anyone's business.'

'I know. But... you have to see that these are extreme circumstances. I've not had chance to tell you yet, but Isla Edwards kept a diary. I looked at a few pages and I found out she and George were scared of someone in the valley. So scared they agreed to sell their cottage. In the diary she referred to the buyers as "that infernal couple". You've just used the same word to describe Susie. Would I be right in saying that it's Susie and Pierce who bought their cottage?'

Aunt Mary's lip's pursed and, rather than speak to break her own code of confidentiality, she gave a slow nod.

'Thank you. Now, who else is likely to know who'd bought it?'

As she waited for Aunt Mary to answer, Fiona allowed her mind to drift along logical lines. It made sense the threat Isla and George felt came from a new source. They'd been in the valley rubbing alongside Craig and Becky, and William and Elsie, for around twenty years, so it didn't seem likely they were the ones scaring them. That left the newcomers, Tom, Leighton, and Pierce and Susie as the prime suspects, yet George and Isla had sold their beloved home to Pierce and Susie.

On the one hand it could be Pierce and Susie were innocents buying the cottage in good faith, but on the other they could have forced the sale through intimidation.

'It was all done on the QT. George and Isla made an appointment to see Mr Cummings and told him they'd agreed to sell their cottage, so he would know. So would the other secretary, but she's a good lass and knows not to gossip about clients' business. The surveyor would know, and I can't say who either Susie and Pierce or George and Isla told. You know what Isla was like. I wouldn't put it past her to throw that information in William's face considering all the rows they had whenever he spread slurry on the fields near their cottage.'

'Why would it bother William if they sold the cottage?'

'William and Elsie had their eye on the cottage. They're not ready to retire yet, but lately William's started talking about selling up in a couple of years, as his daughters both moved away after marrying. You were at their weddings and you don't need me to tell you everything their husbands know about farming could be written on a blade of grass.' Aunt Mary was right about William and Elsie's sons-in-law. Neither was a son of the soil and the idea of either being able, let alone willing, to take on the task of running Scales Valley Farm was a bad joke. 'I've told you often enough Pierce and William don't get on because William feels cheated about the land he sold him. If Isla threw the sale in William's face, he'd be livid.'

'Livid enough to kill her and George?'

Aunt Mary's hand flew to her mouth. 'Fiona MacLeish, how can you think such a thing? You've known William for the best part of twenty years. Yes, he's a grumpy article at the best of times and he's tighter than a duck's you-know-what, but he's not a killer. You can't think that of him, not when you're sheltering in his house.'

'I don't think he's the one who killed her, but I can't let personal feelings cloud my judgement. Someone in this valley is a murderer and it's up to me to find out who.' Fiona looked her aunt dead in the eye. 'I need you to tell me everything you know about Pierce and Susie. I don't care if it's something you've learned at your work or overheard in the hairdresser's. I need that info.'

'They're in a form of semi-retirement. She swans about in that big fancy Range Rover of hers as if she's Lady Muck, but he always seems to be doing something. I've seen his car go away for three or four days at a time, always during the week though. I don't have a lot more to tell you about them than I've already told you.

'I've only been in their bungalow once, it was just after they got here. I took round a wee welcome basket, you know? To be neighbourly. There were lots of pictures of building sites on the walls. So I guess they're proud of what they've done in the past. They've certainly got plenty of money, and while he seems decent enough, Susie is a right one. When she's not complaining about something, she's always talking about whatever expensive thing she's just bought or has her eye on.'

'The building sites in the pictures, were they like one house, or a whole lot of them?'

Aunt Mary's eyes clouded as she trawled her memory. 'They were of several houses, or larger projects such as a school or community centre.'

'Do they have any kids?'

'Pierce has a son, but they hardly mention him as I don't think he gets on with Susie.'

'Remind me, what was the story with the land they bought from William?'

'They bought a large plot, saying they'd build a bungalow and some stables for Susie's horses and use the rest as a paddock. The stables and paddock never materialised and the

next thing there's a planning application for seven more bungalows on the land.'

Aunt Mary gave a little shrug.

'Them building more bungalows doesn't bother me, but
William sees it as a lost opportunity for him. They got their
planning through, but when William tried to get permission to
build some of his own he was turned down. And before you ask,
I don't know why.'

'Because the dumb bastard doesn't understand a thing about
building. Our eco-friendly designs were waved through, as
they're as modern as anything you'd find in a city. He'd likely
tried to build with more traditional methods and materials
because that'd be cheaper for him.'

Fiona hadn't noticed Susie appear at the open door. The
question was, just how much had she overheard?

TWENTY

With their private conversation now interrupted by Susie, Fiona and Aunt Mary made their way back into the kitchen, where they spent a fraught hour waiting as Becky grew more and more anxious. What the worry was doing to her blood pressure, and the baby, was anyone's guess, but the sooner Craig's fate was determined, the sooner they'd be able to remove the element of the unknown and help Becky.

The kitchen door swung open and four sodden men trudged in. Not five. Not four carrying a fifth. Just four. Becky howled as she saw them return without Craig. The tears she'd held back for so long cascaded down her cheeks as her face crumpled at the unspoken message their empty-handed return gave. Fiona knew that until Craig's body was found, and his death confirmed, a part of them all would hope he'd washed up somewhere still alive, but as much as she wanted that to be the case, she was also aware the odds of Craig's survival were so small as to be considered negligible.

Aunt Mary got to Becky first and wrapped her in a hug as she smoothed her hair. Fiona could hear soft mumblings from her aunt, but couldn't make out the words. She doubted Becky would hear them either. Great racking sobs shook all of Becky's body, and when Fiona looked around the room, she found nothing but grim, embarrassed faces avoiding her eye.

William nodded at his wife. 'Elsie. Take the kids through. Get them something to do. They don't need to see their mum like this.'

'Take the kids through. Something to do.'

It made sense William got Elsie to look after the kids. Of all the adults in the valley, their parents excepted, they'd know Elsie the best.

Elsie led the kids off, her soft Borders brogue promising games and sweeties.

Until he left the room, little Jamie's eyes never strayed from his mother, his face tight, except for his jaw, which wobbled as he fought the urge to copy his mother's tears. Fiona had no idea how much he understood, but he was sure to have noticed his father hadn't returned.

Pierce raised a hand to point a finger at William. 'This is all your fault. If you'd not strung that heck thing down by the bridge there'd be no flood. Our house has been ruined and so has our land, and it's all because of you and that damned heck.'

'How dare you sit at my table and blame me for this? That heck has been there for decades. You've only been in the valley for five minutes, so don't give me any of that shite.'

'He's right. It is your fault. My Craig told me last week he was afraid the heck would get blocked as there was a tree caught in it. He told me that you'd said it would be all right and that you would clear it in the spring. It's your fault Craig's missing. Your fault that he may be dead.'

Fiona moved with her best speed to intercept Becky, but was too slow to stop her delivering a stinging slap to William's cheek.

William didn't move. Didn't raise a hand to defend himself and never uttered a word of denial. Fiona could see in his eyes that he believed what Becky had said. The weight of his guilt seemed as if it would crush him flat, like some cartoon character upon whom an anvil had been dropped.

'That's enough everyone.' Fiona wrestled Becky away from William and pushed her into a seat with a mix of assertive force and gentle understanding. 'We need to focus on staying alive. There will be a time for blame and recriminations, but that's not now.'

'Like hell it is. Now seems like the perfect time for me.' Susie was on her feet and jabbing a finger towards William, her expensive attire and styling at odds with the ugly snarl smeared across her face. 'It'll cost us thousands, if not tens of thousands, to get our house sorted and that's not counting on having to find somewhere else to stay while it's being fixed. After this, its value will be halved. And what about all my stuff? I had Axminster carpets, my furniture was hand made to my personal specification.' The finger shifted its aim from William to Pierce. 'And him, he had a vinyl collection worth thousands. Even when the insurance pays out, some stuff is irreplaceable. Are you going to make sure we don't lose out? Are you going to make good on our losses? We had plans for our land and, like Craig, they've all been washed away because you're too bloody lazy to look after the land you own. Can you replace the money we'd make when we—'

Pierce stepped in front of his wife. 'Susie. Sit down and shut up right this minute or so help me—'

'I said that's enough.' Fiona aimed her arm towards the next room and raised her voice as much as she dared without making it audible to Elsie and Becky's children. 'There's kids in there and with their father missing, they're already going to be scared. You lot squabbling like a pack of hyenas won't be helping. I meant what I said before. Now is not the time to point blame. Like it or not, we're going to be stuck here until the flood passes, so we have to put any differences aside and find a way to get along. Mrs Edwards is dead, George and Craig are missing, presumed dead. You lot all falling out with each other isn't going to make anything better.'

Fiona stepped back, her chest heaving with the adrenaline spike she'd felt as she faced down the others. She could feel her nostrils flaring and, while she recognised her own anger was smaller than anyone else's, she still felt outraged that Aunt Mary's home was being flooded because of William's foolhardy negligence.

There was also the dynamic in Pierce and Susie's marriage that had just been revealed. Pierce had been about to lay a threat of some sort on Susie and she'd immediately fallen silent. That was out of character for her, and, while it may be that Pierce knew ways to wrangle his wife's tongue, her first thought was that those ways fell under the heading *domestic abuse*.

As telling as Pierce's unvoiced threat was the reaction of the others in the room at the crass way Susie had spoken about Craig. Leighton had shown horror, while Tom's expression was angry. William's face displayed guilt at Susie's accusations, whereas Aunt Mary's lips went paper thin, as she did what little she could to soothe Becky.

'Fiona's right. What's happening is bad enough without us all slinging abuse around.' Leighton's accent cut through the room like a blunt rapier, but his soft tone was calming enough that everyone slumped back in grumbling acceptance.

Except Susie. She planted a manicured hand on her husband's upper arm and shoved him off the bench at the table. 'I'm not staying here a minute longer than I have to. Get off your saggy arse and go for help. You've done nothing to help so far. Look at you, you're nothing more than a great soft lump. I'm your wife so it's up to you to protect me and I don't feel safe. Go walk over the hills and find a way to get me out of here.'

Fiona felt her top lip curl as her temper broke. Susie needed to be shut down before she caused any more trouble. 'You don't know it, but your husband saved my life earlier, and he helped save Tom's. The wind's picking up out there and asking him to walk over those hills is as stupid an idea as asking him to jump in the river and swim downstream for help. Or maybe you want him to die out there, or at the very least go missing too? After all, the way you've been treating him, it sure as hell doesn't make it look like you care about him in any way.'

Those last bits were too much, but they were out before Fiona could stop them. She re-evaluated her thoughts regarding Pierce beating his wife. While Susie's insistence on Pierce risking his life may be those of an abuse victim looking for a way to escape their abuser, Fiona couldn't see a way any abuse victim would dare be so derogatory about their abuser in public. That meant Pierce may have something on Susie that he used to keep her in check. Like a dirty secret. Possibly one he'd killed Isla and George to keep possession of.

What Fiona hoped Pierce would focus on was her claim that he'd saved her life. He'd certainly helped, but he'd been lax in his vigilance and then slow to react when she needed him. She hadn't yet worked out if he was the useless lump Susie described, or whether he'd been useless on purpose, so there would be a chance Fiona would be yanked into the water and drowned. It was never far from Fiona's thoughts the killer must have seen her either enter or leave George and Isla's cottage. No way did Fiona want Pierce trekking over the hills. If he was the killer, and by some miracle he did make it out of the valley alive, he would then have the chance to disappear.

'Oh, I see. I see it all now. He saved you, but he won't save me. Oh, that's Pierce Normanton all right. You're half his age and that's just what he likes. Have you any idea the number of times I've caught him chasing after younger women? That's all he's good for, acting like a sad old lech. He probably only saved you in the hope you'd feel grateful enough to shag him.' Susie's arm shot in the direction of the door that led to the lounge and the stairs. 'Go on then, take her upstairs and claim your prize. I'm done with you. I want a divorce.'

Aunt Mary uncoiled her arms from Becky to better face Susie, the anger on her face stronger than Fiona had ever seen before. Even the time Fiona had come home drunk and vomited on the lounge carpet hadn't infuriated Aunt Mary as much as Susie's rant. When she spoke her voice was low but as powerful as an earthquake. 'If you speak about my niece in that manner again, I'll personally gag you. She's preaching sense while you're doing nothing but spewing venom. Now will you please sit down and shut up?'

TWENTY-ONE

Susie positioned herself in a corner and, from the sullen expression she wore, Fiona guessed the older woman was in a full-blown sulk. If sulking kept Susie from spilling any more bile, Fiona was happy to let her get on with it.

Aunt Mary rested a gentle hand atop Becky's. 'Come on, love, let's go see how Elsie's doing with Jamie and Adele.'

Fiona was glad for Becky's sake she had Aunt Mary to support her. Calm and caring by default, she was a tigress defending its cubs when needed. Susie had learned that the hard way, but that was only a tiny part of who Aunt Mary was. She was the voice of reason. A shoulder to cry on. A silent listener when all you wanted to do was rage against the injustice of your bereavement. Most of all, Aunt Mary's company was a safe haven when your world was falling apart around you. Fiona owed everything to her aunt, because without her Fiona would have never coped.

As Fiona healed, Aunt Mary had allowed her to grow into the young woman she wanted to be. Even with the weight of grief an ever-present burden, and teenage hormones to deal with, Fiona hadn't once felt the need to rebel against Aunt Mary, such was the woman's steady manner.

It had been different with Fiona's parents. The last time she saw her mother was as she left for school and there had been the usual morning argument about getting out the door in time to get the school bus. The last words Fiona said to her mother were 'For God's sake, will you pack it in? Honestly, you're nothing but a bloody old nag. I don't know how the hell Dad puts up with you. Soon as I can, I'm moving out.'

'And I love you too, Fiona,' was Mum's response. The six words were said with enough false syrup for Fiona to know she'd hurt her mother. At the time she'd taken a childish glee from scoring a point. Now, that final exchange was a ghost. It haunted Fiona's every memory of her parents, shaming her and topping her grief with a thick layer of guilt. What she would give to have that moment again. She'd do what Mum nagged her about and say that she loved Mum as she left for school, so the final time her mum told Fiona she loved her, it would be said with heart not hurt.

Aunt Mary and Becky filed out, leaving Fiona and Susie as the only females in the room. Fiona wanted to be part of the discussions she could sense were coming, and suspected Susie held the same agenda.

It was Leighton who broke the silence. 'Tom, I know you said no to the idea when someone said it earlier, but is there definitely no way you can get over the hills with the quad bike? I'd be happy to come with you, in case you needed any help.'

The offer to accompany Tom might be borne of a noble desire to help, but to Fiona it looked as if Leighton was trying to secure himself an escape route. That moved him two places up her suspect list. A townie such as Leighton would be next to useless on the hills, unless there was a physical element required to the journey. While Leighton was well enough built,

Fiona would bet Tom, with his squat torso, would be far stronger when push came to shove.

In the weeks and months after Fiona moved in with Aunt Mary, she'd walked all the hills surrounding the Scales Valley. There were narrow ravines, scree slopes and even more steep sides. On a summer's day you still had to plot your route up the hills with care or you would find yourself having to double back and plot a new course.

But after two years here, herding sheep on the hills, Tom would know the hills as well as his own face. He'd be able to pick a route over the hills better than anyone, except perhaps William, but it was still a lot to ask of him. Up on the top of the hills, the wind would be stronger, the rain more driven. Visibility would be measured in feet not yards. To try and go over the hills in this weather was a foolhardy idea.

'Too dangerous. Safer staying here.'

The taciturn answer from Tom sparked a thought in Fiona's head. 'Hang on a minute. Let's say that Tom and Leighton did make it out of here and get to somewhere they could summon help. What help could they get us? We're in a house that's keeping us dry. It's still well above the floodwaters so there's no immediate panic about it flooding. I'm sure William and Elsie will have more than enough food in their cupboards to keep us all fed until daylight tomorrow. Yes, there's no heating, but again, I'm sure there are enough blankets and duvets to stop us freezing to death. So other than preventing us having to endure a bit of discomfort, there's nothing anyone can do to help. The road in and out of the valley is blocked. No rescue party will come over the hills when we don't technically need to be rescued. That leaves a helicopter, and in this weather, no helicopter pilot will risk coming to save us when we don't need saving. Yes, Becky may go into labour, but that's a maybe, and while William and Tom are by no means midwives, between them they'll have attended thousands of sheep and cows giving birth. Plus, you can bet the way Odin has been predicted to affect the whole country, every last one of the emergency services will already be stretched to breaking point. Think about it. For all it'd be nice to be rescued, there are sure to be people who are in far greater danger from Odin than we are. Even if Tom and Leighton got to somewhere they could summon help, we'd be well down the list. The risk to them is far greater than the payoff of us being rescued.'

All of this was true so far as everyone except the killer, Fiona and Aunt Mary were concerned. They knew a murderer had struck in the valley, but there was no way Fiona was going to trust anyone else with that information. Either the person she told would blab and then the murderer would find out, or she'd pick the wrong person and inform the killer herself. Whichever course she chose would tell the murderer his crimes were no longer secret, and the only way she could see the murderer not killing again, was to maintain the illusion his kills were unde-tected, and keep everyone in the same place, to deny him another opportunity.

Fiona could volunteer to go instead of Leighton. That might be an option, if she could guarantee her place on the back of the quad bike, but it was never going to be something she would do. Until she'd identified the killer and had them tied up, there was no way Fiona was going to leave Aunt Mary unguarded in the valley. Even if there might be a way of getting help, she *had* to keep the group together lest the killer escape or strike again.

'You're right.' Leighton cast a look at Fiona then moved his eyes to the farmer. 'William, you know this farm best. How are the ground levels? Will this house flood before the water flows over the road?'

The question from Leighton was a good one and it had Fiona trying to picture the landscape in terms of height. The road hugged the far side of the valley against a higher bank than this side, until it curled across the valley floor on a raised bank that kept it more or less level with the bridge. From the bank at the bridge, the road again hugged the valley wall some six or so feet above the level of the fields in the valley floor.

William's face looked aged as he too worked out the levels in his mind. Fiona let him do it in peace. There was nothing to be gained from not allowing him the time to work out the differing levels using his intimate knowledge of the valley. It wouldn't be easy to work out, the road dipped and rose as it followed the contours of the hillside it had been etched into.

'I reckon it'll be within a foot or two.'

'Which way? Higher or lower?'

William shrugged at Leighton's question. 'I don't know.'

'Hang on.' Pierce straightened in his seat. 'I've seen you use a digger on the back of your tractor. Could you cut a channel in the road to let the floodwaters go?'

'Bad idea.' Tom rose from his seat and reached for the kettle that sat on the lid of an Aga hob.

'Why? It'll stop the water getting any higher. You saw how clogged up the bridge was and it's sure to be getting worse. Surely anything that stops the water level rising has to be a good idea.'

Fiona knew the answer, but she left it to William to explain.

'And what about the folks who live below the bridge? As soon as we cut a channel, the water will go pouring through it. The water'll not just pour through the channel, it'll erode either side of it and scour out the base as well. Before long any channel we cut will be ten times the size. All the water that's backed up will go thundering downstream and it'll swamp everything in its path. That's three farms and at least ten cottages or houses. If we release that water, we could end up killing the folks who live downstream.'

'Damn.' Pierce slumped back into his seat. 'I thought it was a good idea.'

'In theory it is, but once you cut a channel, you have no

control of what happens.' Fiona made sure her tone was soft. This was a chance to ease some of the tension filling the room. 'Plus, once that channel is cut, none of us will be able to use the road until it's fixed, and that may take weeks or months unless those of you who live in the valley pay for the repairs yourselves.'

Pierce's face tightened, his lips thinning as he glared at William. 'All this because you're too lazy or too stupid to make sure the heck isn't blocked. This is going to cost me a fortune and you can take this as read, I'm going to sue you for every penny.'

'You can try.' William's face was puce as he returned Pierce's glare. 'I've never seen rains like these before, and don't forget they're on the back of a heavy snow melt. To have any chance of suing me, you'll have to prove the heck was blocked before the rains came and unless you have pictures you can't do that. Anyway, I should be suing you. The land I sold you that you said would be a paddock for your wife's horse, I know you're planning to build on it. I would have never sold you the land if I'd known that.'

'Sod off, that's got nothing to do with it. We're talking about your negligence as a caretaker of the land. Your failure to keep the river free from obstruction is the reason my house has been flooded. It's also the reason I won't be able to ever make a profit if I do build those houses.'

'You tell him, Pierce. We'll sue him. By the time we're finished with him, we'll own the whole farm. Then we can make sure the bridge doesn't get blocked and build as many houses as we like.'

The curl of William's top lip made his thoughts clear before he spoke. 'Shut up, you stupid woman. You were all for divorcing him ten minutes ago.'

'Don't you speak to my wife like that.' Pierce rose to his feet and moved as if he was going to punch William.

'Enough.' Fiona accompanied her shout by slamming the palm of her hand onto the table. 'Are you both so thick that you're squabbling about blame, when two men are missing presumed dead, and we've not long since pulled a woman's body out of the very waters you're arguing over?'

TWENTY-TWO

Everyone wore a sheepish expression apart from Susie. Her face was set in a mask of malevolence and, if Fiona had to bet who'd be the first to restart the argument, she'd put her life savings on Susie.

'Listen up.' Fiona was determined to foster a truce of sorts between the warring parties, and would use whatever methods she had to. It was bad enough they were trapped here with a killer in their midst, to have the group tearing themselves apart would only increase the danger they were all in. 'This fighting and blaming has to stop. In the next room a pregnant woman is probably trying to find a way to tell her two kids their father has been swept away and will most likely have drowned. You're all adults, so why don't you start behaving like it?'

As she looked at each of the room's occupants in turn, Fiona noticed the shame on their faces as they avoided her eyes. Leighton was the only one who returned her gaze. He dropped an approving nod at her as she moved on to Tom.

The shepherd was looking at his feet, the top of his head devoid of all but several hairs. By far the least vocal of the group, there was something reassuring about his steadfast presence.

Whatever happened, Tom remained calm and unhurried. He could be quick when needed, but his measured movements never seemed rushed or panicked.

Like the other men in the room, Tom was on Fiona's suspect list, but he'd maintained his position at the bottom; he'd never allowed himself to be drawn into any of the petty arguments the others seemed to delight in.

Leighton hadn't said a lot either, but there was something about him Fiona didn't trust. Her instincts told her that Leighton was too keen on acting. Whether a trip over the hill, or cutting a channel in the road, he seemed desperate to be out of the house. If Leighton was the killer, the only reasons she could think of for this was that he either planned to escape or claim another victim.

Was that how it was to be? The killer picking them all off one by one until he could escape the valley?

Once the morning came, and with it daylight, there may be a chance of someone getting out and summoning help, but that was a long time off. For the moment it was about staying in a close group so the killer never had a chance to escape or strike again.

Raised voices came from the next room.

Even as Fiona turned her gaze in that direction the door was flung open and Becky waddled into the kitchen as fast as her baby bump allowed. 'If you're not going to look for my Craig, I'll go myself.'

There was a chorus of protestations as people put themselves between Becky and the door. Fiona watched as they argued with Becky. She didn't need to add her own voice to those of the others, there were more than enough of them to deal with a distraught pregnant woman. What she was doing was observing their reactions.

William's face was the perfect portrait of guilt. Fiona could understand that. William would be sure to blame himself on some level. For all he was something of a curmudgeon and was infamously tight-fisted, he was a decent enough man at heart. He'd know he should have cleared the heck; he shouldn't have waited until the waters had risen so high before moving the calves from the low-lying shed.

Leighton and Pierce were reaching for their waterproofs, readying themselves for another foray into the night.

Tom's action was the most telling. He wrapped Becky in his arms and pulled her close as he bent his head so he could whisper in her ear. Fiona had no chance of hearing what he said, but his words hit their mark with Becky. Her legs wobbled and Fiona saw her shoulders tense as she gave Tom a fierce hug.

As Tom led Becky back to the lounge and her children, Leighton and Pierce looked at each other. Fiona reckoned neither wanted to be the first to start stripping off the waterproofs they were in the process of donning, but nor did they appear keen to head out on another search for Craig. William shook his head at them. 'Don't be bothering yourselves. If the poor bugger hadn't got out of the water the last time we looked, he'll still be in it now.'

A thought pricked Fiona's brain and it wasn't one she liked. Tom was taciturn and the epitome of a loner compared to all the others, but there was no mistaking the way Becky clung to him with familiarity. Fiona couldn't help but ask herself if there was a connection between the two of them that they'd kept secret from Craig.

TWENTY-THREE

Fiona took a seat beside Aunt Mary and resisted the urge to deliver a reassuring hug. Aunt Mary was too strong a woman to admit she needed one, and the last thing Fiona wanted was for anyone to think she did herself.

Leighton joined them as the group splintered off into their households. Elsie and William went upstairs to source more clothes and blankets for everyone, and Tom followed Susie and Pierce as they bickered their way to the lounge.

'So, what do you think is gonna happen next?'

The question from Leighton caught Fiona by surprise. She'd been expecting that he'd want to chat, but not that he'd ask her advice. By ending the arguments and preaching what she thought was nothing more than common sense, she'd become the de facto leader of the disparate group.

'Nothing. We'll all stay here until the morning and then, when it's daylight, we can assess our options.'

Leighton's top lip curled into a lazy shrug. 'And if someone else dies or goes missing, what then?'

'What do you mean by that?'

'George is missing and his wife is dead. Craig is missing

presumed dead after being allegedly washed away.' Leighton rasped a hand over his chin. 'When I came here earlier, I saw Tom walking along the lane from George's cottage. He was the last to see Craig. He was the last to get to the farm. He could have been up to anything between me seeing him and him coming into the kitchen here.'

'That's a bit far-fetched, isn't it? You can't seriously think Tom had anything to do with it.' Fiona managed to stop herself from looking Aunt Mary's way. Any kind of eye contact between the two of them would inform Leighton they knew more than they were telling. It was already bad enough that Leighton had jumped from bad luck to suspicions of foul play.

Leighton's testimony about Tom piqued Fiona's interest. He *had* been the last to arrive at the farmhouse, yet Leighton had been there before she and Aunt Mary had returned from their failed attempt to get to Hawick. So what had Tom being doing in that time? Where had he been?

Another, bigger question required an answer. Just how much does Leighton know or suspect?

If he was aware there had been at least one murder, did he think George had also been killed rather than gone missing?

Leighton had also suggested Craig being swept away might not be accidental. That Tom could have caused it. Coupled with the news Tom had arrived at the farm from the direction of the Edwards' cottage, it was easy to suspect Tom was the killer. The time spent between Leighton sighting him and his arrival in the farmhouse kitchen could have given him the chance to knife Mrs Edwards.

The more she considered what Leighton was insinuating, the more she felt she was being played. By casting suspicion onto Tom, Leighton was removing it from himself.

There was a deeper worry for Fiona to consider. If Tom had been along the lane to the Edwards' cottage, why hadn't she seen him? Maybe Leighton was on the level and Tom had concealed himself while she explored the cottage and heaved George on to the bed. But Fiona couldn't picture Tom as the killer. From what she'd seen and heard of him via her regular calls with Aunt Mary, Tom led a solitary life and talked so little it'd be next to impossible to fall out with him. Even the waspish ways of Isla Edwards wouldn't ruffle a man as intrinsically calm as Tom. The rational, unsuspicious part of Fiona's brain believed Tom had been making his way back from a foray on the hills and had joined the road close to the farm, which is where Leighton had spied him.

All the same, if Tom had watched her at the house, he may know what she'd done. That she'd behaved like a copper. If he was the killer and knew or suspected she was a police officer, would he move against her for his own self-preservation?

'You say it's far-fetched, I can tell you, I've heard a lot worse.'

'Go on then, laddie, tell us what you've heard.' Aunt Mary's challenge brought a momentary flash of anger to Leighton's eyes, but it was gone as quick as it arrived.

Susie's voice carried from the lounge as she skewered Pierce with another of her put-downs. While Fiona couldn't make out the words, there was no mistaking the tone.

'There's lots of stories out there of people being bumped off by their neighbours.' Again he shrugged his lip. 'I am really into true crime—books and podcasts, TV shows too—and the one thing most of them stress is that around eighty per cent of murder victims know their killer.'

Fiona filed away the news Leighton liked true crime. Did he see himself as an amateur sleuth? A Mr Marple? Or was he just fascinated by the topic, as so many people were? Either way, Fiona didn't want him espousing theories that may cause greater fissures in the group's harmony. Another point was that if Leighton was the killer, maybe he used the true crime books as research tomes?

'I get what you're saying, but I still think it's far-fetched.' Time to try and learn more about Leighton the person. According to him he was an app developer, but she didn't trust that information, so she would discuss that part of his life in the hope of tripping him up. 'I guess that you do other stuff besides reading true crime. You said earlier you develop apps, what does that entail?'

'Well, it's really just one app at the moment. I built one that allows users to cross-reference trips and events with accommodation and transport providers. In short, say you want to go to a concert in Manchester? My app will be able to give you a single price on your admission ticket, train journey, and a hotel close to the concert venue. I'm currently working on expanding it, so it gives ten hotel price options instead of the current five and breaks your train tickets into segments, if it works out cheaper.'

'That sounds like it'd be very popular. I'm sure it keeps you very busy.' Fiona knew she and her friends would use such an app. She also knew that for the app to collect all the necessary data, it'd have to speak to many other apps and booking systems. Therefore, its creator would have to be a genius-level coder to get the necessary levels of integration required for it to work.

If Leighton was telling the truth, and the pride in his voice suggested he was, he would be by far the smartest person among them.

'I only need to work a couple of hours a day.' The lip shrug made another appearance, causing Fiona to wonder how long it'd be before she was infuriated by his casual dismissals. 'I prefer to paint and write bad poetry.'

The self-deprecation from Leighton about his poetry didn't sit well with Fiona. She always thought people who downplayed their achievements were merely fishing for compliments. Leighton may be insecure about the worth of his poetry, but there was nothing to be gained from showing his doubts.

Another raised voice trundled from the lounge. This time it

was Pierce, no doubt replying to Susie's latest barb. Their fractured relationship might not survive the night. Susie seemed hell-bent on getting Pierce to risk his life, and the statement she'd made about wanting a divorce had been met with no attempt to salvage the marriage. It was their constant arguing that kept Pierce away from the top of Fiona's suspect list. If he was the person who'd killed George and his wife, he'd have been sure to start his killing spree with Susie, as her relentless hectoring and criticism would provide a far stronger motive for murder than anything the inoffensive George may have done.

Try as she might, Fiona couldn't figure out who would want George and his wife dead. The conversation with Aunt Mary had given her snippets of information, but Susie's interruption had prevented her from learning more about Leighton and Tom. Once she knew more about them and their relationship with others in the valley, she might be able to join enough dots so she could identify the killer.

Somewhere in the hidden recesses of Fiona's brain, a synapse fired and she got a picture of what had happened. Under the cover of Storm Odin, the killer had arrived at George and Isla's cottage, perhaps under the guise of offering help. Then when a chance had presented itself, they'd stabbed Isla and pushed her into the waters. George must have seen this unfold and tried to save his wife. The killer would have fought George and then wrapped some twine or wire around his throat. Before the killer could send George's corpse into the river with Isla's, Fiona had arrived, forcing the killer to hide out. What she didn't, and couldn't, know was if she'd been spared because the killer had no motive to kill her, or because they'd not had the right opportunity yet.

'Has anyone even been along to see if George is in his house? Maybe we should go and check. What do you think?'

There it was again. Leighton making a suggestion that would see them leave the relative safety of the farmhouse and head out into the dark. Was he setting up a chance to claim his next victim, or acting from a genuine concern for a good man?

'Their cottage is the lowest lying. The water's got to be chest deep in there by now. I'd say it's far too dangerous for any of you to go there.'

Aunt Mary's words made sense to Fiona, and she appreciated the clever show of support. With her being the one to quash the idea, it shifted the focus away from Fiona. She was backing Fiona without appearing to do so.

'Isn't that all the more reason to go and check if he's there? What if he's trapped in the house by the rising water? He could drown or freeze to death if we don't go.'

Leighton's argument was too good to swat away with a trite answer about danger. George was a lovely man liked by all the valley's occupants. Everyone would want to see him saved.

It was time for an admission. No way could Fiona countenance a rescue attempt that had zero chance of being successful and would only endanger more lives. If there was no risk to life, no killer among their midst, she might go along with the charade, but knowing what she knew, she couldn't allow anyone to go searching George's cottage.

'He's not there. Before Aunt Mary and I left for Hawick, I took a quick run along to see if they were okay. There was no answer at the house.'

'Was their car there? Was the cottage flooded when you were there? Did you go into the house, or was it locked up?'

Damn Leighton and his true crime obsession. He was asking all the right questions. She'd have to be careful how she answered. If he was the killer and he caught her in a lie, the untruth would paint a target on her back. When she had more information, she could use such questions and answers to whittle away at her suspect list until only one name remained, but for now she had to watch every word that came out of her mouth.

'Their car was there and there were a few inches of water in their cottage. The front door wasn't locked and the back one was actually open. I checked the house and George's vegetable garden, but there was no sign of them anywhere. My best guess is that they were standing beside the river watching it rise and one of them fell in, and then when the other tried to help them they were both swept away. I didn't want to believe that. Didn't want to think I was right and that they'd died. I didn't say anything earlier because I wanted to be wrong.'

The lies sat false on Fiona's tongue, but she was watching Leighton's reaction to her words. He appeared to be sorrowful, but her suspicions of him caused her to wonder if he was acting. She'd taken care to create a scenario where George's body may have been carried out of the house by the current.

'How awful for them. I do hope they didn't suffer.'

So did Fiona. Isla had been stabbed and George throttled, but she knew Leighton meant them drowning. She'd had a taste of that herself earlier and it was all she could do not to flash back to the utter dread she'd felt. The urge to yell for help, to thrash against the current. Her head had only been under water for maybe forty seconds at most and she was in decent physical shape, but she'd still emerged with her lungs burning and her mouth gasping for oxygen. That's what would have been the case for Craig too. How long had he been able to hold his breath before he succumbed to unconsciousness and gulped the dirty brown water into his lungs?

'I saw you come back. Why didn't you say?'

The question from Tom startled Fiona. She hadn't heard a sound as he'd returned from the lounge. So he had seen her. Yet he'd kept the information to himself. Why? And, how long had he been there listening in on them?

Fiona kept her tone light; there was nothing to be gained from either man seeing her rattled. 'I guess I should have said, but we all knew George was missing so it didn't really matter.'

'Quick.' Pierce's voice filled the room as he stormed past Tom. 'Becky's gone missing. She asked us to watch the kids while she went for a pee twenty minutes ago. Susie needed the loo and when she went to hurry Becky up, she couldn't find her.'

'Where do you think she is?'

It was a stupid question from Leighton. Becky must have gone to look for Craig because finding him was the only thing on her mind. Now she was out in the storm risking not just her own life, but also the unborn baby she carried, in what was surely a doomed attempt to find her missing husband.

TWENTY-FOUR

'We've got to go and find her.' Fiona pointed at Pierce as she rose and crossed the kitchen to where the waterproofs were stacked. 'Give William a shout, will you?'

The idea of Becky, pregnant and wandering about in the dark, sent shivers through Fiona. All the waterproofs and torches they had were in the kitchen, which meant Becky would have no protection against the elements and, without a torch, she'd be as good as blind in the foul weather.

As they dressed in their waterproofs, Fiona began to plan how she'd like the search for Becky to be conducted. With one of the four men a killer, she preferred they all looked for Becky as a single group. That way there would be plenty of witnesses around to prevent whichever of them was the killer striking again. Fiona got why Becky was searching for Craig, but that didn't stop the tendrils of anger at Becky for forcing them all back outside, into a perilous situation. As quickly as the anger rose inside Fiona, it was battered down by guilt. If she hadn't kept the murders a secret, Becky would have been much more likely to stay in the farmhouse, where she was safe.

The first place to search would be the farmyard, and then

they'd have to check the fields that lay downstream. It would also be worth checking Craig and Becky's home, in case Becky had gone there to look for her husband.

'We've got to check the farm first.' Pierce was on the same page as Fiona. This was good. It meant there was more than one person thinking clearly.

Leighton nodded. 'And their house.'

'If we don't find her in the house or farm, we split up. I'll check from the farm downwards, as I know her best. Tom, you and Pierce take a tractor and the middle section down towards the bridge. Fiona and Leighton can drive down to the bridge and work their way back. If you find her, blare your horn and flash your lights. Take torches and ropes with you and for God's sake, don't take any stupid risks.'

Fiona would have approved of William's logic had she not been paired with Leighton, who was in joint place with Pierce at the top of her list of suspects. If Susie hadn't come through to the kitchen, Fiona would have suggested she accompany Tom or Pierce, but she had, so Fiona had to accept William's pairings. As she zipped up her jacket and stepped towards the door, she vowed to herself that she'd keep Leighton in her sight at all times. No way was she going to turn her back on him, in case he was the killer.

The more she thought about how George and Isla were killed, the more she feared having been watched at their cottage by the killer. Fiona now believed she had a target on her back and she'd have to do everything she could to make sure she never gave the killer a chance to strike against her.

Every face she saw was grim with the anticipation of what they may find. Even little Adele in Elsie's arms wore a stern expression as she rubbed at her eyes with the back of a fist.

Fiona laid a hand on William's shoulder. 'Where do you keep the ropes? If we don't find her at the farm we should each have one, in case, well, you know.'

'They're in the bothy. Tom, you get the ropes.'

'Come on, Fiona, we can check their house while the others look at the farm.'

Fiona stepped aside so Leighton could lead. She wanted him in front of her, where she could see him at all times.

* * *

Leighton set a fast pace as he trudged towards Craig and Becky's house. That was fine by Fiona. The quicker they moved, the better their chances of finding Becky before she was hypothermic or got herself into trouble in the raging floods.

The wind was stronger again than it had been, and where the rain had been pushed to an oblique angle it had flattened further until it was closer to horizontal. Fiona hunched her shoulders and kept her head down as much as she dared without compromising her peripheral vision, but the rain still managed to lash her face with what felt like a dozen hedgehogs per second.

As they neared the house, their torches picked out the murky brown waters of the Scales Burn. Where before the waters had swirled angry knots and formed crested peaks as they rode over submerged obstacles, they now moved in lazy coils, the surface level free of notable undulations. It could only mean one thing: the flow of water coming off the hills was much greater than that escaping under the bridge.

On one hand it would be far less treacherous to anyone caught in its flow, but on the other, it would keep rising until it was so deep it would overflow the road by the bridge. How much of the farm and the buildings in the valley it submerged before it overtopped the road remained to be seen.

They walked down the track to the cluster of houses and cottages until the water was halfway up their wellies.

Leighton's torch picked out the side of Craig and Becky's

house. As it began sweeping towards the door, Fiona arced hers after it. Together they illuminated the front section of the house. It was a grim sight. A large branch protruded through one of the front windows and there was only a foot of the door showing. That meant the water inside would be at least shoulder high, and that was far too deep for anyone to wade through.

Aunt Mary's, Leighton's and Tom's cottages all sat lower than the dairyman's house. The house Pierce and Susie owned sat lower still. They'd all be under at least six feet of water. Everything about them and inside them would be destroyed. Each occupant would have to start over with furnishings, clothes, utensils, crockery. Every last thing they had in their homes would have to be replaced. Fiona's heart went out to them all, but especially Aunt Mary, knowing some of her possessions were family heirlooms that had been passed down several generations.

Fiona blasted her torch at the upstairs window, praying the beam would pick up a human form. It didn't. 'Come on, Leighton. She's not in the house, and even if she was, we couldn't get to her.'

'You're right.'

Neither of them spoke as they made their way back to the farm and the higher ground where the cars were parked.

'I'll drive.'

TWENTY-FIVE

Fiona was content to allow Leighton the masculine illusion of control. Him driving was what she wanted. While he was driving she could concentrate on being vigilant of his actions instead of navigating in near-zero visibility.

Leighton's car was a VW. From the limited amount of the car's styling her torch picked out, Fiona could see it was a high-performance vehicle, although she didn't care enough about cars to recognise the exact model. It was the kind of car that sat an inch from your rear bumper whenever you drove in the fast lane. To Fiona it was a man-child's car, yet Leighton wasn't old enough to have suffered a mid-life crisis, and was too far past his teens to be a boy racer.

The car's engine rumbled into life, its exhaust notes deep enough to thrum menace. For rutted and potholed country roads between here and the A7, Leighton's VW would be as much use as a rail card.

As Leighton drove towards the bridge, Fiona kept one eye on him and another on the road ahead. It was too much to hope that Becky or Craig would appear in the tunnel of illumination the VW's headlights seared through the gloom.

When they reached the bend where the road turned to cross the valley floor and track over the bridge, Leighton turned the car around until it was aimed back at the farm and cut the engine.

The first thing Fiona did when she climbed out was flash her torch down the banking until it found the surface of the water. As best she could judge, the water had eight feet to climb before it overtopped the road.

Leighton appeared at her side causing Fiona to curse to herself. She'd been lax and not tracked his movements. Her back had been to him. Either he wasn't the killer, or if he was, he didn't suspect her of knowing half of what she did, because if either of those ideas was wrong, she'd have been his third victim.

'Better check right over to the bridge.'

Fiona aimed her torch along the road and made sure she stayed a pace behind Leighton. Both of them were scanning the bank and the water as far as their torches would allow. On two occasions Fiona's torch picked out a shape in the water, but when she focused in on it, the shape turned out to be nothing more than a tree that had been uprooted by the surging waters.

At the bridge, Fiona could hear the roar of rushing water. After making sure Leighton was several paces ahead, she crossed to the downstream side of the bridge and cast her torch beam downwards.

Murky brown water frothed and seethed its way downstream, but the river was carrying less than its normal level. The heck must have gathered so much debris a near-impenetrable dam had formed. The suction from the waters that gushed through it would draw more and more debris into the dam further restricting the flow of water.

A look ahead at Leighton saw him leaning over the farm side of the bridge parapet, his torch pointed downwards.

Fiona aimed her torch at the trees on either side of the bank to which the wire rope supporting the heck was tethered. Both stood firm and strong, although each seemed a tad less upright than usual.

If either of those trees were to be pulled over, or the wire rope was to give out due to a strain they'd never before been subjected to, all the pooling waters would cascade under the bridge and decimate everything in their path.

If the telephones worked there would be a way to warn those downstream. Or if there was a path they could take, they'd be able to trek down there and forewarn them. But William had been right earlier when he said there was no way to travel downstream without going over the hills.

As much as Fiona didn't want anyone to leave the valley until she'd identified and arrested the killer, she knew she also held a duty of care to those who lived downstream. It was the mother of all conundrums and one she couldn't answer without more thought.

Leighton walked over, his face red from the constant assault of the driving rain. 'She's not in there. The water is above the top of the bridge's arch. Some's getting through but obviously not enough.'

'I know. I had a look downstream. There's nowhere near enough of a flow to get the water away.' Fiona whipped her torch back towards the farm. 'Come on, let's work our way back.'

Leighton sidled into the lead and Fiona resumed her position two paces behind him. Every now and again a light ahead snuck its way through the downpour, but there were no audible horn sounds to indicate Becky had been found.

After the first hundred yards or so, the fields widened with a higher section that had yet to be engulfed by the rising water. The widening fields meant their torches struggled to pick out the edge of the waters, so they clambered down the bank and over the stone dyke. In the field the short grass was so sodden that every step was an exercise in maintaining balance, the waterlogged earth causing their feet to slip and slide with every forward step.

They fanned out, Leighton taking the left side so his torch could sweep out over the water and cover half the field's width. Fiona was ten feet behind and twenty yards to the right of him, the beam of her torch covering the other half of the field and the bank.

There was no sign of Becky in the first field, so they scrambled over the stone wall and into the next field.

Fiona's hands and face were numb from the spikes of icy rain, but she gritted her teeth and kept trudging forward, her eyes scanning left and right as they followed the arc of her torch.

Ahead and to her left she kept getting glimpses of Leighton doing the same thing. Further ahead the flashes of light from Tom and Pierce were more frequent and held greater intensity as the gap between them narrowed.

At the furthest reaches of Fiona's torch beam another stone wall was picked out. As she moved forward she was able to scan its length, and at the foot of the wall she found Becky.

With a shout to Leighton, Fiona powered into as much of a run as her wellies and the slippery earth allowed. How Becky had managed to get so far while pregnant was a testimony to the woman's drive and desire to hunt for Craig.

Becky sat with her back to the wall, her face crumpled as tears and rain cascaded down her face. Both arms were wrapped around her body and she was trembling from cold, shock, grief or a combination of the three. Becky looked beaten down, exhausted by the emotional and physical toll of her failed mission.

Leighton arrived at the same time Fiona did. He'd already removed his waterproof coat and was draping it over Becky's shoulders as Fiona bent to speak to the distraught woman.

'Becky. It's Fiona. Leighton's here with me. Are you hurt?'

A sob was followed by a nod. No words escaped Becky's mouth, but she pointed at her left ankle. Clad as it was in an UGG boot, whatever injury she'd picked up would only be worsened by Fiona removing the boot and probing with inexperienced fingers.

Fiona raised her gaze upwards and took a blast of the elements in her face. 'Get the others, Leighton. We're going to have to carry her back to the road and your car.'

Leighton did as he was bid and climbed the wall to retrieve Tom and Pierce.

While she waited for them, Fiona asked the question, though she dreaded the answer. 'Becky, is baby okay? You didn't fall on your belly, did you?'

Becky's hands moved until they were cradling her bump and then her head shook. 'Baby's fine. But... Craig. My Craig is gone, isn't he?'

Fiona's training had stressed the importance of not giving false hope, but until Craig's body was found, Becky would never know for sure what became of her husband. 'I'm so sorry, Becky, it looks like he's gone. Maybe by some miracle chance he's got himself out of the water, but you do know that's not likely, don't you?'

'I know. But I also know my Craig. He is so big, so strong. He makes miracles happen.'

The words and the emotion behind them set off a fresh bout of sobs. Fiona could do nothing except cuddle into Becky, to offer support and a little shelter from the driving rain.

TWENTY-SIX

The thunderous rumbling of a tractor engine announced the arrival of the three men. As she heard it approach Fiona raised an arm high enough that her yellow waterproofs would identify their location.

A minute after hearing the engine Tom, Leighton and Pierce were all huddled round Becky, a mixture of relief and concern distorting their rain-soaked features.

Fiona stayed where she was, on one knee at Becky's side. 'Becky, we're going to get you back to the farm, back to your children and some warm clothes. Can you stand on your good leg?'

A nod.

Between them Leighton and Fiona got Becky upright. She clung to them for support, but her head was scouring the darkness as she continued searching for Craig.

Tom removed six of the pointed stones from the top of the wall, creating a more level area. After dropping the last stone at his feet he patted the level part of the wall and then pointed at the tractor.

As much as she liked Tom's idea, Fiona wasn't sure it was

the best course of action. After everything Becky had already endured, being bounced around in a tractor with a broken or sprained ankle would be agony. Much better to get her to Leighton's car.

'Pierce, swap with Leighton. Leighton go get your car and bring it to the road there. Tom, take your tractor as near to the road as you can get it, so Leighton knows where to stop.' Fiona gave Becky's side a gentle squeeze. 'Come on, let's get you back.'

'No. I've gotta find my Craig. He's out here somewhere. He needs me.' Becky squirmed to be free, and as she clutched the woman's top in her hand, Fiona could feel the drenched material oozing water over her fingers.

Fiona knew that one way or another, she had to snap sense into Becky before she further endangered herself and her baby. Once back at the farmhouse, there would have to be a concerted effort to watch over her, in case she tried another stunt like this one.

'That's enough, Becky. Jamie and Adele need you too.' Fiona hated the idea of using tough love on someone in as much physical and emotional pain as Becky, but there were times when dirty deeds had to be done. At Becky's next squirm Fiona allowed the arm over her shoulder to wriggle free so she could look into Becky's face. 'If the worst has happened to Craig, you have to be there for Jamie and Adele. It'll be bad enough them losing their father, but if anything happens to you, they'll lose their mother and baby brother or sister too. Is that what you want?'

'Arrrgh. Ow, ow, ow.' Becky's arm snaked back over Fiona's shoulder as her injured ankle protested the brief period of weight bearing it had to endure. Becky's head nudged Fiona's and she felt a frozen nose pressed above her ear. 'You're a right bitch, you know that?'

Fiona let the insult slide; she took that kind of abuse and

worse every time she donned her uniform. In Becky's position she'd hate the voice of reason too.

It was a slow laborious process getting to the dyke at the bottom of the road; though Fiona and Pierce supported Becky, she could only plant one foot on the ground at any time. On several occasions Becky's hops forward caused her one good leg to slide away from her, thereby transferring all her weight on to Fiona and Pierce. It didn't help that Pierce was a good six inches taller than Fiona, which led to an imbalance to the support they could give.

By the time they'd hopped, trudged and slid their way to the dyke, Tom had positioned the tractor so the bright lights beaming out from the top of its cab were illuminating both the dyke and the banking alongside the road, and Leighton had brought his car along, coming down the slope to meet them.

Tom repeated his trick of removing several of the dyke's capstones and waited at the other side with Leighton.

The bank up to Leighton's car was only a few feet high, but it was steep and layered with long grass that had never been cut nor munched upon. Fiona and Pierce rotated themselves and Becky so she could plant her bum on the level area Tom had cleared.

Becky's resistance to being taken back to the farm had vanished. She was now nothing more than a shrunken, shivering figure looking for direction. Had she possessed any religious leanings, Fiona would have thanked God or another deity that she wasn't in Becky's position.

It was bad enough that Becky had lost her husband, but to lose him needlessly would worsen her torment. The faint hope that he may have somehow escaped the floodwaters would haunt her until the day his body was found.

Fiona knew only too well how unanswered questions about the death of a loved one could plague a grieving heart and mind. She'd never had the closure of knowing who had snuck into her home and knifed both her parents as they were redecorating the spare room. Nor had she known why, as nothing had been stolen. The detectives assigned to the case had offered the theory the killers had broken into the house intending to burgle it and had overreacted when confronted by her father, but Fiona had never believed that idea. The killers hadn't taken a thing from the house, not even a kitchen knife was missing, therefore they'd brought their own. And if they'd brought a weapon, they were anticipating the need to use it. Fiona believed her parents had been targeted for a specific reason. And learning what that reason was, and who the killers were, had fuelled her. The drive to become a detective was everything, and the only thing in the world that could compel her to try to conquer that most debilitating of enemies: the exam room.

For now, for Becky and her children, she had to make sure that, dead or alive, Craig was found. But first, to get Becky up the slope, the four of them would have to work as a team.

Fiona pointed at Leighton and Tom and raised her voice so it could be heard over the rain battering at their waterproofs. 'You two get Becky's arms over your shoulders. Pierce and I will lift her legs. Go slow at first and when her calves are on the wall, we'll jump over and help you get her up the slope. You got that, everyone?'

There were three nods of varying manliness and an uncomprehending blank face from Becky.

They all took their positions. 'On three.'

Fiona did the countdown and hefted Becky over the wall until she was in the designated position.

It wasn't until Fiona went to clamber over the wall too that she realised how much of her reserves she'd used. Her tank was running on fumes. After everything she'd been through in the last few hours, there was little left to give.

Yet she had to give more. Becky needed her to dig in and

there was no way she was going to let her old friend's wife down.

With a scream that was three parts primal, Fiona dug her toes into the bank and pumped her legs. Ahead of her, Tom was forging a path upwards with his typical metronomic stability. Every step he took left a foothold Fiona could appropriate for her own use.

Just when the two men lifting Becky by the arms were cresting the slope, Leighton slipped, his left leg sliding away from him. He went down to a knee, but his sideways movement jerked Becky enough to force Tom to also take a knee.

Fiona felt her own balance faltering and, rather than risk toppling onto Becky, she bent a knee to prevent any greater injury.

Something in Becky was awakened by the rough treatment and she gave a brief thrash as she was dumped onto the bank. Becky's thrash was nothing more than a single convulsion of each limb, but it was enough to drive a knee up into Fiona's descending face.

A starburst replaced the tractor's lights. Instead of the yellow waterproofs Tom wore, all Fiona could see were tears. Her nose was a bulbous explosion of aggrieved nerve endings and her eyes filled with tears as blood ran down the back of her throat.

Fiona dug in. Deep. Deeper than she ever had before. Deeper into reserves she'd never known she'd possessed. 'On three.'

They all lifted on three, and together they crested the bank, and, with an uneven share of grunts and swearwords, they managed to get Becky into the passenger seat of the Golf.

Tom made his way back down the slope to the tractor, as Fiona and Pierce opened the back doors of Leighton's car.

Leighton drove back to the farm at a slow and steady pace. Fiona wanted him to go fast so she could get warmed up, but said nothing as he was doing what he could to make Becky's journey comfortable.

Fiona's thoughts had taken an ugly turn. It had been Leighton who'd slipped causing Becky to be dropped onto the bank. Had the slip been genuine, or was he trying to cause injury to Becky? Such a fall wouldn't do her too much harm, but it might jolt her into labour. If Becky started to give birth, the need for outside help would massively increase, and then Leighton could renew his offers to get help as a ruse to allow him to escape the valley and imprisonment.

What she needed was facts rather than suspicions. But with Isla's diary lost in her car, the only source of information Fiona had left was Aunt Mary and what she could pick up from the others.

As the farmhouse came into view, Fiona could see disaster had struck again. The rising winds had torn a mighty bough off the ancient oak in the garden and dropped it into the roof of the farmhouse.

Aunt Mary was Fiona's first thought, and when she heard Pierce whisper Susie's name in a tone that carried every ounce of the concern she herself felt, she realised that despite the constant barbs Pierce still loved his wife.

TWENTY-SEVEN

William was waiting for them at the kitchen door when they returned. There was relief in his eyes when he saw Becky in the passenger seat, but every part of his body language spoke of the stress he felt.

Fiona was out of the car first and she marched up to William. 'Is everyone okay?'

'Aye. They're all shaken, but okay.' He gave a backward nod. 'They're all in the kitchen now. How's the lass?'

'She's hurt her ankle and she's soaked and frozen. We really need to get her warm and dry as soon as we can.'

Together with the others, Fiona lifted Becky from Leighton's passenger seat and carried her up the path into the farmhouse.

Even by the flickering light of the Tilley lamps, Fiona could see the faces of Aunt Mary, Elsie and Susie were ashen. Adele was snuggled into Elsie's side, her pink cheeks stained with tears and snot trails from where she'd obviously wiped her nose with the back of a hand. Little Jamie stood at Elsie's side, a soft toy cuddled against his chest. Fiona took a wad of kitchen roll and used it to wipe as much of the blood off her face as she could. Her nose throbbed from the impact with Becky's knee, but it had stopped bleeding, so as far as Fiona was concerned all was good.

Jamie ran to his mother, his little face crumpling further with every step, yet he shed no tears. 'Mummy. Mummy, where have you been? A tree fell in the house. Adele cried but I didn't. I was big and brave just like Daddy.'

Becky lifted a hand to cup his head. 'You *are* big and brave like your daddy.' Silent tears ran from Becky's eyes, and her teeth chattered as she spoke, but the sight of her children seemed to lift her mood.

Fiona aided Becky into a seat and helped lift her leg onto a separate chair as William laid a cushion onto it. Fiona looked around the room. 'Does anyone have any first aid training?'

As a police officer, Fiona had training, but she wanted to see how they responded.

Nobody stepped forward. Instead they all slid looks back and forth. Fiona glanced at Elsie. With farming being such a dangerous occupation, Elsie no doubt had to treat all manner of cuts and sprains over the years, but there was no offer from her beyond a brief twitter about bandages.

'Okay, I don't know much, but I know a little. We've got her foot elevated, which helps, but we should bind it as well.' Fiona looked Becky in the eye. 'I'm going to have to take your boot off. I'll be as gentle as I can, but it's going to hurt.'

Becky's answer was the closing of her eyes and the setting of her jaw. The sodden UGG boot clung to Becky's foot and ankle as Fiona teased it free. There were no sounds from Becky, who was probably being stoical for the sake of her kids, but the twisting of her face showed the agony Fiona was inflicting.

'Here.' Elsie dumped a cardboard box on the table beside Fiona. The box was filled with plasters, bandages and dressings of various sizes.

Fiona's fingers were numb as she selected a bandage and

began to wind it around Becky's ankle. With a muted sense of touch she almost dropped the bandage on several occasions, but after a couple of minutes she had Becky's ankle strapped tight enough to offer compression, but not so tight as to restrict the blood flow.

That was only the first part of the treatment Becky needed.

'Elsie, have you more dry clothes for Becky? Some towels?' Fiona turned her head to Susie and Aunt Mary. 'Susie, can you take the kids? Aunt Mary, sort out a cuppa or some soup for Becky, please. We need to get her warmed up.'

All three women sprang into action, but William blocked Elsie from going through to the stairs.

'We need to check out the damage before anyone goes upstairs.'

With her focus on looking after Becky, it had slipped Fiona's mind about the tree that had fallen onto the house. William was right. Who knew what damage the tree had done and whether or not it was poised to do more?

'You stay there, Elsie. I'll go and see what the craic is. I'll get some towels and clothes for Becky as well.'

Pierce stepped forward. 'I'll come too if you want. When I started out, I made my money doing up distressed properties, so I know what to look for safety-wise.'

The olive branch from Pierce set Fiona's suspicions jangling. He and William had been at loggerheads all night, yet here he was offering to help. The idea of parties of two went against Fiona's instincts, and with there being the potential for danger when checking out the damage caused by the fallen tree, it would be easy for Pierce to engineer a way to harm or kill William that looked like an accident.

'I'll come too.' Fiona pointed at the waterproofs that still clad her body. 'I'm still dressed for the weather and I'm sure Becky would rather a woman got her some dry clothes.'

William gave a sharp nod. 'That makes sense.'

It didn't escape Fiona's notice that Tom was kneeling beside Becky, her left hand in his right and his thumb stroking her knuckles.

'What if it's not safe? What do we do then?' Susie had the grace to keep her tone light, as she had Adele on her knee and Jamie at her side, but there was no mistaking the gravity of her expression.

Fiona looked at William and saw he had no answer. 'We either move to a shed that's above the water line, or we get in our cars. They're all topside of the road so there's no fear of them getting caught in the floods.'

Susie didn't look happy at the answer, but that wasn't a surprise. The house wasn't very warm now, but it would be a lot warmer and more comfortable than a shed or car.

Becky's teeth started to chatter again, so Fiona pointed at the door leading to the lounge and staircase. 'Come on, let's get this done. Tom, can you go out and take a look at the tree? If it's likely to blow over, let us know at once.'

'Wait. Before we go up there, you need to listen to me.' Pierce's tone was soft, but serious. 'We need to be quiet when we're up there. Gentle too. There's no saying what's hanging ready to drop. We don't want any unnecessary vibrations to carry through the house.'

TWENTY-EIGHT

The upstairs of the farmhouse was a place Fiona had never been. She'd expected it to be dated, but not by this much. The wallpaper was either a sixties style, or painted woodchip. Underneath her feet, the carpet was worn to the point of threadbare. Fiona could tell it had once been a quality weave, but she'd bet a week's wage it was at least as old as she was.

Pierce's warning was uppermost in Fiona's mind as she padded after William, one of the Tilley lamps in her hand. A shelving rack displayed several ornate thimbles, the greater part of their number now strewn on the carpet with at least three broken. William bent and used a careful hand to sweep them aside, his head shaking as he straightened. It was a rare show of tenderness from the gruff farmer and Fiona expected the collection of thimbles belonged to Elsie, or perhaps William's late mother.

Ahead of them a bedroom door swayed back and forth in the wind that was now coursing into the farmhouse through the damaged roof. Fiona could hear water dripping and there was the occasional clatter as a slate tumbled down the roof.

William advanced through the doorway in a series of half

steps, his torch picking out the great branch that had speared through the roof and into the bed. If anyone had been asleep in that bed, they would have been impaled.

When William's torch examined what was left of the ceiling, it picked out a mess of broken timber. Fiona had no idea whether the timbers were joists, struts or spars, but she did know that it looked as if it could collapse at any time. Most of the ceiling had already fallen to the floor, and the parts that hadn't were hanging from the timbers of the ceiling. Water cascaded in at the top where it ran down the undamaged roof, as well as that blown in by the wind. Everything in the room would be ruined and very soon the water damage would extend down into the room below.

A soft bump at Fiona's back informed her Pierce wanted to join them in the bedroom, so she pressed her back against the wall and allowed him space to complete his assessment.

Pierce's torch was focused on the roofing timbers, not the branch or the remains of the ceiling. The beam carried along every exposed member as he worked out the extent of the damage.

'This your bedroom, William?'

'Aye. What about it?' William turned to look at Pierce, his hands balling into fists and his tone defensive.

Pierce's long arm gestured at the bedside table, where a pair of photo frames were knocked flat. 'Do you want me to get those for you? They're by your bed so they must be important to you or Elsie.'

'Please.'

Fiona could hear the grudge in William's tone, and had a little suspicion Pierce had read his anger and changed what he was going to say about their dated home.

As Pierce skirted the fallen branch, a touch on her arm made Fiona look to William, to find his torch was on a wardrobe at the far side of the room. Fiona cast her torch at the ceiling above the wardrobe and didn't like what it showed. A large section of plaster hung from a pair of thin wooden strips that looked as if they could give way at any time.

Fiona swapped the Tilley lamp for William's torch and moved towards the wardrobe. Beneath Fiona's feet the fallen parts of the ceiling were strewn, uneven hazards with exposed nails ready to pierce her foot, or simply send her sprawling. What should have been three easy steps ended as a half dozen shuffles. With the torch gripped between her thighs Fiona reached up for the hanging section of ceiling. Either she'd be able to pull it free and remove the danger, or determine if it was secure that she could step beneath it. As soon as Fiona's hands made contact, tiny pieces of bone-dry plaster tumbled onto her face and into her eyes. She ducked her head forward, allowing the tears that were forming to wash the offensive plaster away.

A section of ceiling flopped over in Fiona's hands and as it came down thumped into her leg, shattering into pieces that cascaded onto her foot.

Fiona dropped the pieces she still held onto the pile at her feet and opened the wardrobe. It was filled with heavy sweaters, thick shirts and pairs of jeans. A set of small drawers at the left revealed socks and women's underwear. Fiona didn't waste time on ceremony; she grabbed a few of everything until she could carry no more.

Pierce used his torch to illuminate her way out of the bedroom and back down the stairs. At their heels, William followed, his arms laden with towels taken from a closet.

When they returned to the kitchen and had all the clothes on the table, Fiona left Aunt Mary and Elsie to help Becky change into dry clothes, while she followed the others to the lounge.

Every eye was on Pierce, as he was the most experienced builder among them. What he had to say would determine whether or not they'd be safe in the house.

'Well?' Of course, it was Susie who was pushing for an answer.

'This part of the roof is buggered, but the rest of it looks sound. The branch fell between the trusses, but it's smashed two purlins and all the battens and counter battens.'

Having seen the innards of the roof, Fiona worked out the battens and counter battens must be the smaller timbers that ran up and down the purlins and then horizontally so slates could be fixed to them. But all that mattered was that the whole roof wasn't going to fall in on them.

'So it's safe?'

'Yes and no.' Pierce faced William as he answered Susie's question. 'There's enough of a hole in the roof for the wind to really get in. It's already started to strip some slates off and I'm sure that if it stays as strong as it is now, it'll strip the rest of the roof off. There's also the tree to consider. More of that could easily come crashing into the house. From what I could see, the part that came through the roof has broken off and is half in the bedroom and half sticking out of the roof.'

'The tree's solid.' Leighton's tone was assured. 'I went with Tom and it looks like a major part of the tree was rotten and it snapped off in the wind. Tom said there's not enough branches left on the tree for it to topple.'

Fiona caught the look that passed between William and Tom. The silent accusation on Tom's face said everything she needed to hear. Like the clogged heck, it appeared William had been warned about the dangers of the rotting section of tree, but had chosen not to do anything about it. Was it his legendary tightness again? Or had he simply too much to do and too little time to do it?

And what was behind the expression on Tom's face? Was it censure? Or regret for not being more insistent?

'What are you saying, Pierce? Is this house safe or not? Can you do a quick fix to make it safe?'

Fiona's eyes were rolling before Susie had even finished her question. Did she really expect her husband to scale a ladder and fix a broken roof in this weather? To Fiona it seemed Susie was determined to have her husband killed or seriously hurt just to make her feel better.

'If you've nowt sensible to say, shut up.' William's nostrils flared as he spoke, and while Fiona agreed with his sentiment, the belittling tone he used was likely to send Susie off on one again.

'Susie's not too far wrong. We can't fix it, but there may be a way we can sheet it over.' Pierce looked at William. 'Do you have a chainsaw, a tarpaulin and some heavy weights to tie the tarpaulin down?'

'We've got a tarpaulin that'll be big enough to cover this part of the roof, plenty of rope to reach to the ground so it can be tied off, and a chainsaw. You could use the ploughs at the front of the house to tie it down with.'

'And the fallen branch at the back.' Leighton jumped into the conversation. 'It'll be better than any weight.'

Tom was already heading for the door when Leighton joined him.

TWENTY-NINE

The buzz of the chainsaw seemed extra loud in the house as William cut away the branch that had pierced his roof. Fiona held the Tilley lamp to give him some light to work by. Becky, Elsie and the kids were in the kitchen, while the other men were trooping in with supplies for the fix.

Aunt Mary and Susie stood in darkness at the far end of the hallway. They were both keen to help, but there wasn't anything for them to do yet.

The smell of fresh cut timber mixed with petrol fumes filled the air as the chainsaw spat a stream of sawdust across the room.

So far William had been trimming off the smaller branches from the great bough, but he was now cutting at the bough itself. Fiona could see the cut opening up as the weight of the branch still outside sagged towards the ground.

The next part of their task was hardest. With the chainsaw set in a corner, William rolled the remains of the bough until it was nestled against a wall.

Fiona helped him drag the bed to the centre of the room, then place a chair onto the bed. As soon as it was there William clambered on top of it and started pulling at the loose pieces of timber the branch had smashed. It took him ten minutes to clear away a sufficient amount of the debris that he'd exposed, opening enough of the hole for them to feed the tarpaulin through.

Despite William's best efforts to reach up, his hands barely made contact with the lower part of the hole. The upper part was a good eighteen inches from his fingertips so he pointed at Pierce. 'You're the tallest. You'll have to do what's needed in here. Mary and Susie can help you. The others will need to be outside with me.'

Tom and Leighton hefted the heavy tarpaulin into the bedroom. It was old and stained and stank of damp, but it looked to be intact enough to stop the wind and rain entering the house. Tom fussed with the tarpaulin until it was set in a particular way.

'Here.' Tom handed Pierce a series of ropes to which he'd tied heavy tools. The ropes were of different colours and when Fiona looked more closely, she saw there were three spanners and three hammers.

'Spanners to the front of the house. Hammers to the back. Red, green, blue.' As Tom said the colours he indicated the gable of the house, the centre of the hole and the far side.

Tom's plan was a good one.

'Good stuff.' Pierce clambered onto the bed and reached up, his hands going through the hole but only by a few inches. 'Susie. Grab that chair and come up here to hold it steady.'

Susie did as she was told without speaking or pulling a face, placing the chair onto the mattress for her husband to step onto. This was Pierce's domain and it was obvious that, when he was working, she would always respect his skills and superior knowledge of the task at hand. It was an insight into how their marriage had survived as long as it had.

The chair from Elsie's dressing table was a sturdy affair, but on the unstable mattress it threatened to pitch Pierce first one way and then the other whenever he shifted his weight. Susie's knuckles on the chair back turned white as she fought to keep it steady enough that Pierce wasn't toppled to the floor.

'First rope, please.'

Tom lifted the red rope with the spanner on it and handed it to Pierce with just enough rope left that it wasn't tugging at the tarpaulin. As Pierce lifted the rope through the hole, Fiona ducked out of the room, calling to Aunt Mary as she went.

Fiona understood the power shift in the room. No longer were the group looking to her or William to lead or make suggestions. Now it was about Pierce's experience coupled with Tom's practicality. Common sense told Fiona everyone was sensible enough to leave things to those who knew best, but she was on high alert in case one of the group said something that didn't gel with what she knew, or they did something that endangered another.

Instead of going downstairs, Fiona made her way to a front bedroom. It was filled with junk and she had to pick and fight her way to the front window.

'Stay in the doorway, Aunt Mary. You're my contact with the others.'

The window slid up with relative ease. Rather than lean out and risk being hit by one of the spanners, Fiona aimed her torch through the gap and swung its beam from side to side.

A vertical red strand flapped in the rain. When Fiona traced down it, she saw a spanner lying atop one of the horse-drawn ploughs decorating the garden.

'Tell them red is good.'

Aunt Mary hadn't finished relaying the message when a green rope arced into the garden.

'Green is good.'

The next thing Fiona knew, the window was smashing in front of her eyes. Instinct made her wheel away, eyes screwing shut. When she'd got her initial fright and reaction under control, she turned back to the window. The spanner on the blue rope hung in front of it. As the farmhouse windows were sliding sash, the lower portion Fiona had raised acted as a barrier to the spray of broken glass from the upper window.

Fiona could easily work out what had gone wrong. The third spanner hadn't travelled as far as the others, and when it reached the end of its trajectory, its rope pivoted on the gutter, slamming the spanner into the window.

The question was, had Pierce thrown the last spanner less far on purpose, in the hope of injuring her? It was an unknown, but because she was passing information back to him, he'd be sure to have worked out that she was by a window. For now there was no way of knowing if it was a deliberate act, or a simple mistake. More than anything, it made Fiona realise that regardless of how dangerous Storm Odin might be, the greatest threat to them all was the unidentified killer in their midst. There had been that moment when Pierce had sought to retrieve a sentimental item for William and Elsie; on the surface it could have been done out of kindness, but it could also be the act of a man desperate to hide his true intentions.

The spanner was nestled against the broken glass, but that didn't deter Fiona. She lowered the inner window back to its original place and used her torch to knock out any loose pieces of glass. She took hold of the rope and gave it a gentle tug. It moved but only a foot or so until it seemed to jam.

The gain of a foot was all Fiona needed; the spanner now hung against the lower portion of the window. She slid it back up and wrapped both hands around the spanner.

As she pulled down whatever had jammed the rope surrendered its grip and she'd soon hauled enough rope down that the spanner was on the ground.

Aunt Mary was still reporting what had happened as Fiona closed the window and drew the curtains. The curtains wouldn't stop either the wind or rain from coming in, but they'd at least lessen its reach into the room.

Back in the master bedroom, Tom was handing Pierce the other ropes for the back of the house. These throws would be easy as the hole was no more than six feet from the wall and there was no ridge to clear with the hammers.

By the flickering light provided by the Tilley lamps, there was no chance to read expressions with any surety, but Fiona could tell the tension in the room came more from their collective animosity to each other than the situation they were facing together.

Once the hammers were all thrown, William clapped his hands together. 'Right, listen up. Leighton you stay here and help the ladies pass the tarp to Pierce. As soon as he's got it through the hole, get yourself to the back of the house. The wind's coming from that direction.' William pointed at the corner of the room where the outside wall met the gable. 'So it's that side we'll need to do first. Tom, you'll be with me. Fiona, you go to the front of the house. The wind'll push the tarp your way, so it'll be our job to stop it. Mary, show me your torch at the window when Pierce starts to feed the tarp out. We'll be watching for it at the back.' William gave a stern look at Leighton and Fiona. 'Whatever you do, don't wrap the rope round your hands. If the wind gets it, you'll be going where it's going.'

Leighton snapped a salute William's way. 'Sir, yes, sir.'

'Really?' Aunt Mary's tone was strong enough to put shame onto Leighton's face. 'You're taking the mickey when he's outlining a plan? How old are you?'

Fiona sent a hard look at Leighton.

'Never mind that, let's just get on with it before the wind gets under the roof.'

With his nod sent Tom's way, William headed for the door. Fiona followed.

The sooner she got the front ropes tied off on the ancient ploughs, the better. With all the tensions starting to spill over, Fiona wanted to do her part as quickly as she could, because it hadn't escaped her notice that William's plan would isolate her at the front of the house.

Either he was innocent and unaware of George and Isla's murders, or he had killed them and was engineering a chance to get her alone.

THIRTY

The first thing Fiona noticed as she stepped out of the house was the new intensity with which the wind was blowing. Where before it had been growing in strength with sporadic gusts showings its true intent, it was now a steady mass, pressing against her as it flung icy raindrops sideways. The cuffs and collar of Fiona's jacket were no barrier to the driving rain. Unless she kept her back to the wind, the jacket's hood was pulled off her head.

One by one Fiona tied the ropes off on the ancient ploughs. Each time she had to grip her torch between her knees to free up both hands. The knots she tied weren't pretty, but they were secure. She'd made sure to arrange the ropes in the right order. Red at the gable end, then green and finally blue.

As soon as Pierce fed the tarpaulin out, she'd haul each rope in turn and tie it off in a more final position.

With the last rope tied off, Fiona set her back to the wind and her eyes to the window. With the branch punching through the roof and all the work and chaos it had created, she'd not had a chance to think any further about the killer's identity. She had a moment now, but she was too busy playing her part while also scanning for any threats that may come her way. By her best reckoning, one of the four men who'd be engaged in securing the tarpaulin with her was the killer, and she was isolated at the front of the house.

A part of Fiona wondered if this was a sensible use of their energies. Rather than push themselves to try and save the farmhouse, would they not have been better off using the last of their strength to decamp to a barn or their cars?

Fiona knew the answer before she'd finished asking herself the question. Even Susie hadn't suggested abandoning the house and she was as selfish as they came. If not for themselves, the others had to try and protect Becky. She needed the warm dry environment the farmhouse provided. After the soaking she'd had and the time she'd been exposed she was sure to be suffering, possibly from hypothermia. For Becky to spend the night in a freezing, draughty barn, or a car, could be the difference for her baby, if not Becky as well.

Fiona saw a shape emerge from the kitchen door and run past her. A second taller shape followed. Leighton and Pierce were now also outside and, even though she saw them run past her and round the corner of the house together, she gave a shudder of dread at the thought of either of them coming for her.

The red rope in front of Fiona was whipping back and forth so she dropped her torch and grabbed the rope tight. It threatened to pull her from side to side until she began to haul on it. Hand over hand she reeled the rope in. When she had it tight against the tarpaulin, she tied it off with a rudimentary knot and moved onto the green rope.

As she dragged the green rope down, Fiona found herself without the handles to aid her efforts, so she looped the rope through the plough's metallic frame and hauled away until she could get no more purchase.

The blue rope was a different matter. With a series of hefty pulls she managed to loop more and more twists of the rope around the handle of an aged sharpening wheel until she could reel no more in.

With that done Fiona picked up her torch and set off to help the others at the back of the house. Upon rounding the corner, a quick sweep of her torch found William on the ground beside the red rope, both Tom and Pierce on the green, and Leighton wrestling against the blue one.

All four men were locked in a battle against the tug of the ropes. William and Leighton were hanging on but were unable to do anything beyond using their combined weight to anchor the tarpaulin. On the central rope, Tom and Pierce were having even less success, as they were actively being dragged by the rope until they could regain their footing and haul it back.

Rather than join the men in hauling on the ropes, Fiona located the end of the red rope and fed it under the splintered bough that had been riven from the tree to crash into the house. William couldn't do anything except hang on, and there was little light to see anything as everyone had dropped their torches so they had two hands free to grapple the ropes.

With the rope fed under as far as she could reach, Fiona clambered over the bough and pulled the rope through. Twice more she repeated this move until she was confident the friction of the rope on the bough would match William's efforts. Next she brought the rope over the bough, fed it round and back under the bough, and tied it off against itself.

William put his mouth to Fiona's ear, his breath a series of warm heavy pants, but when his head bumped hers, she felt the sticky kiss of a bleeding wound. 'You help Leighton. I'll sort the middle.'

Fiona moved on, the dropped torches offering almost enough light to guide her passage. Twice she encountered parts of the fallen tree. The first time left her with a stubbed toe, the second a barked shin.

THIRTY-ONE

Fiona limped to Leighton's side and groped around for the end of the rope. As soon as she'd located it, she felt it being hauled forward as one of the periodic gusts gripped the tarpaulin. She dug in and added her own weight and strength to Leighton's efforts.

It was no good. They were both dragged forward and she heard Leighton yelping in pain. A hefty gust pressed her against Leighton, and the next thing she knew he was being lifted from the ground. She clung to his jacket, letting her knees sag to add her full bodyweight.

A pained yowl fled Leighton's mouth only to be followed by a stream of profanities, each more vicious and derogatory than the last. Fiona imagined the curses were aimed at the storm and the rope, but she also caught the word bitch and woman. It was always the same; a person's true nature would be shown in moments of adversity.

Fiona didn't know if the gust subsided or her efforts to save Leighton worked, but he dropped back to earth with swear-words still tumbling from his lips.

Let him swear if that's what he wanted to do. She grabbed

the rope at Leighton's feet and crawled away from the house, her hand waving in the darkness as she sought out the branch.

As soon as Fiona's hand collided with the fallen bough, she traced it downwards ready to feed the rope under it. The further down her hand went, the less confident she became. Not only was her spatial awareness telling her she'd soon touch the ground, but the bough was showing no signs of curving away from her.

Numbed fingers collided with wispy grass and then Mother Earth. Not only was this part of the bough tight against the ground, but it also felt to Fiona as if it had embedded itself in the rain-softened lawn.

Fiona changed tactics as the rope was pulled through her fingers. Unable to feed the rope under the entire bough, she was now searching for a smaller branch protruding from the main bough. She found one on the far side. It was maybe six inches in diameter and it had been broken off a foot from the main bough. Perfect.

Twice Fiona wound the rope around the stumpy branch. The moss on the branch and the sodden rope didn't create much friction, but when she pulled on the rope she could reel in the slack created by Leighton's position four feet away.

Light bled from the farmhouse as someone inside had the good sense to bring a Tilley lamp to the window. There wasn't a lot of light, but enough that Fiona could see Leighton had ignored William's warning about wrapping the rope around his hand. No wonder he was being jerked off his feet. Or that he was swearing so much. The rope would feel like a vice as it tightened around his hand.

Another gust lifted Leighton from his feet, but Fiona hung tight, her strength more than enough to halt the slide of the rope around the stumpy branch. She prevented the latest gust from lifting Leighton several feet in the air, but his feet were clear of the ground for a few seconds and she could see him squirming around in agony.

When he dropped back to earth, he thrashed at the rope until his hand was clear then cradled the hand into his body.

Fiona wasted no time. She overhanded the rope to draw in as much of it as she could before another gust came. Whenever she felt the pull against her increase, she stopped pulling and held tight. Mossy and slick as it was, the stumpy branch offered enough resistance that she was able to reel the rope tighter and tighter.

Pierce's lanky figure loped over, his hands grasping the rope and hauling downwards to aid her efforts.

When they could get no further tension onto the blue rope, Fiona tied it off, and clambered over the main bough to approach Leighton.

'Come on. Let's get inside and get warm.'

Leighton flashed a look Fiona's way. She expected him to be grateful for the help. To feel shame at being caught disobeying a warning and having someone aid him. That would have been understandable. The fury in the look he gave her wasn't.

And then the look changed back to Leighton's normal passive face as he accepted the hand she offered to help him to his feet. 'Thanks.'

Before Fiona had a chance to process the slipping of Leighton's mask, as she stooped to pick up a torch, the other men joined them, each of their faces showing a different tableau. Tom's was pensive as he checked the knot Fiona had tied, while Pierce wore the expression of a man who'd rather be anywhere else. But William's face was thunderous as he fronted up to Leighton and Pierce.

'Which one of you ungrateful buggers was it?'

'Was what?' In the half-light it was tough to read Pierce's expression, but there was no mistaking the bewilderment in his tone.

'As you and the soft lad went by, one of you thumped me in the back, sending me flying.' A finger pointed at the wound above his eye. 'I was damn near knocked out when I hit the path edging.'

'It wasn't me.' Pierce gestured at where Leighton was still cradling his hand. 'Ask him, and before you say another word, let me tell you this, if I had hit you, you wouldn't have got back up so fucking quick.'

Both of William's hands slammed into Pierce's chest, driving him back. Before the fight could properly start, Fiona got between the two men and planted a hand on each of their chests to keep them apart. 'That's enough. William, I kicked a branch when I passed you. It could be that was what thumped your back. Pierce, calm the hell down, right now, you need William's help a damn sight more than he needs yours.'

Both men glared at each other, their chests heaving. It was clear to Fiona neither wanted to be the first to back down, so she aimed her torch at where William claimed to have been thumped, illuminating a short branch that lay on the ground. 'See? Now let's get out of this rain.'

Fiona made sure she was the last in the group as they trudged back to the house. Her claim about the branch could be correct, but she didn't think so. To her knowledge, no other branches had rained on them while they were grappling with the ropes holding the tarpaulin, and with Pierce and Leighton occupying the top spots on her list of suspects, she was wondering if one of them had deliberately shoved William, in the hope of causing enough injury to leave him incapacitated.

THIRTY-TWO

The farmhouse kitchen was crowded to the point where personal space was a thing of the past. Pierce, William and Tom had dragged a mattress from the spare bedroom and laid it on the floor for Becky and her kids. Becky was swaddled in blankets and a duvet while her kids nestled in against her. Adele was asleep, thumb in mouth with fingers splayed across her cheek. Jamie was at Becky's other side, his eyes closing and re-opening as he fought sleep. Aunt Mary was busying herself winding bandages around Leighton's injured hand. His face was a picture of stoicism interspersed with agonised winces.

Above them Fiona could hear the tarpaulin flap in the wind. Before they'd come back into the house, they'd all cast their torches upwards to check out the job they'd done of covering the roof. It had been a makeshift fix and it was a long way from perfect, but it did stop the worst of the wind and rain from getting into the house. With luck it would hold until the storm had passed and they'd be able to escape the Scales Valley.

Like the men who'd also been outside, Fiona was standing as close as she could get to the Aga, absorbing the last of its heat.

Susie was with them, having made no bones about the way she'd placed herself between Fiona and Pierce.

'Does anyone want anything to eat? We've got cereal, biscuits, scones, and crackers and cheese.'

It was typical of Elsie to try and feed them. Like so many farmers' wives of her generation, she was known for being a feeder. Anyone in their house at a mealtime would have a plate of food offered to them. Whether a visiting rep, family friend or a contractor helping with a harvest, food would always be pushed their way in large quantities.

Most shook their heads at Elsie's offer, but Fiona felt the growl of her stomach. Whatever was to come, she'd need to keep her strength up, and getting some food into Becky wouldn't be a bad idea.

'I'd love some cheese and crackers, thanks Elsie.'

As Elsie rose to her feet, William walked towards the door leading to the stairs and the lounge.

Predictably, the cheese Elsie cut was doorstop thick and the crackers slathered with enough butter to have a pathologist reaching for his artery scraper. Being a farmer's wife, Elsie didn't make enough for just those who'd asked for some, she made enough to heap a plate high.

When William returned he held a bottle of Grouse and a stack of tumblers.

A nip of whisky might be his nightly routine, but the last thing Fiona wanted was for the bottle to be shared round. Alcohol was disinhibitory, and with a killer among their midst there was no way she wanted anyone's inhibitions lowered. While a couple of whiskies may cause the killer to say or do something that revealed their identity, it may also make them more confident about killing again. It could also cause someone to do or say something to make them a target of the killer.

The same also counted for the strife rending the group apart. Other than William or Craig, Fiona wouldn't have chosen to spend any time with the others beyond a neighbourly greeting. Susie and Pierce had issues of their own, with Susie seeming hell-bent on falling out with everyone except Becky and the kids. Leighton was a strange character, and the flash of anger he'd shown outside sat uneasily on Fiona's mind. She was trying to work out whether it was a product of the pain he'd felt, or a reflection of an inner anger that he usually kept hidden.

Elsie was doing the rounds with her platter of crackers. 'Pierce?'

'No thanks. I'm lactose intolerant.'

William's snort was audible across the room. 'You whisky intolerant?'

'No.'

'Thought not.'

William followed his wife handing out tumblers of whisky. True to his thrifty nature, there was only a single finger to each measure.

Fiona refused his offer. Whisky was a drink to be savoured in a relaxed environment, and as much as it might warm her in the taking, it would also thin her blood, plus she had to keep all of her faculties sharp. Tonight wasn't finished by a long way; she had to unmask the killer. When the endless questions came from detectives about this night, she wanted to be clear of memory and also unimpeachable from blame. When it came out that as a cop hunting a killer, she'd drunk whisky from a potential, if unlikely, suspect, her credibility would be shot, and the already long odds of her ever making detective would further lengthen.

The cracker crunched in Fiona's mouth as she worked over a few points. George and Isla had been killed for a reason that was as yet unknown to her. Craig's death could have been an accident or a third murder. That too was unknown. What she did know was that since Craig's disappearance into the waters of the Scales Burn, there had been no confirmed attempts to harm anyone else, although she was still suspicious about whether someone had thumped William in the back.

This gave Fiona two options: either the killer had completed his objective with the murders of George and his wife, and Craig's plight was an unfortunate accident, or Craig had seen something that meant the killer had to silence him.

A third idea plucked at Fiona's brain and, even as she was thinking it, she could feel her stomach coil in disgust at the thought.

What if Craig's determination to risk his own life to save the calves stemmed from something other than a love of animals, a duty of care to his stock? What if it was fuelled by guilt? Craig was more than big enough and strong enough to strangle poor George. And like everyone who worked on a farm, there would always be a folding knife in his pocket. If Craig was the killer it explained why nobody else had been harmed since his disappearance.

This reasoning led to a new set of thoughts. Each less palatable than the previous. To follow them Fiona tried to put herself in Craig's shoes. First of all, if Craig was the killer, he'd want to escape the confines of the valley before he was caught. If it had been a spur of the moment act, he'd fear forensic evidence once the adrenaline rush of the kill subsided. Perhaps he'd seen Fiona's return from the Edwards' cottage. If so, he'd fear being caught more than ever. He'd be jailed, losing his wife and children.

This was where Fiona hit a roadblock, as there was little for Craig himself to gain from the rescue of the calves other than a sense of having done the right thing. Fiona's later teen years had been spent hanging out with Craig when he wasn't working or playing rugby. Like all farmers and farmworkers, he mourned an animal's passing, but in an abstract way, as death was a part of farming life, and livestock was never mourned the way a pet would be. This truism coupled with the fact he had a pregnant wife and two young children counting on him made it less and less probable he'd take such a risk, unless fuelled by something else.

It could have been guilt, but the more Fiona thought about it, the more she was zeroing in on another theory. What if Craig had backed his mighty strength and had faked the fall into the Scales Burn? If that was the case he could have pulled himself out of the water a few yards upstream of the calf shed and nobody else would have known.

Once free of the water, he'd be able to make his escape over the hills. That was a long and dangerous trek, but to a man desperate to evade capture for murder, such a route would seem like a yellow brick lifeline.

Fiona kept her final cracker in her hand rather than feed it into her mouth. The last one she'd eaten had tasted bitter as her thoughts led her down a path of betrayal. She'd known Craig for nigh on twenty years and he was someone she'd always thought of as a good person. Yes, he was rough and ready. Yes, every third word from his mouth was a swearword, but, in essence, at the very heart of his being, Craig was kind and caring. He'd do someone a good turn rather than a bad one, and to think of him as a callous killer who'd abandon the family he adored was to insult his memory.

Yet, in detective work, there was no room for feelings. It was all about the evidence, and the theory she had stacked up in terms of evidence. There was no evidence to prove Craig's death, only his disappearance. Likewise, there was no evidence indicating he'd killed George and Isla Edwards, but the halting of murders after his disappearance pointed its own finger.

What she didn't have in her reasoning was a motive. Unless, she thought, the closeness between Tom and Becky was something Isla had noticed. It would be typical of Isla Edwards to delight in goading Craig about how close his wife was to another man. Craig had a fiery temper and was hugely possessive about his wife, but even then, it was a stretch to see him resorting to murder in the face of Isla's taunts.

To counter all these unpalatable suspicions, Fiona turned her mind to the others in the kitchen with her. Each had their own issues with others. All were neighbours, but none were neighbourly. According to Aunt Mary, Leighton had a bad habit of parking his car in a way that made access to the field behind his cottage awkward. Pierce and Susie had an agenda with the land they'd bought from William, and William himself was struggling to keep the farm profitable as his fitness decreased with age.

William drained his whisky and lifted his jacket from the pile by the back door. 'I'm away to check the water levels.'

And with that brief statement, he was gone.

Aunt Mary rose to her feet. 'Elsie, please may I use your bathroom?'

'Use the bathroom. Of course.'

Fiona saw an opportunity and seized it. 'I'll go too if that's okay?'

'That's okay.'

Elsie's repeating of other people's words was endearing in small doses, but the more time she spent in the woman's company, the more Fiona found herself with gritted teeth. She'd never say anything, it was her hang up, but there was only so much empathy her fractured nerves could give in a short period of time. Fiona was hunting a killer; since five o'clock she'd been soaked by icy water numerous times, almost killed twice, and it wasn't yet midnight.

Everyone else would have their own petty annoyances. Susie was strung out and even the calmer members of the group would be distraught about the destruction of their homes and possessions.

Fiona made sure she led the way to the bathroom. As much

as she was guarding Aunt Mary from danger, she was also engineering a chance to finish picking her aunt's brains.

With Aunt Mary in the bathroom holding their only torch, Fiona listened to the flapping of the tarpaulin. Every few seconds there would be a snapping sound as its fabric whip-cracked under the influence of the wind. At first the sound had been worrying as they'd all thought the material was tearing, but as time went on the sound had become a background noise, like the ticking of a clock.

Upon Aunt Mary's emergence from the bathroom, Fiona led her along the passage until they were as far as they could be from the stairs. She'd only have a few minutes to grill Aunt Mary before someone came looking for them, and she wanted every second to count.

'Quick, tell me about Leighton. I need everything you know about him and how he gets on with the others in the valley.'

Aunt Mary's face went blank as she organised her thoughts. Fiona knew better than to push her aunt, but she was conscious of not appearing to be away from the group for too long.

'He has his post delivered to Cummings and Co rather than his house. Once or twice a week I'll drop it off for him. He gives me the odd box of chocolates for doing it, but it's never a bother. He told me that he does this because he went through a bitter divorce and he doesn't want his ex's family knowing where he lives. Since his app thingy was launched there have been letters asking for a share of it as his ex-husband is claiming he made a contribution.'

'Okay, that's good.' And it was good to learn Leighton was trying to hide in the valley. That spoke of a guilty conscience and the story about the divorce could be just that, a story. 'What else do you know? He said he's an app developer, is that right?'

'So far as I know. He works with computers is all I know, but there's no shortage of money about him. There's always delivery vans coming to his house, and I know he bought his cottage outright without a mortgage.'

Everything she'd learned so far was setting alarm bells ringing in Fiona's mind. Leighton could be telling the truth, but she didn't trust the man at all, and what Aunt Mary was saying was just deepening her suspicions of him.

'Do you know if he's seeing anyone? If he has kids from his marriage? How does he get on with the others in the valley? You seem to be on good terms with him, but William and Tom don't seem to have much time for him, and neither do Pierce and Susie. What's he done to upset them?'

'I don't know if he's seeing anyone and I've never heard tell of him having kids. His ex is claiming half of his income from something he created. As for how he gets on with the others, his cottage doesn't have its own parking space and because he's a townie who doesn't understand the country, there was this one time he was walking up the valley and he'd left his car blocking the gate to the field past George and Isla's cottage. William and Tom had driven some sheep up the track and they were going to put them in that field but couldn't. William was furious and was in the process of attaching a chain to drag the car out of the way when Leighton came back. It was Tom who told me about it, but the way he told it, Leighton and William almost came to blows.' Aunt Mary shook her head. 'Why is it men always resort to violence?'

'Probably from the time they were hunter-gatherers.' Fiona didn't have the time or energy to enter into a debate about the reasons some men acted like Neanderthals. She'd broken far too many Friday night brawls to understand the logic behind beating another human to a pulp. 'How does he get on with Pierce and Susie?'

'Not bad so far as I can tell. I used to see him chatting to Susie quite a bit, but he doesn't do that as much as he used to. You know they're planning to build more cottages, well it's not broken the surface yet, but he's planning to sue them, as the cottages will spoil his view and devalue his cottage. He's got a land agent involved as well to help stop them getting planning permission.'

'Really? Now that's interesting.' The more she learned, the more Fiona realised the Scales Valley was a tangle of hidden agendas. Could it be that, desperate to thwart Pierce and Susie from developing those extra cottages, Leighton had killed George and Isla, to stop the sale of their house going through? It was a weak motive, at best, but so far it was as good a motive as she'd come up with. 'Is there anything else you can tell me about him?'

'Not really. He's pleasant enough to me, but then, I've never had cause to cross him.'

'Okay. Now tell me about Tom. He's not been in the valley very long either.'

Aunt Mary's mouth twisted. 'You can't think Tom has anything to do with those murders, can you?'

'I'm not ruling any of the men out.'

'Oh, Fiona, rea—'

A man's voice clumped up the stairs and along the passage. 'Are you pair all right up there?'

'Yeah, Pierce, we're just coming.'

Coupled with Aunt Mary's information, Fiona's assessments of the group were helping her rearrange the order of her suspect list. Dave Lennox had always praised her ability to read people and divine their intentions and agendas from what they did and didn't say. It was this skill she was now using to whittle away theories and suppositions until she uncovered the killer's identity.

When William came back to the kitchen and dumped his gear by the door, his ruddy face was ashen and his breaths were ragged. Whether it was age, whisky or the elements that were exhausting him, he looked as if standing was all he could achieve.

'Don't just stand there, man, what've you found out?'

William was too spent to even send a glare at Susie.

'It's not good. The water is about two and a half feet away from coming into the house.' He took a pair of deep breaths and pointed to where Becky and the kids lay on the mattress. 'I think we should reconsider cutting the bank. With the roof damaged it's not safe to be upstairs, and a night in the shed'll not do them three any good.'

And with that suggestion, William sprang two places higher on Fiona's suspect list.

THIRTY-THREE

Fiona kept her mouth shut and let the arguments rage back and forth. Everyone had an opinion and nobody could agree. Pierce and Susie were on opposing sides, which was no surprise, but it was only the wail from little Adele, when their shouting woke her, that calmed them down.

Some people argued that whatever was best for Becky and the kids had to be their course of action, while others were insistent they had to consider the risks to the people downstream, if they released the newly created dam.

Becky had sat up and was pulling at Fiona's arm. 'Please, Fiona, don't let them do it. Please, I don't care how much my ankle hurts. If we have to move to the barn or our cars, that's what I want to do.'

Fiona couldn't speak as she viewed the pain in Becky's eyes and heard the catch in her voice. Becky's bravery and spirit were admirable; she was the perfect soulmate to accompany Craig through life. While Fiona herself had once felt something for Craig, she'd always been aware she was damaged and in desperate need of a male presence in her life after the loss of her father. Craig might only have been a year older than Fiona, but, for a brief time, the distraction of his presence filled an aching void.

What Craig had with Becky was different from what Fiona had had with him, or wanted for herself. Becky completed Craig's ambition of being a farmhand, with a wife and kids, whereas Fiona had always known her future lay a long way from the Scales Valley. Fiona had been at their wedding – a drunken affair with lots of dancing and the obligatory fight in the car park between three of Craig's cousins – and sent gifts on the births of their children, but she'd always known Becky's acceptance of a rural life wasn't for her. The love Becky displayed for Craig was understandable, although Fiona had never felt it herself.

Back and forth the arguments raged. Voices were increasing in volume and when Fiona spied angry fingers being jabbed, she knew she'd have to defuse the situation, although a part of her wanted to let the argument continue, in the hope the killer made a mistake she could use to identify them.

'Enough.' Fiona clapped her hands together until she got their attention. 'We've all got our thoughts on what William's saying, but instead of acting like a pack of wolves turning on itself, let's try and act like adults.' She looked around the room and hoped the anger she was trying to suppress wasn't contorting her features into a glower. 'One by one, we all get our say and then we take a vote. Let's be democratic about this.' Fiona gave a nod to William who was immediately to her left. 'You think we should cut the bank for Becky and the kids' sake. Do you have anything to add to that?'

'He just wants to try and save his precious farm. That's what he wants.'

'Susie. Will you be quiet? We've all heard far more than enough from you, or shall we count that as you having had your say?'

Fiona sent a look of thanks to Aunt Mary for silencing Susie and turned to William. 'Anything to add?'

'Just that the safety and wellbeing of people ought to be our first concern. Elsie is a pensioner, Mary's no' far behind, Becky's still frozen and that's before you consider the bairn she's carrying and the two wee ones. If we cut the bank right, it should allow a slow trickle at first that, should it get to any of the houses down by, it'll be shallow enough they can get out safely. 'Sides, the valley widens out a mile or so down. Wider the valley, the shallower the water.'

William sat back and looked to Fiona, who couldn't help feeling a little spark of pride that they'd all fallen into the habit of letting her lead at times like this. She looked to William's left. 'Leighton, what are your thoughts?'

'I dunno. If we have to spend a night in the barn, I can handle that, but like William said, it's about the women and kids. I'm not sure he's right about what would happen in terms of the volume of water. I watch a lot of stuff on YouTube and I saw this one video about flooding in India, and when the soil dam broke, the water rushing through a narrow gap didn't waste any time in making a much bigger gap for itself to get through. I think we could end up unleashing a tsunami downstream.'

When he was finished speaking, Leighton nudged Pierce's arm.

'I say we release it. William knows the terrain around here and if he reckons it'll be safe, we should listen to him.'

Susie didn't wait for anyone to indicate it was her turn. 'And that, ladies and gentlemen, is yet another example of my husband showing his stupidity, trusting in William. We're already screwed. Our home and possessions ruined by William's negligence and flat-out lazy way of farming his land. If he'd cleared the heck, this wouldn't have happened. If he'd trimmed the tree, we'd be able to go upstairs and not have to think about the possibility we might end up killing people

because of one man's selfishness. You can all please yourselves
but I won't be stupid enough to vote for something that may
lead to a murder charge. I want it on the record that I am
opposed to cutting the bank and accept no responsibility for any
decision the rest of you make.'

The fold of Susie's arms and the way she slammed them
into her belly was enough for Fiona to shift her gaze to Tom.

'I'm with William.'

'Aunt Mary?'

'First, William Green, you're older than either me or Elsie so
don't give me any of your nonsense about us being old. You've run
around all night getting constant soakings, but so has Fiona, while
Becky here has birthed two children into the world – no small
thing, so anything else you've got to say that might infer women are
the weaker sex and need looking after is a waste of words. On the
other hand, I agree with the others, if you think cutting a narrow
channel to create a slow release will work, then maybe that's what
has to be done. Although I can't help but wonder, if there is a
sudden release, whether all the water that's backed up will rage
through all the flooded homes and do even more damage than it
would by rising slowly. Susie,' Aunt Mary's tone hardened as she
shifted her gaze in Susie's direction, 'William and Elsie have taken
you in, given you shelter, food and drink in your hour of need. To
rage at them the way you have been is worse than bad manners, it's
downright rude, and if I hear you threaten or castigate them once
more, I'll throw you out of their house myself. Anything to add?'
She speared Susie with a lanced glare that dared her to respond,
and waited a full thirty seconds. 'I didn't think you would, and I
suspect I'm not the only one that's glad you haven't.'

It wasn't often Aunt Mary got her dander up, but it was
always spectacular when she did. The indecision about how to
react coloured Susie's face like a kid's drawings on a fridge door.

'Elsie?' Fiona was quick to move things on in case Susie was foolish enough to try and take Aunt Mary on. While it'd be good to watch, it'd eat into whatever time they had left before the water started coming into the house.

Elsie's head turned until she was looking at William. At his nod she opened her mouth. 'Narrow cut will be fine.'

As Fiona looked down to Becky she heard Elsie's voice again. 'Mary's right, Susie. You were rude. You conned me and William and yet we still helped you. And you were rude. You're a rude woman.'

'Okay, Else, that's enough now.' William circled his wife in his arms and repeated Aunt Mary's warning look at Susie.

Fiona felt a pang of jealousy for William. After finally seeing Elsie speak her own mind, she too wanted to hug the woman. 'Becky?'

Before Becky spoke she checked her kids. Jamie was fast asleep on her left while Adele was snuggling in trying to get back to sleep.

'Please don't cut the bank. My Craig may well be holing up in some branches or on a tree. If that water floods out it could take him with it.' Her eyes closed as her chin dipped to her chest. 'And if he's... he's... I'd like to think there's a chance his body will be recovered. You know... for the funeral. I don't care how much my ankle hurts, please don't release that water.' Becky circled a hand over the bump in her stomach. 'The baby is fine. I can feel him kicking me just like normal. Please, please don't take away my Craig's last chance.'

As everyone took a moment after Becky's plea to contemplate her words, Fiona used the time to weigh up what each option might mean to the killer. By releasing the water, they'd all be able to stay in the farmhouse, which, if Craig wasn't the killer, meant there would be too many eyes for another murder to take place. On the other hand, maybe the killer wanted them to cut through the road bank, so he'd be involved in the cutting process and could either make his escape or claim his next victim.

As for letting the water continue to rise, that would mean an uncomfortable night in the barn, but as much as that may not trouble her or most of the others, there was Becky's condition, the two young kids and three elderly people to consider too. No matter how quickly they could decamp to a barn or their cars, they'd all get a soaking.

Try as she might, Fiona couldn't work out whether cutting the bank would be something the killer would want.

When the silence was broken it was by Aunt Mary.

'Fiona, what are your thoughts?'

Fiona could have done without the question, as she was leaning towards cutting the bank. William had made sense about the wider area, and although Susie's warning about them committing murder was overhyped, a manslaughter charge may still arise. Of course it wouldn't be their intention, and it may never come to pass. All the same, if anyone downstream was hurt or killed by a flood she'd had a hand in sending their way, it would be the end of her police career. A full stop on her journey to detective. Becky's plea tugged at Fiona's heartstrings. It would be a cruel person who could listen to such an entreaty and vote against it. Fiona knew she had a duty of care to everyone. Those in the room, the people downstream, even the killer. The more Fiona considered it, the more she realised her initial thoughts were wrong; not cutting the bank was the best course of action.

Except, Becky was showing signs of both shock and exposure. For all she said the baby was kicking away as normal, without proper medical tests there was no way of knowing whether or not the baby was in distress.

The faces looking Fiona's way were unreadable in terms of canvassing opinions, but from what people had said, it may be that she had the casting vote. When push came to shove, Fiona couldn't be a party to extinguishing the last of Becky's hopes. 'You've all made a lot of good points. Both for cutting and not cutting the bank away. How about an alternative plan though? Instead of cutting the bank away, we try using the digger to clear some of the debris blocking the bridge. That ought to let enough of the water away to stop it reaching the house while also limiting the flow so as not to endanger anyone downstream.' Fiona looked down at Becky. 'It will also mean the flow won't be strong enough to trouble Craig if he's still alive. And it'll leave the road intact so once the water's gone we can still get in and out of the valley.'

William sent an approving look her way. 'Sounds like a good idea. It'll be a sight more comfy for Becky in here. That gets my vote.'

Tom lifted a hand. 'And mine.'

'No. I vote to not release any of the water.' Becky pointed at Adele and Jamie. 'They're asleep so I'll vote for them. They agree with me.'

Fiona looked at Elsie who nodded as she cast a glance in William's direction. 'I vote to clear the dam.'

Three apiece. As each vote came in, Fiona was scanning every face, trying to see beyond opposition or agreement to the given vote so she could assess each person's inner feelings. It was what she'd been doing all night, watching for the little clues, the chinks in the killer's mask of normality.

With William, Elsie and Tom having voted, Fiona looked at Leighton and Aunt Mary.

'I say we clear the dam.' Leighton folded his arms and looked everywhere but at Becky.

'Aunt Mary?'

Fiona could see Aunt Mary deliberating as she let her gaze drift round the room, locking eyes with each person in turn. Nobody except Tom held her stare. 'I'm going to hold my vote until you've voted, Fiona. I don't know what to think, but I trust you to make the right choice, so whatever you decide, that's what I vote for.'

It was a lovely show of support, but Fiona could do without the added weight of responsibility that Aunt Mary's vote would place on her. The fact Aunt Mary was more than smart enough to know her own mind meant she had an agenda.

To avoid having the casting vote – or votes, with Aunt Mary's backing – Fiona opened her mouth to give her verdict, but was drowned out by Susie. 'And what if the dam breaks? All that water will go raging downstream and flatten anything and everything in its path. Anyone who votes to release any amount of that water is an idiot and I'll say it again, I'll not be held responsible for any decision you idiots make. I vote that we start moving to the barn.'

'By voting you've become a part of the democratic process and, as such, you'll be associated with any decision we make.' Aunt Mary's tone was granite hard.

The vote stood at four-all. However Pierce voted, Fiona, with Aunt Mary's support, would be whose vote sealed their decision. With luck Pierce would choose to stay true to form and do the opposite of what his wife wanted. That way Fiona's vote would be an unnecessary addition to an already winning vote. So far she'd seen nothing to suggest the killer's identity, but that didn't mean she wouldn't keep looking. Perhaps a strong opposition to their vote would be revealing.

Pierce gave a shrug; he'd know his vote counted for little. 'I vote we cut the road. That water is going to keep on coming and sooner or later it'll overtop the road. You might be able to clear some of the debris from the dam, but there's no way you'll clear enough of it. And that water is going to have to be released at some point, better that it happens now. We've got Becky and the kids to think about. That's four each for clearing the dam and doing nothing beyond moving to the barn, and one vote for cutting the road. What's your thoughts, Fiona, are you going to cast a winning vote, or agree with me and tie the vote so there's a recount?'

Pierce's choice to waste his vote and urge her to tie the ballot set off alarm bells in Fiona's mind. If, as she suspected, the killer had seen her at George and Isla's cottage, it stood to reason that before leaving he'd cast George's body into the waters. By unleashing all of the dammed water there was every chance George's corpse wouldn't be found, or was so abused by its journey in the water all signs of murder were obliterated. If that happened, then the eventual inquest into Isla's murder would conclude it was George who'd murdered her and had died trying to escape justice.

Fiona kept her face as neutral as she could. If the killer knew she'd been in the cottage after George and Isla had been killed, she'd be sure to be a target. For the time being, she had to act as if she knew nothing about their murders.

Pierce's comment about them not clearing enough of the dam to make a difference made a certain amount of sense, but the way he was goading her made him every bit as toxic as his wife. The good thing about them being married was that their behaviour would only make one marriage miserable instead of two.

'I vote we try to release enough of the dam that the water stops rising. When morning comes, we can revise our plan accordingly, or simply see what the dawn brings.'

From her seat on the bench behind the long kitchen table, Aunt Mary sent a contented smile Fiona's way that gladdened her heart. The decision might be opposed by almost half the voters, but Fiona had the approval of the one person on earth she loved.

THIRTY-FOUR

Fiona trooped out of the door at the back of a line of stooping figures. William had given them all a series of instructions as to what he wanted each of them to do, and while a lot of what he wanted from them seemed unnecessary to Fiona, she trusted him to know what he was talking about.

Due to his injured hand, Leighton was left behind in the farmhouse. This left Fiona wishing she'd thought to warn Aunt Mary about Leighton and the temper he kept hidden. On the other hand, Aunt Mary was a good judge of people and a calming influence. So long as the group all remained in the same room, she hoped their combined presence would act as a deterrent to nefarious behaviour.

The rising water had swamped the farmyard with a murky brown malevolence, its surface rippled by the ever-falling rain. The wind was showing no signs of dropping, but it felt as if the temperature had fallen several degrees since the last time Fiona had left the house.

William's tractor rumbled into life and he navigated it across to where his digger stood. The back lights of the tractor floodlit the ground as he reversed up to the digger.

The digger was little more than a mechanical arm attached to a frame that connected to the back linkage of a tractor. On the top of its frame a metal seat faced a series of levers. To look at this digger and compare it to the mighty ones used on building sites was a joke. To Fiona it was spindly and weak, but the tractor William drove was huge and, as it was the digger's power source, she supposed it would have more than enough power to achieve what they were going to ask of it.

Between William's accurate driving and Tom's familiarity with hitching implements to tractors, they had the digger attached in no time at all.

When Tom pushed the coupling of a hydraulic pipe into a socket on the back of the tractor and stepped back, William hoisted the digger and set off down the road.

Tom led them to the bothy where they gathered up a selection of tools such as sledgehammers and a heavy pinch bar. Fiona couldn't fathom the reason such tools might be needed, but was smart enough to recognise it wasn't her area of expertise. As each tool was collected, Fiona couldn't help thinking that in the hands of a killer, they could easily be used to inflict fatal wounds.

Pierce hoisted the makeshift grapple hook. 'Is there a chain or metal rope anywhere? We can fix this to the digger bucket and use it to haul out, or at least loosen some of the dam.'

To Fiona, Pierce's idea was a good one, but she caught a look of disdain on Tom's face as he pointed to where the chain was. She bent her mind to work out what was wrong with the idea. So far as she could guess, Tom didn't have faith in the grapple hook withstanding the huge forces the powerful tractor would exert on its improvised construction. All the same, Tom grabbed a couple of meaty shackles from a bench and added them to the pile of tools they'd take with them.

With the tools loaded into William's pickup, they climbed in and set off after the tractor. Neither man spoke to the other, and Fiona couldn't help but wonder if it was the tensions that existed in the valley before the flood that kept them silent, or if one of them was working out if they could engineer a chance to kill again. For all she'd espoused the theory of the falling branch having thumped William in the back, it wasn't one she believed.

At the bend where the road curved to cross the valley, William turned the tractor and reversed until his rear wheels were a few feet short of the bridge.

At once, Fiona saw the first of many problems they'd have to face if they were to release some of the dammed material.

The huge tractor was a foot narrower than the roadway it rested upon. Not a problem for the tractor, but a sure-fire one for the digger, as its stabilising outriggers folded outwards from the frame of its body, making it wider than the tractor.

If William tried lowering them, they'd rest atop the bridge's parapet, lifting the whole apparatus at least two feet higher. With the bridge several feet above the water level, and the dam below the surface, every inch would be precious.

William parked the tractor and climbed the small ladder to the digger's seat. Even over the roar of the water and the thrumming patter of rain on her waterproof hood, Fiona could hear the steady deep rumble of the tractor's engine.

One by one, William set the outriggers and pulled at levers until the digger arm unfolded itself and reached out into the area illuminated by the tractor's rear lights. The bucket attached to the digger was three feet wide and William's first move was to set the bucket behind one of the parapet's capstones to exert some pressure. The capstone moved and, with deft use of the controls, William soon dragged it off the parapet onto the road.

The next three capstones all moved with the same ease, but when he swung the arm across to the other side of the bridge, the first capstone resisted all his efforts to remove it. When he'd swung the digger's boom out of the way, Tom stepped forward with a sledgehammer and the pinch bar.

The sledgehammer was handed off to Pierce while Tom kept the pinch bar in his own hands. With a careful deliberation, Tom placed the tip of the pinch bar into the mortar joint beneath the centre of the capstone and gestured for Pierce to start swinging the sledgehammer. In some ways Tom was showing a lot of trust towards Pierce, as one badly aimed swing could smash into his flesh, but the analytical part of Fiona's brain couldn't help but think that it just showed Tom was unaware two people had been murdered.

The plinking metallic sound cut through the air as Pierce used blows from the sledgehammer to drive the pinch bar into the joint. Clad as they were in waterproofs, it seemed a laborious task, but after a series of heavy swings, they'd popped the capstone free. As they set themselves to repeat the process, Fiona decided to seize the moment their industry had given her and clambered down the bank of the downstream side of the bridge.

Fiona's torch picked out the river with ease. It was a bubbling maelstrom of murky brown water that frothed and thundered. From what she could judge, its flow was more than normal, but nowhere near as much as it should have been considering the volume of water it needed to disperse.

When Fiona cast her torch under the bridge a gasp escaped her mouth. She'd expected to see water flooding over the top of the rudimentary dam, but that wasn't what she saw. Instead she was looking at a dense thicket of trees, branches, roots and other debris that bled dirty brown water from a thousand orifices.

For all the dam seemed secure, Fiona scrambled back up the bank lest it suddenly burst and wash her away to a watery death. A part of her had been looking for a splash of colour. Craig's waterproofs were bright orange and made of PVC, so durable the waters would never stain the colour out of them until they degraded with age.

The only colours she saw were the brown of the water and the branches and the white froth where the water squeezed its way through the dam.

Back at the top, William was hauling the capstones out of his way so the tractor had a clear path. Pierce was panting while Tom wore his usual inscrutable expression as he climbed into the tractor.

Once the capstones were dumped on the downstream bank, William lifted the outriggers and signalled to Tom to start reversing.

This placed a lot of trust in Tom, as William's position on the digger's seat exposed him to disaster should anything go wrong.

THIRTY-FIVE

Tom inched the tractor backwards at a steady pace, no matter how many times William waved at him to hurry. He'd be feeling the weight of responsibility, as one wrong move from him could easily kill William.

When William reached the end of the removed capstones, Tom halted and stayed where he was as William set the outriggers. Tom's foot on the brake added a red glow to the lights beaming out from the back of the tractor.

William planted the outriggers on the heavy stones of the parapet wall and gave them enough pressure the weight was lifted from the tractor's spongy rear tyres.

Fiona got herself into position. Her job was to monitor the digger's footing, and seeing how it was set; she knew it was a job that needed doing. The bottom stone of the parapet ought to prevent any lateral movement, but there was no telling whether or not the stone had been loosened by the removal of the capstones. And with the dam being on this side, every attempt to clear it would mean the application of Newton's Third Law: every action or force having an equal and opposite reaction.

As Fiona watched the arm of the digger extend towards the

water, she aimed her torch at where the bucket would enter the swirling mass. There were a multitude of swirling whirlpools as the water was sucked down to pour through the breaches in the dam, but compared to what it was like a few yards to the left as it thundered downstream, the surface of the dammed water was serene.

The tree anchoring the heck was to Fiona's right and out of reach of the digger's arc, but that was a good thing; they weren't trying to destroy the whole dam.

The bucket disappeared into the water, the arm of the digger descending with it until Fiona could see the arm curling back to the bridge. The engine note deepened as it met resistance, and William changed his tactics and lifted the arm instead.

When the bucket broke the surface, water streamed from all its drainage holes and a meagre collection of small branches nestled in the bucket itself. William swung the arm over until he could empty the bucket on the bridge and then take it back for another attempt.

In the water a small number of thin branches loosened from the pile rotated lazily in the current before being sucked underwater. Fiona didn't know much about vortexes and how they worked, but to see the buoyant sticks dragged beneath the surface was a frightening sight. If any of them fell in, they wouldn't stand a chance against the sucking of the water as it sought a way out of the growing reservoir.

Pierce was on the far side of the tractor detailed with the same task, while Tom stood on the bridge. He had the chainsaw with him, but there wasn't yet a need for it, as the branches William had cleared were small enough Tom could easily toss them over the parapet into the waters cascading downstream.

William kept working the controls and to Fiona it seemed he was making headway, as the underside of the digger's boom was getting ever closer to scraping the top of the parapet stone.

An animalistic sense told Fiona she wasn't alone. When she turned, she found Pierce standing behind her, the grappling hook and short chain in his hands. She got it at once. Pierce had grown impatient with their meagre progress and wanted to try his idea. To do so he'd abandoned his post and sought out the items he needed to put his plan into action. His actions could be viewed as a dereliction of duty, or a wise alternative to a plan that wasn't working.

To get William's attention he'd had to come around to this side of the tractor. When William saw Pierce and what he was holding he shook his head violently.

Pierce rattled the items in his hands, clearly unwilling to have his idea dismissed. William abandoned the controls, dismounted the digger, and came at Pierce with fury written all over his face.

'That's a stupid idea. And how dare you stop keeping watch? I need your eyes on that outrigger to keep me safe. Do you understand that? If that outrigger slips, the tractor will be unbalanced and could fall into the water. It'd be a miracle if I wasn't killed. I bet that'd suit you right down to the ground, wouldn't it?'

'Don't give me that. I may not like you, but that doesn't mean I want you dead.' Fiona saw the way Pierce towered over William, translated the menace in his body language and prepared to intervene between the two men should things turn physical. 'Why is it such a stupid idea? Come on, oh wise farmer whose neglect has led to this mess, tell me, why is using the grapple a stupid idea?'

William's arm extended towards the water. 'Because if it gets snagged on something too big for the digger to lift, the only way to get it free will be to crawl out and disconnect it from the bucket. If you're prepared to do that, then go ahead, attach it. If not, go back to keeping an eye on the outrigger and stop delaying me. This is slow enough as it is.'

With his piece said William turned and started back up the digger's ladder. For a moment it looked like Pierce was going after William, so Fiona made sure she was positioned where she could stop him.

From Pierce's face Fiona could see the internal battle he was experiencing and she wondered if she'd made a mistake. It wouldn't be hard for a man of Pierce's height to shove her aside, and if he did that she'd end up in the water. The thought she might be blocking a killer while exposed to danger sent tingles of dread throughout her very being.

Fiona could feel her body reacting to the situation, adrenaline coursing through her veins, and she found herself reaching out and taking hold of one of the tractor's steps as her subconscious prepared her body for what may come.

Pierce's face twisted and he threw the chain and grapple to the roadway with enough force for Fiona to hear them despite the proximity of the roaring tractor engine.

As Pierce stalked off, Fiona returned her focus to the task at hand, but she was now casting occasional glances over her shoulder in case Pierce returned.

William's reaction to Pierce moving away from the outrigger tweaked at Fiona. The fact he'd suggested Pierce might want him dead hinted at William knowing more than he was letting on. So far as she knew, only herself, Aunt Mary and the killer were aware two people had been murdered, but William's vague accusation set her on a different train of thought.

If William was the killer, could their cottage have been William's motive? It had an extensive garden that was more than large enough to house another cottage. William had held designs on buying the Edwards' cottage, so maybe he'd planned to build another cottage, and either sell it, or rent it out as a holiday let.

Instead of selling to William, the Edwards had sold their cottage to Pierce and Susie. It was no secret Pierce had designs on building several properties on the land he'd bought from William and Elsie; therefore, a furious William could have killed George and Isla out of spite for selling to someone he felt had screwed him over.

Yet none of this fit with what Fiona knew of William's character. Leighton and Pierce were her prime suspects and, with what she'd learned about Leighton from Aunt Mary, she couldn't help but strongly suspect he was the killer. Pierce's comment to William when accused of pushing the farmer while they were securing the tarpaulin spoke of a familiarity with violence.

There was also the question as to why a couple such as Pierce and Susie had moved to such a remote area as the Scales Valley. It was clear both liked the finer things in life, and while Hawick was one of the larger towns in the Scottish Borders, it lacked the boutiques and fine restaurants that would be important to a couple such as Pierce and his wife. Hawick boasted no Harrods, no designer stores selling Louis Vuitton or Prada. Had they, like Leighton, had an ulterior motive for leaving their former life behind?

In her rant earlier, Susie had intimated that Pierce had a wandering eye. Had he strayed and been caught? It crossed Fiona's mind that accusers often attributed their own failings onto others. Therefore, Fiona wondered if Susie had been the one to stray.

There was also the question of Pierce having a son he rarely saw. Could it be that Pierce had left his son's mother for Susie and the boy was siding with his mum? In her police career Fiona had seen this scenario more times than she cared to count, but it was a matter for Pierce and Susie to work out between them.

A headache began to develop at the front of Fiona's brain as she tried to work out all the different reasons why any of the men might be the killer she was hunting.

In the water, the arm of the digger was moving with far less care. Before the argument with Pierce, William had used steady measured movements to guide the bucket, whereas he now jerked and slammed the digger's arm around. When he lifted the bucket from the water, a small tree was gripped between the bucket and the digger arm.

It looked for all the world that the bucket would never manage to lift the tree onto the bridge without dropping it, but by using a more tender touch on the controls William managed to deposit the tree atop the bridge, where Tom could then attack it with the chainsaw.

With the more aggressive tactic bearing the best fruit so far, William launched another violent attack on the dam. So abrupt were the movements of the digger, Fiona could see the arm sending splashes of water as it was directed back and forth with sharp movements.

Again, the bucket snagged on something underwater, but William worked the levers with abandon as he fought to lift whatever he'd caught. As his movements became more violent, the pad of the outrigger started to slide across the parapet wall.

Fiona backed away as she monitored the pad's journey across the stone parapet. The last thing she wanted was to be trapped between the tractor and the wall. As the pad neared the edge of the parapet wall, she flashed her torch up at William to warn him things weren't good.

William left his seat and leaned out to take a look, so Fiona illuminated what he needed to see. First the pad, which was four inches from the edge of the stone block, and then the tractor tyre, so William could see it was almost touching the inside wall of the stone.

With a brief thumbs up, William returned to his seat and resumed his attempts to lift whatever the bucket had captured. As she watched, Fiona saw that whatever William tried, he could neither lift the object, nor move the bucket to get a fresh grip. The more William tried, the less success he had.

The tractor tyre was drawn across so it rested against the parapet stone and the pad was right on the edge. William jerked at the levers; a section of the stone crumbled beneath the pad and the forces applied to it.

Fiona signalled William only to be waved away. Whether it was guilt, self-recrimination or a residual anger from the argument with Pierce, William was throwing caution to the wind as he tried to free the bucket.

The tractor's note deepened as he again tried to haul up on the digger arm. Fiona could see it straining as more parapet wall crumbled and then, with a whooshing hiss, one of the hydraulic pipes on the digger burst, sending a stream of oil back towards William.

The reaction from William was instant. He abandoned the levers with a howl and shook his hands as he tried to dislodge the oil.

Unsure of the cause of William's injury, Fiona laid a hand on one of the digger's hydraulic pipes. It was hot to touch, and considering how much the icy rain would be cooling the outside of the pipe, the oil inside it must be scalding.

When the shaking didn't work William clambered down the ladder and plunged the backs of his hands into a water-laden pothole on the bridge. His next move was to scoop some of the water up and splash it onto his face. The water wouldn't wash the oil off, but it would at least cool it down to salve the burns on William's flesh.

William returned from the pothole, his face set hard as he clambered back onto the digger and reached for the controls. He was working the other levers with an increasing abandon, but nothing was happening. The digger was stuck and, with a burst pipe on the lifting arm, there was no chance of freeing it until they could replace the pipe, or the water subsided and they could cut the bucket free from whatever it had snagged on.

William, it seemed, had other ideas. He released the pressure on the outriggers and folded them up, the rear tyres of the mighty tractor squishing down under the load of the digger and whatever it held.

William climbed into the tractor's cab and when his intent became clear, Fiona scrambled along the road and positioned herself under the pickup's raised tailgate, which afforded a crumb of shelter from the wind and rain.

THIRTY-SIX

Pierce joined Fiona, his head stooped so as not to bump on the tailgate. 'He's a bloody idiot. The way he was carrying on he was always going to break something. That digger is probably older than you are. The lazy old fool has caused all of this, and by God me and Susie will make sure he pays.'

Fiona kept silent. While she agreed William might hold a certain amount of culpability for the valley flooding, to lay all the blame at one door when there was a freak weather front causing chaos was plain wrong. It was also wise to not get drawn into the middle of their animosity by showing support for either party. Their relationship had been toxic long before the first raindrop had fallen. She'd got that information from Aunt Mary as a running commentary whenever they'd spoken over the last few months.

The comment from Pierce about him and Susie working together to make sure William paid nagged at Fiona. Could the couple be working in cahoots, with Susie fully aware of Pierce's actions? It wouldn't be the first time a couple had conspired to kill, and while it was rare, it wasn't unique.

Ahead of them, William was trying to drive the tractor back

and forth to free the digger. He was moving inches at a time, the massive tractor leaning heavily due to the displaced load of the submerged digger arm. The tractor's engine roared as its tyres clawed at the slick road, trying to find enough grip to pull its way out of trouble. From the slow rate the rutted tyres were rotating, Fiona could work out William had selected one of the tractor's lower gears to gain maximum pulling power.

Whether William was going forwards or backwards, the results were the same. He'd travel a foot or more, and then the anchoring effect of the trapped digger arm would slew the tractor sideways, forcing him to stop before the whole apparatus was pulled into a situation that would cause further damage or outright disaster.

When the tractor door flew open, and William stomped out, Fiona knew that she had to get to him before Pierce did. Even so, she grabbed at Pierce's arm. 'If you've any sense, you'll not say a word about this.'

With the warning delivered she followed William's path to the back of the tractor. The first thing she saw was that the digger's arm was now twisted from the forces exerted by William's attempt to drive out. As a digger it'd never be serviceable again and, although it wouldn't be the most expensive thing to lose, its loss on top of everything else would be sure to eat at William.

William was at the back of the tractor with Tom and one of the sledgehammers. Together the farmers worked to disconnect the digger and tractor. As soon as the final bolt was released the digger scuffed a foot sideways as it was drawn by the load countering the pressure the tractor had exerted.

William handed Tom a length of baler twine and pointed to the top hitch of the tractor's linkage.

Tom collected the twine and held out his hand. 'Gie's your knife.'

'Where's yours?' William's hand moved to his pocket.

A shrug. 'Lost.'

'Hey, City Boy, go get that chain.'

William's instruction to Pierce was a shout, but other than the barb about Pierce's native home, there was no anger in him anymore. Only defeat.

Even in these horrible weather conditions, Tom took his time and made a neat job of tying up the top hitch. His actions spoke of a professional pride in his work that would see him do nothing but his best regardless of circumstance.

Pierce got the chain, but instead of handing it to William, dropped it at his feet, and stalked away.

It was Tom who picked up the chain. He gave a nod to William, and the farmer clambered back into the tractor as Tom hooked one end of the chain around the frame of the digger.

The rear arms of the tractor descended as William lowered the whole hitching mechanism. A halting gesture from Tom saw William release the appropriate lever, while Tom dropped the eyed end of the chain over the trailer hook.

Fiona reached for Pierce, pointed to the middle of the bridge, and set off after Tom. She knew from the times she'd attended RTAs, nobody with any sense stood near a rope or chain that was under stress.

William revved the engine and trundled forward. There was a dip in the engine note when the chain went taut, but that was followed by a roar as William increased the revs and the tractor hauled on the digger. Inch by inch the digger contorted forward until it would move no further and the tractor's tyres were spinning on the damp tarmac. William eased back a foot and dropped the hitch. He might not have retrieved the digger, but he'd at least moved it far enough it was no longer blocking the road.

Tom retrieved the chain while Fiona and Pierce gathered up the chainsaw and the other tools.

With the tools stowed in the pickup, Fiona went back to the

downstream side of the bridge and took another look at the face of the dam. From what she could judge, their efforts hadn't made even the slightest difference. The water flow seemed as intense as before, but there was no discernible increase caused by their removal of part of the dam.

When she rejoined the others, William and Pierce were engaged in a shouting match as Tom watched on. Neither man was backing down, and it was only a matter of time before they came to blows. The disharmony of the group was going to lead to further problems, and they had a bigger issue to deal with.

If they abandoned the house to the rising waters and transferred to the barn they'd be consigning themselves to darkness until morning came. With the weather as horrible as it was, that would be at least nine hours. No way could they risk using the candles or Tilley lamps when resting on top of straw bales. She had to take charge of the situation, and if that meant separating these two men, then so be it.

Fiona strode forward, planted a hand on each of their shoulders and pushed each away from the other. 'That's enough. Like it or not, the pair of you are going to have to work together for the greater good. Instead of falling out, start acting like the grown-ups you are and use your heads. This idea failed, so what? We move on to the next. William, your house has stone floors, right?'

'Aye.' There was puzzlement in William's eyes, but explanations could wait.

'And the vents in the wall, how high are they?'

William held his hand four inches above his knee.

'That's higher than you think the water will get, right?'

'Maybe.' The puzzlement was now understanding.

'Then do you think we can seal off the doors and the vents and stay in the house?'

'Aye.'

And with the one-word answer given, William was rushing

away to the tractor, leaving Fiona wondering about Tom's lost knife. He'd had it after his ducking, which told her he kept it in a pocket he deemed safe, but somehow he'd conspired to lose it when doing nothing close to being immersed in the tumultuous waters. It could be that he'd laid it on a bench in the bothy when attaching the ropes to the tarpaulin and forgotten to pick it up.

Was this what detectives did all day? Second guess their every thought?

Fiona pondered the question a moment and then realised detectives had to second guess themselves. It was what prevented them from making mistakes, and what she must do now, as there were lives depending on the decisions she made.

THIRTY-SEVEN

Back at the farm, Fiona was knee deep in water as she explored the bothy. Right where Tom said they would be, she found a roll of plastic sheeting, a mastic gun and two tubes of mastic. At Tom's request she picked up a weird contraption he'd called a slate knife. It was a little over a foot long, its blade offset to the left of the handle by an inch, and when Fiona tested its edge she found it to be a lot blunter than she expected. How it was supposed to cut slates was beyond Fiona, but she imagined Tom would have a good reason for requesting she bring it.

When she deposited them at the farmhouse, Fiona saw Tom had collected a half dozen slates and Pierce had delivered the first straw bale from the barn.

'How does this knife thing cut slates? They're stone, aren't they?'

It was a rubbish question, but Fiona wanted to engage with Tom. For all she knew who he was and what he did, she knew little about him and she hadn't yet had a chance to learn anything about him from Aunt Mary.

'They are. Don't know how it works, just that it does.'

'Do you think sealing up the house will work?'

'Dunno, but gotta try. Night in the barn's not good for Becky and her bairns.'

That he'd mentioned Becky and the kids as his primary reason for protecting the farmhouse said a lot. Of course Becky was uppermost in all their concerns, but Aunt Mary had mentioned that Tom was often seen chatting to Becky, and this sat at odds with the taciturn behaviour he usually displayed. There was also the suspicion Fiona had had earlier, about Tom and Becky being more than friends. That didn't sit with the love affair that was Craig and Becky's marriage, but, as a police officer, she'd long ago learned that nobody really knew what went on behind closed doors.

It could be nothing more than Tom being sweet on Becky, but when looked at in a different way, that filtered into Tom shoving Craig at the calf shed and removing a love rival. Like the theory about William, it was a stretch, as there was no guarantee Becky would entertain Tom; also, if Tom killed Craig for Becky, what was his motive for killing George and Isla?

Like every other theory she'd had, Fiona found nothing but holes in this one.

Tom hefted the slate knife in his hand and offered a slate up against one of the vents. The slate knife was used to scratch dimensions onto the slate and then Tom was on his knees at the front step. With the slate knife rising and falling like a butcher's cleaver, Tom trimmed the slate to the desired dimensions a half inch at a time. After checking it fit in the opening, Tom used the slate as a template and scratched the next one ready to cut it to size.

Leighton appeared at the door. 'Need any help?'

'Yes. Come with me and we'll get some bales.'

Fiona led the way to the hay barn and went to pick up a bale. Isla Edward's body still lay where they'd left it, her face more pleasant in death than Fiona had ever seen it in life.

As tragic as it was to see the corpse of a one-time neighbour, what Fiona saw was a reminder that one of the people in the valley was a killer.

Unlike Pierce and Leighton, who had head torches, Fiona had to stuff her torch into a pocket to free up both hands to carry the bale. This meant she had to navigate her way back to the farmhouse by following the head torches of the others.

The bale wasn't too heavy at first, but as she waddled her way across the yard with it bumping against her legs, its weight grew with every step. The coarse twine enveloping the bale ate at her fingers and she knew that if she carried many more across the yard, her fingers would end up raw and blistered.

Leighton had a different tactic. Maybe it was to protect his damaged hand, and maybe it was a flash of genius, but he'd hoisted the bale up so it was resting on his shoulder.

By the time Fiona had deposited the bale by the front door, William had returned. When he started to follow Fiona to the barn she stopped him. 'Have you a flatbed trailer?'

'Aye. But what does that matter?'

'Park the trailer in the bit of your garden between the kitchen window and the road. It should be about window level and it'll give us a platform to easily get from the house to the road, if we have to evacuate the house for any reason. Plus, once the doors are sealed up, that's how we'll have to get back in.'

The way they were all separated into different areas right now niggled at Fiona. The old saying about there being safety in numbers was accurate, and with everyone in one place, the killer wouldn't have the opportunity to pick off another victim unseen. Fiona knew that she had to get everyone back together as soon as she could.

'Right.' And with that William was heading off back to his tractor.

A stack of bales would have done the same job, but the trailer would be sturdier and much easier to install in place than lugging a couple of dozen extra bales.

When first built, the farmhouse had two doors, a front that was rarely used and a back door into the kitchen which was only locked on high days and holidays. Were there only these doors it wouldn't be too bad, as four bales per door would more than suffice. At some point, William had added a large patio and installed a double set of sliding doors. To shield these doors from the rising water would take at least a dozen more bales.

With the slates cut and the trailer in place, William and Tom joined in the relay of people carrying bales from the barn to the farmhouse. Fiona found it impossible to keep track of who was where, as flashes of light scythed through the darkness and shapes drifted in and out of the night.

Together they piled up enough bales to blockade all the doorways – two bales high and two bales deep.

'Where's Pierce?' Leighton looked at the door as if accusing Pierce of ducking inside to avoid helping out.

Rather than dig into a debate, Fiona opened the kitchen door and looked Aunt Mary's way. 'Is Pierce in here?'

'No.'

Fiona shut the door behind her before Susie could enter the conversation. Pierce would no doubt turn up in a minute with another bale.

Outside, Tom was etching a thick bead of mastic around the face of the door opening. Down one side he traced, across the ground and then up the other side. With the knife he'd borrowed from William, he sliced a section of the plastic sheeting free and pressed it onto the mastic with the care of a decorator finishing wallpaper. William flumped the four bales into place so the pressure between the sealant and the sheeting was kept constant.

Pierce still hadn't returned, so with a fey feeling balling in her heart, Fiona plucked at Leighton's arm. 'Come on, we better check for Pierce. If he was getting another bale he should be back by now.'

Leighton strode off towards the barn and Fiona was content to let him lead. It meant she could keep her eye on him.

There was no sign of Pierce by the bales, but when Fiona directed her torch to the far reaches of the barn she saw Pierce. Or rather she saw Pierce's body slumped face down in a dark corner.

THIRTY-EIGHT

'Go and get the others.' Fiona yelled the stark instruction to Leighton as she rushed over to Pierce, her run slowing as her torch picked out the wound on the back of his head.

Her first thought was to preserve life, so she knelt and squirmed a hand under him until she could press her fingertips to his throat. She felt nothing. No life-affirming beat, no faint throb of a still-beating heart pumping blood through veins, and no warmth, although they were all so cold that she doubted she'd find warmth on her own body.

To safeguard herself against a wrong diagnosis, Fiona lifted Pierce's left hand and repeated her search for a pulse at his wrist. As she expected, the results were the same.

After a deep, steadying breath, Fiona cast her torch at the back of Pierce's head and looked at the wound. It was fresh enough the blood still glistened, and while she'd be the first to say she knew little about trauma-induced wounds, Fiona could guess from the depth and width of the wound that Pierce had been hit hard with a heavy object.

Fiona rose to her feet and took two steps back from the body, her mind already working on the who and why. She also assessed whether Pierce was killed by the same person who'd murdered George and Isla. The odds of there being two killers in the valley were tiny, but there was a lot of animosity between them all, and while she didn't think it likely there were two killers, she knew better than to rule it out before she had evidence to prove otherwise.

Whomever had struck this blow hadn't been trying to stun or incapacitate Pierce; they'd been flat out trying to kill him. Each of the three remaining men had had the opportunity to deliver this blow, but it was impossible to know which one. With the raggle taggle nature of their trips with the bales, and some people not being able to carry a torch as well as a bale, it was anyone's guess as to who was where at any given time.

The why was also an unsolvable puzzle. After all their arguments, and Pierce's threat to sue, William certainly had a motive to kill Pierce, and the two had been at loggerheads most of the night, but she doubted that he'd have done it in such a way. Of the three suspects, William was the one whose character she knew best. William was a hothead who was all bark and little bite. If he was going to snap to the point of murder, he'd have done so at the bridge and thumped Pierce there and then, not calmed down and bided his time. However, Pierce's murder tied in with her theory that William had exacted a revenge on George and Isla for selling their cottage to Pierce.

Before the others returned, Fiona had two tasks she must do: the first was to search the body for clues. It wasn't a pleasant task, but she cast her torch over and around Pierce's corpse and looked for anything that may indicate why he was in this corner when he had no need to be. The waterproof leggings Pierce wore looked baggier than usual in the crotch, so using a single finger, Fiona lifted the base of Pierce's jacket. As she suspected she'd find, the top of the leggings was below the bones of Pierce's hips.

While the plastic waterproof leggings had a habit of riding

down, Pierce's hands would have been free at this point, enabling him to hitch them back up. Except they were lower than they ought to be, and he was in a dark corner he had no reason to be in. To her mind that gave only one answer: Pierce had walked to the dark corner so he could have a piss. The leggings were pulled down so he could access his fly.

Flashes of light indicated the others were on their way. Fiona recognised she didn't have much time left alone at the crime scene, so she made sure she used it wisely and directed her torch anywhere that may have been deemed a good place to dispose of the murder weapon. Nowhere her torch looked showed itself as the new home of the weapon. Some were possibilities that bore a greater examination in the future, but that would require being alone and having the correct amount of time to conduct a thorough and proper search.

Tom pointed in Pierce's general direction. 'He dead?'

Fiona took a deep breath before answering. 'I'm afraid so.'

'What happened?'

'He was murdered. Someone caved his head in while he was having a piss.'

For a man whose every movement was a study in slow deliberate intent, Tom could move with great speed when he wanted. The punch he threw caught Leighton square on the cheek and sent him staggering across to the bales.

Before Leighton could recover enough to mount a defence, or Fiona could stop Tom, the shepherd had planted a punch into Leighton's gut that doubled him and left him gasping for air.

'Enough.' The shouted word came from both Fiona and William as they forced themselves in front of Tom.

William planted his hands on Tom's shoulders and pushed him back. 'Calm down, Tom. There's no need for this.'

As much as Fiona was compelled to help Leighton, she was more concerned with listening to what William and Tom had to say to each other. It wasn't often Tom said more than a word or two, so when he did speak it was usually worth listening.

'Someone killed Pierce. Wasn't me. Doubt it was you. That leaves Leighton and the lass. Doubt it was her.'

Tom's words were a game changer for Fiona. Now everyone would find out there was a murderer in their midst, they'd all suspect each other. As she knew about the first two murders and was quietly trying to solve the case, she'd never given thought that when the murders became public knowledge, her name would be on some people's suspect list. Not for the first time, she questioned her decision to keep George and Isla's murders from becoming public knowledge.

Come on, Fiona. Don't be naïve, you should have worked that out for yourself. Of course others will think you're a suspect in Pierce's murder. Everyone who had the opportunity to kill him was a suspect. Now get a grip of yourself and start acting like a bloody police officer and not a guppy. The words were only a low mutter in her mind, but they came out with enough venom that they spurred Fiona to take charge of the situation.

'Will you guys pack it in? Is it not bad enough that Pierce is dead without you lot fighting?'

'He clearly killed him.'

'Tom.' As much as Fiona tried to put a stern tone into her voice, she could tell Tom wasn't paying her any attention, as his eyes were locked over her shoulder.

Fiona took it as a warning, although when she turned she found Leighton still doubled over, a stream of bloody spittle hanging from his mouth. Tom must have been watching for any signs of retaliation from Leighton, but the younger man hadn't yet recovered enough from the first two punches to do anything about it.

'What do we do with him?' William nodded towards the pile of bales. 'Same as Mrs Edwards?'

This was a question Fiona had already asked herself.

Which course of action would cause the least damage to the crime scene? Moving the body, or leaving it where it was and hoping the waters didn't rise high enough to interfere with the scene?

One option was to leave Pierce where he lay for now and then, if the waters threatened to rise that high, lift him onto the bales alongside Mrs Edwards. It was the best option apart from one thing – to do it, there would have to be constant monitoring of the water level and that would mean entering and exiting the house on a number of occasions: each opening of the kitchen window that was now their doorway would leech warmth from those who needed it most.

Fiona made her decision. Due to the way they'd all been huddled up against one another at some point during the evening, Pierce's body might well have traces of all their DNA. There was little harm to be done in the four of them doing what they could to preserve Pierce's corpse. Not only for the pathologist, but for his wife and estranged son. 'We can't leave him here. If the floodwaters get this high, goodness knows where he'll end up. That's not right.'

'That was assault that was.' Leighton's arm passed Fiona's side as he pointed at Tom. 'When we get outta here, I'm gonna make sure you get done for that. William and Fiona are witnesses.'

Tom didn't respond to Leighton's threat. Not with a glance, a retort, not even a shrug.

Fiona didn't blame him. Leighton had stood behind a woman to issue his threat. To a man as tough as the hills around him, Leighton was an insignificant fly he could swat at a time of his choosing.

William and Tom grabbed one of the trailer sides that were stacked in a heap by the barn door and, with Fiona's help, rolled Pierce's corpse onto it. Fiona's eyes scanned the ground where Pierce had lain, looking for anything that might incriminate his killer, but other than a few pieces of loose straw and a smattering of small stones, there was nothing to be seen.

All four of them took a corner, although Fiona made sure to position herself so that Leighton was at the opposite corner from Tom. Since landing the second punch, Tom had shown no further desire to attack Leighton, but that didn't mean he wasn't biding his time until he got a better opportunity.

With Pierce's body on the makeshift stretcher, they trudged off to the same part of the stack of bales where they'd laid Mrs Edward's corpse. They'd shielded her behind a few loose bales and no one bothered looking that way.

Fiona did.

Pierce's murder had raised way more than one suspicion in her mind, and she was now seeing if there may be an extra motive at play. That's why she was checking in on Isla Edwards.

Except she wasn't there.

Fiona's first thought was that they'd got it wrong and Isla had somehow survived her immersion in the waters and had risen Lazarus style. The idea only lasted a fraction of a second. The knife wound to Isla's chest would have been fatal on its own. As would the way she was found face down in the water.

She hadn't risen, she'd been moved. It stood to reason the killer was trying to cover his tracks, and Fiona now suspected Pierce had seen or heard something that led to him being bashed over the head to ensure his silence.

After placing a few bales around Pierce's body they all trooped back to the farmhouse, where Tom continued sealing up the doors and the air vents.

Fiona and Leighton hung around doing minor tasks like using their torches to provide light, while William got himself fully involved.

As they lined up on the bed of the trailer so they could clamber through the window, the looks they exchanged all asked the same question. Who was going to tell Susie?

THIRTY-NINE

With everyone back in the kitchen, and four of them wrestling their way out of restrictive waterproofs, the kitchen was jammed tight.

'Where's Pierce?' Susie was in William's face, a manicured talon ready to gouge him.

'The barn.'

To Fiona's ears William's words were true, but they were no answer. Instead they were a cop-out, an easy thing to say that could have no comeback. To Susie they'd sound like a world class body swerve.

Susie's eyes flitted to the window they'd just crawled through. 'You've just done the latch on the window. Where is he? Where's my husband? What have you done with him? Why have you left him in the barn?'

Fiona laid her jacket on the pile by the door and crossed to Susie. There was no seat behind the older woman, so Fiona took both of Susie's hands in hers and held them tight. Half to provide support and half to prevent Susie lashing out in response to the news she was about to receive. 'I'm so sorry to have to tell you this, Susie, but Pierce is dead.'

Susie didn't speak. No words poured from her mouth. There were no denials of the bad news Fiona had just delivered. There wasn't even a shaking of the head. She just stood there, statuesque and every bit as talkative.

'Did you hear me, Susie?' Fiona had to make sure Susie understood what she'd just been told.

The dipping of Susie's chin wasn't enough to class as a bob of the head, much less a defined nod, but Fiona took it as confirmation.

To see another human being in such shock they were numb to everything around them was always something Fiona found tragic. Whatever thoughts were cascading around Susie's mind right now, they were probably trapped in a cage of disbelief as her brain tried to make sense of what she'd just been told.

Elsie appeared with a tumbler of whisky that she put to Susie's lips. As Susie took a sip the first tear snuck from the corner of her eye and ran down her cheek. Her expression remained the same as that first tear was followed by others.

After another sip of the whisky, Susie's eyes began to move. Slowly at first, then they started flicking from one man to the next, and back and forth they went, taking in Fiona as well.

'How? You were just waterproofing the house, weren't you? How was that dangerous compared to everything else you've done tonight? What happened? Pierce is a good man. He loves me and I love him. He can't be dead. He isn't dead. You're lying to me. Lying, you callous little bitch. You probably want to steal him away for yourself. That's it. Isn't it? *You* want him, so you're telling me he's dead when you've probably got him outside somewhere, waiting for you after you've told him lies about me.'

The uncomprehending nature of Susie's thoughts was understandable.

Pierce, of course, had been reinvented in death. Instead of the useless lump she wanted to divorce a few hours ago, Susie now had her husband on a fast-track to sainthood. Fiona had seen this countless times before. Many were the times she'd heard a wife extoll the qualities of a deceased husband despite having suffered various forms of abuse at his hands. It was a social norm not to speak ill of the dead, but in some ways it felt abnormal to see Susie's pendulum swing so far in the opposite direction, considering the way she'd spoken to, and of, Pierce earlier. Except it wasn't. Despite banging heads on a daily basis with her mother when she was still alive, Fiona had never once not loved her. Susie's behaviour was stripping away the artificial front she put on and showing how she really felt about Pierce.

Leighton's shoulder brushed Fiona's as he stepped in front of her. 'She's not lying, Susie. I'm sorry, but Pierce *is* dead.'

'I want to see him. Want to see him myself. I don't believe you.' Susie's eyes flicked behind Fiona to where she knew William and Tom stood.

Fiona knew from the widening of Susie's eyes they'd both added a confirming nod to what Fiona and Leighton were telling Susie.

'What happened? Please, will one of you tell me what the hell is going on?' Susie spun to face Fiona. 'Come on, Fiona. Will you tell me how my husband died?'

Susie's legs faltered, but Fiona and Leighton caught her and eased her into a seat. Fiona crouched down until she was eye to eye with Susie. Compared to what she had to say next, the first part of breaking the news of Pierce's death to Susie had been easy. Horrible, but easy, as Susie's reaction was understated, shock insulating her from the most savage parts of the news. 'We were all getting bales from the shed, but Pierce wasn't at the house with the rest of us when Tom decided we had enough bales. I thought he'd be along any second with another bale. When he wasn't, me and Leighton went looking for him. We found him in the corner of the barn where the bales are kept.'

'What, so he'd collapsed? Maybe he's not dead. Maybe he's just had a mild stroke or a heart attack and he's in a coma. He's not used to all the running about you've done tonight. That's what it is. You've got it wrong, he's not dead, he's in a coma.'

'I'm afraid that's not the case, Susie.' Fiona couldn't help but pause to take a steadying breath before saying the next words. She was already holding Susie's hands in hers, but she tightened her grip. 'I'm so, so sorry to tell you this, but the back of Pierce's head was caved in. It's not a medical issue, he was murdered.'

'Liar.' Susie wrenched her hands free of Fiona's and went to deliver a slap as a stream of abuse flew from her mouth.

Fiona blocked Susie's arm to prevent the blow landing. But another followed on its heels and, although Leighton was using his good hand to try and restrain Susie, the older woman wriggled free and pushed Fiona back.

Susie's next target was Leighton. He too was pushed back until he and Fiona were within a couple of feet of William and Tom. Susie was between them and the valley's other occupants as she screamed accusations at them all. William got the most vitriolic comments, but considering the underlying animosity between the two couples, that was no surprise.

'One of you four killed my husband. It had to have been one of you, and my money's on that tight sod.' Susie's hand was trembling as it aimed at William. 'You couldn't help yourself, could you? You thought we'd conned you, but you'd just been your usual stupid self. We never conned you. When we bought that land from you, it was always in the agreement that we had your permission to build houses on it. You've went and killed a good man. The best man ever, and all because you're too stupid and lazy to properly read a contract. Either that or you were too tight to pay your solicitor to read it for you.'

After getting to know William over a twenty-year period, Fiona could believe that last part. He'd want to keep the billable hours down and would rush any meeting with services that charged by the hour.

'It wasn't me. I swear it. I'll be honest and say I never liked your husband, but I didn't kill him. I think Leighton did.'

'Did I hell, you liar. You're the one who's got a reason to kill him. We all know you're pissed off because he's a smarter businessman than you, and that you hate him because he got one over on you. You're the one with the motive, not me.'

For a second Fiona thought Leighton was going to fly at William, but the younger man didn't do anything beyond glower at William. Susie, on the other hand, went berserk and threw herself at Leighton, her nails hooked and reaching for his eyes.

Fiona grabbed Susie's left arm as Leighton blocked her right. Susie writhed and swore until her anger lost intensity.

Aunt Mary stepped in and, with an arm draped over Susie's shoulder, guided her back to her seat.

The look Aunt Mary shot Fiona needed no interpreting. This is what they'd feared since Isla Edwards had been found. The killer striking again, and everyone in the group fighting and accusing each other.

Susie reared from her seat. 'The police. We need to get the police here so they can arrest all four of them.'

'The police are already here. Fiona is a police officer.'

Everyone in the room looked at Aunt Mary, then Fiona, upon hearing that statement.

FORTY

'Yes, I'm an officer for Police Scotland.' Fiona paused, more because she needed a moment to choose her next words. What she said had to reassure the innocents that she'd protect them, but not strike enough fear into the killer that he decided she was a real threat to his liberty. Aunt Mary's statement had painted a target on her back and, while Fiona wished she hadn't, she could understand why Aunt Mary had revealed her occupation. 'But that's all I am, a regular constable. I'm not a detective.'

As she spoke Fiona was watching each man for the same three signs. Reaching for a weapon, getting ready to make a run for it, and hints of guilt in their body language. All the men remained still, apart from Leighton, who was shaking his head. That could be guilt, or it could be disbelief.

'Don't just stand there, arrest them. Arrest them all.'

The men didn't move. It was as if they were waiting for Fiona to follow Susie's instruction.

In any other circumstances, Fiona would have arrested them all. Except she couldn't get them to a police station anytime soon. It could be at least twelve hours before they could leave the valley, and there was no way she'd be able to watch over all three men while summoning help. Like it or not, she had to let them enjoy their freedom for a while longer.

The PACE Act didn't help. After being arrested, a suspect could only be held for twenty-four hours unless charged. Extensions to this could be applied for, but as the twenty-four hours may pass before Fiona got them to the police station in Hawick, arresting them now may well scupper any chances she had of securing a conviction.

One of the three men was guilty and the other two innocent. With them all being trapped in the valley, she'd need the innocent men's help to alert the outside world to their plight.

'Well? Are you going to arrest them? Or are you going to let my husband's killer walk free?'

'Susie.' Aunt Mary laid a hand on Susie's shoulder. 'What do you think will happen if Fiona arrests them all? She's off duty so she doesn't have her handcuffs, police baton or any of the other things she'd normally have when making an arrest. Three on one is nobody's idea of a fair fight. And say they do all let her arrest them. They let her tie them up. What then? Who's going to go for help? With those men tied up, we're on our own. Two women who'll never see sixty again; a heavily pregnant woman with a sprained or broken ankle and two young kids, and that leaves Fiona and you. As a police officer, Fiona won't be able to leave arrested suspects in the care of a civilian. That leaves you as the person who'd have to go for help. So, come daylight, it'd be you who has to find a way out of the valley. You who'll have to trek along the road. You're young enough and seem to be in decent shape, so I don't think walking a few miles should be that tough for you. But who knows what the journey will be like. If the water keeps rising until it overflows the road, then you're going to have to go over the hills. That's several miles in what won't be very favourable conditions. I've never seen you walking these hills, so there's a chance you might get lost. Or at the very least, end up walking many more miles than are necessary. Tom might know a route he could safely take the quad bike on when it's light, but I doubt you do. However you leave the valley to go for help, you'll be in for a long and dangerous trip.'

Fiona wanted to applaud Aunt Mary for the way she destroyed Susie's wishes with solid logic. She didn't though. There was no point in being antagonistic for the sake of it. Everything Aunt Mary said made sense. If she could only identify the killer and arrest him, then she'd be able to enlist the other two to help her guard the prisoner and summon help. With all three men arrested, there was no way anyone but Susie could go, as leaving a bereaved wife to guard their husband's killer was a recipe for disaster.

'I'm innocent but if you want to arrest me, I won't resist.' Leighton didn't go so far as to hold his hands out ready for cuffing, but it wouldn't have surprised Fiona if he had.

'Innocent my arse.' William shoved at Leighton. 'He's bluffing. There was only four of us there. I know *I* didn't kill Pierce, I'm more than happy to vouch for Tom, and Fiona is a cop, therefore it has to be him. I've never trusted him, he's a Scouser. Have the milk out your tea that lot.'

Fiona pulled a face. That was all they needed, lazy regional stereotyping that further raised tensions. From the corner of her eye she could see Elsie moving to the pantry. She guessed the farmer's wife was going in search of more food, as that seemed to be her default position.

'Oh please, will you just listen to yourself, William. You think that because I'm from Liverpool I must be a thief, and that because I'm a thief I must be a murderer. I've never heard such bigoted bollocks.'

'That's enough.' Fiona crashed her hands together in a loud clap. 'As I see it, there are three known suspects for Pierce's murder: William, Tom and Leighton. However, we don't know for certain that there isn't a fourth person out there who killed

Pierce. I'll admit the idea someone else is in the valley is unlikely, but there's no proof against any of the suspects at this time.'

'So get some. You're a copper, aren't you?'

Fiona ignored the jibe from Susie. The woman was caustic enough when not recently bereaved, and the shock of her loss would loosen what few shackles there were to restrain her tongue.

'Who is this fourth person? I don't remember seeing any strangers in the valley and my Craig never mentioned anyone.' A hand flew to Becky's mouth. 'Could it be George?'

Sideways glances slid around the room as everyone assessed Becky's theory. Most people pulled a face as they tried to equate murder with the kind and gentle George.

Aunt Mary's face was neutral as she knew better, but typically it was Susie who had something to say on the matter. 'You're right, Becky. Nobody is as nice-seeming as George. He'll have a dark side, mark my words. He must have, how else could he stay married to a woman like his wife?'

Even as the eyes of the three suspects were widening at Susie's twisted and hypocritical logic, Fiona was coming to the realisation she'd have to reveal a lot of what she knew.

'There's no way George killed Pierce. Because George is dead. Before we struck out for Hawick, I went down to see if he and Mrs Edwards were okay. Their cottage was already a few inches deep in water, and when I searched it, I found George. There were ligature marks around his neck from where he'd been strangled. There was no sign of his wife. If you remember, when her body was found I stayed with her a moment after we'd put her in the barn to say a prayer for her? I used that time to give her a quick examination. She'd also been killed. She wasn't strangled though. She'd been stabbed in the heart. Pierce isn't the first person to be murdered in this valley tonight, he's the third. And what's more, Isla's body isn't where we left it on the bales. Nor is it anywhere else in the barn. My suspicion is that the killer dumped it back into the water, and because they thought Pierce had seen them, they killed him to cover their tracks. I reckon they'd have dumped his body too, but didn't have time.'

As the others looked at each other in stunned silence, Fiona picked up the block of knives from the kitchen counter, took a step towards the lounge door and hooked a finger at Aunt Mary. She needed the last pieces of the puzzle to confirm her suspicions about the killer's identity.

'I'm going to go to the lounge where I'll use Aunt Mary as a sounding board. I'd advise you all to keep a close eye on one another. If one of the men tries to leave, there's a good chance they're the killer. I'd suggest the other two men stop them.' As each man eyed the other two with suspicion, Fiona fixed Susie with a glare. 'I know you're suffering unimaginable grief right now, Susie, but you need to stay calm and not make matters worse. If you can do that for me, and I can find a way to safely do so, I'll take you to see Pierce.'

* * *

In the lounge, Fiona positioned herself at the far side of the room where she could see the door to the kitchen but was far enough away to not be overheard.

'Right, we don't have much time, so think of this as a quick-fire round. What do you know about Tom? Has he any kids, is he divorced? Widowed?'

'He was married but she left him for someone else. It was about eight years ago if I remember what he told me correctly. From what I gather it was quite acrimonious, as she went back to using her maiden name. O'Neill I think it was. Tom has two daughters.' Aunt Mary's eyes hit the floor. 'Actually, he had two. The youngest took her own life four years ago. Both his daughters took his mother's side and changed their names too. He was rebuilding his relationship with Keira when she, well... He told me that when she was at Colchester University studying to be a quantity surveyor, she got herself entangled with a married man and had her heart broken when on a placement. He said Keira ended up being drummed out of uni and her name was trashed within the industry down there. Personally, I believe that's what he wants to think caused her to do what she did. Deep down I think he puts as much blame on the breakup of his marriage and his behaviour at the time. That's such a burden of guilt for someone to carry, Fiona.'

'It is.' The words were a platitude as Fiona digested what she'd learned. Tom's story was as tragic as they came and it was no wonder he'd chosen to escape the world and spend his days on the hills surrounding the Scales Valley. All day long he'd be left alone with his thoughts. His mind tormenting him about the mistakes he'd made that led to his daughter's fateful decision. 'How did he get on with the others in the valley? He seems sweet on Becky, is there anything in that?'

'He got on fine with Craig and William, he likes Becky but there's nothing going on between them, if that's what you're thinking. Trust me on that one.'

'What about Leighton? Pierce and Susie? George and Isla?'

'He doesn't have much time for the first three. I've seen him having the odd blether with George in the past, but Isla never took to him. About six months ago she came to Cummings and Co wanting to get a restraining order against him, so he couldn't go within a half mile of their cottage.'

'Why?'

'She claimed he was, of all things, spying on her, trying to see into her bedroom when she was getting changed. What a ridiculous thing to say. Anyway, it was dropped when they sold the house to Pierce and Susie. I guess the hassle of getting it wasn't worth the short time they'd still be in their cottage. Mind you, knowing what Isla could be like, I'm surprised she didn't pursue it out of spite just to make life hard for him.' A hand flew to Aunt Mary's mouth. 'Oh, Fiona. I didn't mean it like that.'

'I know.' And Fiona did. Aunt Mary had the odd minor fault, but crassness wasn't one of them. 'What else do you know about him?'

'That's about all of any worth, but Fiona, don't be fooled by the fact he doesn't talk much and always seems to be assessing what's going on. He's a kind and decent man who's trying to overcome a terrible bereavement.'

In an ideal world, Fiona would like time to write lists of pros and cons for each of the three suspects. Her colleague Heather Andrews had always extolled the value of standing in front of a whiteboard and marking connections between motives, means, opportunity and suspects. Heather was lucky, she had other trained officers to bounce ideas off. Had forensics to provide cast iron clues. Fiona had none of that. Just her wits, and a pressing need to identify the killer before he claimed another victim.

Now the killer knew a cop was already on their trail; they'd become desperate, and desperate people made bad decisions.

'Okay, I've a few more general questions that I want you to answer as quick as you can. If you need a longer answer, give it, but we're pressed for time.'

'I'll do my best.'

'How do the newcomers get on with Craig and his wife?'

'Not bad with her, but there's always been tension between them and William, so Craig's never got on with them either.'

'What about with Tom?'

'Same as Craig.'

Aunt Mary was warming up to the rapid-fire questions, which was good. First answers were so often the ones given by instinct rather than thought, and it was in those that gold could be mined from a witness.

'You said before Pierce and Susie were once closer to Leighton. Any further thoughts about why they fell out?'

'No.'

'What about Tom and Becky? Friends or something more?'

'Friends. She adores Craig.'

'How angry was William about getting ripped off by Pierce?'

'Furious. He ranted for days, but eventually calmed down.'

'Does he harp on about it?'

'From time to time, but less often and with less intensity than he used to.'

'Come on, Aunt Mary. We have to get back in there, right now.'

FORTY-ONE

With Aunt Mary's information in her head, Fiona returned to the kitchen. Soft clumps emanated from the pantry where Elsie was busying herself, but otherwise the room was silent enough for Fiona to hear the tick of the clock.

Susie was waiting, an expectant look in her eye. 'Come on then, Fiona, which one of them is the killer? Which one of these bastards made me a widow?'

The temptation to leap straight to the answer was strong, but Fiona resisted it. When the killer was revealed, Fiona needed the two innocent men to have her back. Without any of her usual police gear to aid her, she'd have to make an arrest that may turn into a one-on-one situation, and the man she'd be arresting was a lot stronger than she was, plus he'd be desperate to evade capture and that would make him dangerous. To list the reasons why each suspect was guilty or innocent would be grandstanding, like in those Miss Marple and Poirot dramas that Aunt Mary loved to watch, but she needed to make the accusation so inarguable that the others were ready to spring to her aid. Plus, she was only ninety per cent certain of her theory, and needed to finalise her thoughts by drawing reactions from the three men.

'Let's look at William first. He has the motive to kill Pierce. They've been at loggerheads over the land Pierce bought from him. I'm sorry if this offends you, Susie, and I certainly don't want to speak ill of the dead, but there's no denying Pierce pulled something of a fast one there. Would this be enough to warrant murder? I'm not sure, the farm has been in William's family since forever and he'd not like the way Pierce tricked him.'

'What about George and his wife? You've covered Pierce but that's only one of my alleged victims. What about the other two, why would I kill them?'

'Because you found out they'd agreed to sell their cottage to Pierce and Susie. At the risk of speaking ill again, Mrs Edwards wasn't an easy woman to like, and it wouldn't be hard to picture her throwing it in your face that she'd sold her home to a man you despised.'

'You what? They'd sold their cottage to that pair of robbing gits?' Incredulity decorated William's face, but that didn't phase Fiona. He could have already known about the sale and was acting this way to deflect suspicion from himself, or he was unaware and reacting normally.

'Yeah, we bought it. So what? From what I heard you tried to get it for a song, probably so you could sell it on. Fat lot of use it is to anyone now. My husband and that old couple are dead because you're a shit farmer. If you'd taken care of your land, Pierce and me would be at home watching the telly right now.'

'That's enough, Susie. You need to hear me out.'

As Susie slumped back to her seat Fiona rounded on William. 'My guess is George and Isla came to you, to ask if you wanted to buy their cottage, but you being as careful with money as you are, you didn't offer them market value. The Edwards chose another buyer, that's life. However, you were not the only potential buyer, a fact you may or may not have known. It would be a bitter pill for you to swallow on top of being tricked by Pierce and Susie. The Edwards had a huge garden, more than big enough for another cottage. I dare say you and Pierce had the same plan. How it must have galled to learn the man who tricked you had also stolen a march on you over the sale of the Edwards' cottage.'

'You don't know what you're talking about. Some copper you are. I didn't kill any of them. Not George and his wife, and not Pierce. Yes, I hated him, but I didn't kill him. I think Leighton did.'

'It's okay. I know you didn't kill him. I also know that you're planning to sell the farm in a couple of years. I guess the plan was that you'd live in the Edwards' cottage as long as you were able. It makes sense that you wouldn't want to leave the Scales Valley, and I've heard that you don't trust either of your sons-in-law to take over the farm. That's why I don't think you killed anyone. Yes, I've known you for years and I could never see you as a killer, but that's a personal instinct and, as much as I trust my instincts, I trust facts and logic more. You had the means and opportunity to kill three people, but your motive is weak. As I said, I've known you for years. You're not a rash man, nor are you a vindictive one. You grumble and curse all the time, but I've never known you to fly off the handle. I may be wrong and you could have snapped, but I don't see it. You're looking to wind down into retirement, and the odds of you spending the rest of your life in prison for murder are too great for you to risk it.'

Elsie padded back into the kitchen from the pantry. One hand was empty – the other down by her side, out of view, until she raised it and handed William a shotgun.

William whipped the shotgun up and aimed it at Leighton. 'In the corner, murderer.'

FORTY-TWO

The shotgun was a game changer. William was holding it level and steady with the barrel aimed squarely at Leighton. From his position in the corner, Leighton held his hands up and, even in the dim light provided by the Tilley lamp, Fiona could see the trembling of his body.

'William, be calm. I don't believe you've killed anyone yet, and you really don't want to start now. Not when we are all witnesses. Think about it, you'd have to kill us all so word never got out and, even then, as the only survivors you and Elsie would become suspects the minute the detectives investigating what happened realised you weren't here.'

Fiona watched as William digested her words. There was a chance he'd believe he could dump their bodies in the water and have them lost downstream, but she didn't believe he'd go so far as to kill them all. Still, if Leighton moved in a way William deemed as threatening, or made an attempt to escape, he might pull the trigger.

A glance at Leighton showed sweat on his brow and a constant licking of his lips. With luck he'd have the sense to keep both still and quiet.

'Okay, everyone take a breath, please. We don't want any accidents. I don't believe William killed anyone, which leaves Leighton and Tom as my main suspects. While there's a chance someone else is the killer, I think we can all agree it's not at all probable.' Fiona took a step towards the centre of the room, half because she wanted to have a closer view of Tom's face as she gave the reasons he was on her suspect list, and half to distance herself from Leighton and the blast area should William fire the shotgun. 'I want to start with you, Tom. You've only been working for William for two years now, which means, after Leighton, you're the most recent newcomer to the valley.'

'Aye, so?' Tom's tone was patient and his face looked unconcerned, but there was a minute tic at his left eye that spoke of his worry about being a murder suspect. It could be a sign of guilt, or it could be a natural reaction to being accused of a heinous crime, the fear of wrongful arrest and imprisonment.

'In itself, that doesn't mean much. But it does mean you've had less time to integrate than the others. You don't say a lot, so it's not like you'd be the first name on a list of dinner party guests. Aunt Mary tells me that you keep yourself to yourself and rarely say anything more than hello or a comment about the weather.'

'Don't believe in speaking about nowt important.'

'That's your way and that's fine. The point I'm making is that none of us really know you. But Leighton, do you know Tom has a daughter? Susie, are you aware that Tom's wife left him eight years ago? That their split was so toxic that his wife reverted to using her maiden name and that his daughters followed suit?'

Both shook their heads, although Leighton's shake was at quarter the speed of Susie's. That was a good sign; he wasn't making any sudden gestures that may concern William.

'No. But he has and they did. That's a fact.' Fiona took a deep breath.

William gave a slow nod. 'I knew. He told me and Elsie one night when he was full of whisky.'

'So? My business is my business.' Tom's tone was that of a sullen teen being challenged by a weary parent.

'Absolutely it is. But it's common knowledge that you'd often be seen chatting to Becky. Sometimes with Craig there, but mostly when Craig was in the milking parlour.'

'Yeah, I seen him. Bit creepy if you ask me, him being old enough to be her father and all. But what does it matter if he's divorced? Leighton's divorced too, and I was married when I met Pierce.'

Fiona shot Susie a glare. 'If I may continue. Tom, why, when you hardly speak at all, were you often chatting with Becky?'

William's sawing head and caustic tone spoke of exasperation. 'Isn't it obvious? He had a thing for her. She's attractive and she always dresses in a way that shows herself off. Craig knew about it and laughed it off with me. He trusted Becky and thought Tom was just lonely. Tom only ever leaves the valley to go to market and the shops. So what if he views Becky as a bit of totty?'

'Bit of totty.'

Elsie's repetition of William's words held a different edge than usual. Instead of the bland imitation she gave so often, there was now an undercurrent of disappointment and betrayal. William had just fessed up that he paid attention to how a younger woman dressed and viewed her as attractive totty. A confession that would rankle with any wife, but for one as downtrodden as Elsie, the confession was yet another instance where the man she'd married disrespected her.

For her part, Becky gave a half-hearted shrug as she smoothed Adele's hair.

'Tom, I asked you a question.' Fiona gave him a look, hoping he'd give her a noncommittal answer she could pry at to learn a deeper truth.

'Reminds me of my daughter's... age, I mean. About the same age.'

And there it was. A deeper truth that exposed a searing loneliness. Tom was around twenty years older than Becky, which meant he must have fathered his daughter in his late teens or early twenties. After what Aunt Mary had told her about Tom's daughter, it was no wonder he sought out the company of a woman his daughter's age. If he was estranged from both his ex-wife and remaining daughter, a friendship with Becky and glimpses of her domestic life may be a soothing balm on the wound of his isolated life in the valley.

'That's all very sweet and twee, but I don't believe it. He was hanging round her like a lech. You should have seen him in the summer when she wore those vest tops all the time. There was never a day went by without him hanging around her. He killed those people, not me. And think about it, he was with Craig when Craig went into the water. What if that was him getting Craig out of the way? He was already Becky's friend. He could be there to be a shoulder to cry on and, when the time was right, he'd make his move.'

Leighton's accusation was a fair one, but Fiona had facts he didn't.

'You make a good point, Leighton. However, let's take a look at you as a suspect for a moment. All night you've been quiet about George being missing. That leads me to think you've known all along he was dead. That suggests you're the killer. You're the last person to have moved into the valley and, as such, little is known about you. Yes, we know you developed an app, but that's only because you told us earlier. Before that, we knew nothing about you. Except Aunt Mary. She knew about the divorce. Being divorced in itself isn't remarkable, what is odd though is the circumstances leading to the divorce, and the claims being made against you for a half share of the proceeds from your app. Your ex wants his share, and it's my guess that you moved here to start over. A valley like this is a long way from a metropolitan city like Liverpool; and for some reason you felt you had to hide your sexuality from everyone. I have to say, though, that while attitudes in a place like this aren't as forward thinking as in cities, there's still plenty of acceptance. My guess is that Isla saw a guy you'd hooked up with leaving your place and threatened to expose you. Maybe she tried blackmailing you, either about your sexuality or the fact that your post all goes to a solicitor's office in Hawick and is then delivered to your cottage in the valley by Aunt Mary. That speaks of someone trying to hide themselves. If she threatened to expose you on either front then you'd have reason to kill her. Of course, being gay means nothing these days, but Isla was very old-fashioned and devout in her opinions. She'd see being gay as a sin. You then saw the storm as your perfect chance. You went there, killed her and then her husband. What do you say to that?'

Leighton turned his eyes towards Susie. 'What have I told you about my sexuality?'

'That you are bi.' Susie looked at Fiona. 'He told me his husband caught him in bed with their neighbour's wife. That's why he's divorced. The neighbour beat Leighton up and has vowed to kill him. It's why he moved here and does the whole post to the solicitor's thing.'

This was just the kind of information Fiona had been hoping to unearth, but she still had to cross check it. 'When did he tell you this?'

'A couple of months after he moved in, he invited me and Pierce over for dinner. We all got a bit drunk that night.'

The way Susie's eyes wouldn't meet hers, and the fact her voice was subdued, told Fiona them all getting a bit drunk after the dinner party maybe wasn't where the night had ended. It remained to be seen whether that would be a key fact, or an irrelevant piece of gossip.

'I'm bi. So what? I've never hid who I am and I've never been ashamed of it. Why should I be? As for me paying a black-mailer not to expose me, that's the biggest load of crap I've ever heard. And what about Pierce? Why would I kill him? What's my motive there?'

'That's an easy one, although there are a couple of possible answers. After what happened at the dinner party, you wanted more. Maybe from him, and maybe from Susie, or maybe from them both. It doesn't really matter which, so long as you saw Pierce as an obstacle that had to be removed. If that isn't reason enough, I know that you've engaged a land agent to protest on your behalf against Pierce and Susie building any houses in front of yours and thereby spoiling your view and devaluing your house.'

'I knew it. I bloody knew it.' The way William lifted the shotgun to his shoulder made Fiona fear what his next action would be. No way could she allow William to pull his trigger.

After a quick look Aunt Mary's way, Fiona stepped in front of Leighton and found herself staring down the twin abysses of the shotgun's barrels.

FORTY-THREE

Fiona could see the shotgun was steady in William's hands as he aimed over her shoulder at Leighton. It didn't matter that it was steady. Nor that it wasn't aimed directly at her. At this range a cartridge being fired would leave her with life-changing injuries if the spread of shot didn't kill her outright. There was no greater danger to be had by moving until the barrel was aimed directly at her, so that's what Fiona did. 'Leighton, stay behind me. William, lower the gun. Nobody's going to be shot.'

Uncertainty crept into William's eyes, so Fiona stayed both still and silent as he ran his thought processes. After what seemed like an age, he lowered the shotgun from shoulder to waist, but kept it trained her way. That was okay with Fiona; she'd presented herself as a shield for Leighton, and the longer she did so, the less chance there was of William or anyone else in the room trying to harm him.

'I didn't do it. I didn't kill any of them. Please, you have to believe me.'

Fiona didn't bother turning. 'Shut up, Leighton. In fact, everyone be quiet.'

'To hell with being quiet. That prick killed my husband.

Tom, William, will you start acting like men and tie that bugger up, so we're safe from him and his murderous ways until we get out of here?'

This time Fiona turned. 'I won't tell you again, Susie. Shut. Up. There's a lot more to this than you know, and I still have some questions. You can be the first I ask. Have you ever felt Tom was being inappropriate with the way he looked at you?'

Susie's head shook. 'Nope. I caught him looking down my top once, but I don't blame him for that.'

'Aunt Mary, have you felt Tom was being inappropriate around you, maybe trying to look through your windows as you changed clothes?'

'Not once.' Aunt Mary tuned to Elsie. 'What about you?'

'No, not once.' Elsie's tone was as bewildered as her expression.

Fiona pointed at Becky. 'We know he had at least a soft spot for Becky, but what none of the rest of you know, is that a few months ago Isla Edwards was in the process of taking out a restraining order against Tom for stalking. According to her statement he's been peeping through her windows. She'd caught him wiping his hands on a blouse of hers that she had put out to dry.'

'Urgh, Tom. How could you fancy that dried-up prune?' As William turned to face Tom the barrel of the shotgun turned with him, causing all the people in its arc to press themselves lower.

'Didn't. Wiped my hands as payback for her accusations.'

Fiona shook her head at this explanation. 'I hear what you're saying there and we all know that Mrs Edwards was quick to blame someone without evidence to back up her accu- sation, but as innocuous as that piece of petty revenge may be, it was the tipping point that drove her to get the restraining order. I have no doubt she rubbed your nose in it, and that she made sure you knew you wouldn't be able to go within a half mile of her. Am I right?'

'Aye.'

'I'm sure Isla would have told you about the restraining order. So, you're facing the fact a restraining order's coming your way. If it's successful, and with George backing her up like the loyal husband we all knew him to be, it's likely to be granted. You don't need me to tell you the track beside their cottage is the only way to access the top of the valley. If you couldn't go within a hundred metres of her, you wouldn't be able to use the track. As the track also gives access to the best route up the hills you'd be of no use to William, as there's no way he could employ a shepherd who wasn't allowed on parts of his land; therefore, you'd have to leave the valley and start over somewhere else. In normal circumstances that would be a pain, but from what I've heard, you're good at what you do and would soon get another job somewhere else.'

'He would. He's a good shepherd and a good man. Where the hell are you going with this?'

'Patience, William. I'm almost there. Tom doesn't want to go and get another job. He wants the one he's got here. Not because it's a particularly good job, or that he likes it here. Both of those things may be true, but they don't matter to Tom, because he has a particular reason for being in this valley. Call it an ulterior motive or an agenda if you like, but he didn't come to this valley by chance.' Fiona took a look at Aunt Mary and caught the terse nod that was thrown her way – affirming that she had worked it out correctly. 'He came to this valley to avenge his daughter.'

'You what? Avenge his daughter? You make him sound like a gunslinger from the Wild West, not some gnarled old shepherd from the arse end of nowhere.' Susie's tone dripped as much scorn as her words. 'How's he going to avenge his daughter? Did old George get her up the duff? Or maybe his wife upset her precious nature. Jesus wept, if this is the standard of policing we have nowadays, it's no wonder the country's in such a mess. Come on then, Miss Marple, who's he avenging his daughter from?'

'From you and your husband.'

'Now I've heard it all. And just what are we supposed to have done to this daughter we never knew existed until tonight?'

'Does the name Keira O'Neill mean anything to you? I'm sure it does, but let me explain so everyone else knows. Keira is Tom's daughter. She changed her surname from his, Urquhart, to her mother's, O'Neill, after they divorced. Four years ago, Keira was a university student who got a summer job as a trainee quantity surveyor at your husband's firm. I've been told you have pictures on the walls of your bungalow that depict construction sites. Some of the sites are large enough that it makes sense, as the contractor, you'd employ a quantity surveyor. It also makes sense that you seized on the chance for cheap labour by accepting a student on a placement. At some point, Pierce seduced Keira, or maybe it was the other way around. No matter—when you found out, you made him fire her. I don't think you stopped there though. That wasn't enough for you, was it? You got Pierce to give the university a scathing reference and to ring all his mates in the industry to badmouth her. Instead of Keira being able to move on and learn a lesson from the mistake of sleeping with her boss, you forced Pierce to make her life hell, while also ruining her future prospects.'

'Bitch deserved everything she got for leading my husband on. But... I didn't know she was his daughter.'

'Shut up, Susie.' Fiona looked for a reaction from Tom but his face was implacable. 'I speak with Aunt Mary at least once a week. A few months ago she told me about over-hearing you arguing with Pierce in the garden. It seems that you've been every bit as unfaithful as Pierce. And, I'm not sure if you know this, or even care, but Keira took her own life four years ago. Because you'd moved, it took Tom a couple of years to track you down. He then came to this valley just so he could get revenge on the two of you, and tonight he got his chance to kill Pierce—a chance he took. Leighton was never the killer. No way did he care about any threat Isla Edwards may or may not have made. Poor George and his wife were only killed because they were in the process of forcing Tom out of the valley, and he couldn't have that. When I asked Tom about his friendship with Becky earlier, his answer was that she reminded him of his daughters. He used a plural—Becky, William, you two were closest to Tom. Did he tell either of you about his family? His daughters? Earlier he said "his daughters". Then he stopped himself. Pretended he was saying "his daughter's something…" That's right, isn't it, Tom?'

'I knew his wife had left him and that he never saw his daughter, but he never said anything about a daughter who died.' William's eyes clouded. 'I think he said his daughter's name was Claire.'

'There's more. Isla Edwards was killed with a stab wound to the heart. Earlier Tom was carrying a knife. So were you, William. But do you remember that he had to borrow yours when we were down on the bridge?'

'Aye what of it? He got a ducking earlier. He probably lost his knife then.'

'That makes sense, but he had it after that. I saw him use it. So, if he didn't lose the knife then, it wasn't likely he'd lose it at any other time. I reckon that after we retrieved Isla's body, he realised he was carrying the murder weapon and, as soon as he could, he made sure the knife was thrown into the river. From the surprise on your face when he asked to borrow your knife, I'd say he's never been without one in all the time you've known him.'

'Fancy idea. Not true and you've no proof.' Tom's eyes held Fiona's, but she could see the bluff in them.

'I've been a police officer for over a decade now. I've never been a detective, but I've worked with plenty. One of the things they, and all experienced cops, say is that the minute a suspect says the police have no proof, they know that suspect is guilty.' Fiona aimed a finger at Tom, pistol style. 'You've just said I have no proof. Well, you may or may not know this, but Aunt Mary works as a legal secretary for Cummings and Co in Hawick. She was the one who typed up a transcript of the meeting you had with one of their solicitors. A meeting where you tried to get the restraining order overthrown. You were also trying to get a defamation claim against Pierce and Susie for what they did to your daughter before her suicide. I'm no expert, but I don't think it's likely the claim would have stood. However, I understand your true aim with the lawsuit was to scare Pierce and Susie into offering to settle out of court. I'm sure you thought that by getting them to pay you off, you'd be proving they admitted driving your daughter to take her own life and then you could take that to the police. Those statements are on record and will count as proof with regards to your motive. Aunt Mary also typed up your will. Everything you own is to be left to your remaining daughter, Claire. I should tell you, Tom, that Aunt Mary and I took a walk up the river yesterday. What I'm sure I don't need to tell you is there's a copse about a half mile past the Edwards' cottage. When we were at that copse, I saw a whole bunch of treetops that had been dragged to one side. It's my guess they were left after someone had thinned out the trees. Am I right, William?'

'Aye, you are. But we never dragged them off to one side. We just left them where they were lying. Craig said he'd retrieve them next year for Bonfire Night. What are you getting at, Fiona?'

'The treetops and a lot of large branches were all arranged

by the riverbank. Tom was seen walking back to the farm from that direction. That copse is high enough up the valley that it'll never be touched by the flooding waters, so the treetops and branches should still be there. They won't be though, because Tom went up there and threw them all in the river, knowing they'd get caught up in the heck and would form a dam. Maybe he never expected the dam to grow so large, or maybe it's just as he planned it. Either way, a significant portion of the trees forming that dam are only there because Tom made sure they went into the river.'

'My Craig's missing because of you, you...' It was only the stirring of little Jamie at her side that prevented Becky from delivering the finale to her insult.

'Anyone could of done it.'

'That's another regular utterance from the big book of clichéd sayings by guilty suspects trying to prove their innocence. As you say, anyone *could* have done it.' The pedant in Fiona couldn't let the grammatical mistake go uncorrected. 'Except, Craig was either with his wife and kids or William. William was with Craig or Elsie. Pierce and Susie were together, as were Aunt Mary and I. Apart from you, Leighton is the only other person who doesn't have someone to vouch for his whereabouts during the hour or two leading up to the time we all evacuated our homes. However, we've already established Leighton has no real motive. Not compared to yours. Being spurned by a lover or two, or not being happy about losing your view, doesn't come close to the motive you have, considering what happened with your daughter.'

'Even if I did the rest, they'd have just driven off. Couldn't cause the landslide, could I?'

'As it happens, that's exactly what you did. I've been travelling that road for years now. The others too. Right where the tree blocked the road, is an area that's always been stable ground. The roots of the trees really helped hold the bank together. And the place where the water was streaming over the road, there's a drain around there somewhere that runs beneath the road. I never paid much attention to it at the time because I was concerned with getting myself and Aunt Mary to safety, but now when I picture the tree blocking the road, I can't help but focus on the roots. Instead of them all being jagged where they were ripped apart or pulled from the ground by the tree toppling over, three or four of them had nice flat ends, like they'd been cut with a saw. I'm sure you gummed up the drainage pipe with a few stones so the water would run down the hill, eroding away the bank beneath the tree. With its roots partly severed, it wouldn't take long for the tree to fall across the road trapping us all in the valley.'

'I couldn't predict the storm or make it happen.'

'You're a shepherd, Tom. Are you seriously trying to tell me you spend your days out on the hills and never look at the weather forecast? Storm Odin has been predicted in every news outlet you can think of for the last week. Trying to say you didn't know Storm Odin was coming is like saying you didn't know water is wet. Everything you're saying now is nothing more than desperate attempts to deny the undeniable. You knew the storm was coming in and planned to use it to cover your tracks. First you killed Isla Edwards because she was making it impossible for you to stay in the valley, her husband George because he had seen you kill her. And Pierce for what he did to your daughter. You're guilty as sin, so, Tom Urquhart, I'm arresting you for—'

Fiona didn't get to finish her sentence, as Tom grabbed William, spun him round and tore the shotgun from his boss's hands. As soon as it was in his hands, Tom shouldered the weapon and aimed it straight at Fiona. She could see his finger curl around the trigger as he yelled at her to stay put.

FORTY-FOUR

Fiona saw eyes filled with hate.

As much as she knew it wasn't all directed at her, Fiona was compelled to recoil away from it such was the intensity of the anger streaming her way. As a police officer Fiona had seen killers before, but they were people who'd killed in the heat of the moment. Tonight she was staring into the eyes of someone who'd made a cold-hearted decision to take the lives of three people.

Worst of all, Fiona was looking into the eyes of a killer from the wrong end of a shotgun.

She'd never once thought William would pull the trigger when he'd pointed the shotgun at her, but with Tom's finger on the trigger, it was far more probable. He had nothing left to lose. His grabbing of the shotgun confirmed his guilt to everyone in the room.

'Tom. Listen to me. Don't do anything stupid. Give the gun back to William. Shooting me is just going to make everything worse.'

'How?'

'There are five witnesses. You can't kill us all, not with a double-barrelled shotgun. William, Leighton and I will be on you as soon as you fire that first shot. Give the gun back to William. It's the only sensible thing to do.'

'You've ruined everything.'

Fiona saw the knuckle of his trigger finger turn white as he applied enough pressure to send one of the firing pins against a cartridge. All Fiona was working on was an unspoken message from Aunt Mary.

When Elsie had appeared with the shotgun and given it to William, Fiona had glanced her aunt's way. Aunt Mary's face had been so indifferent it was as if William held a cheese sandwich rather than a weapon that could blow a hole clean through someone.

Fiona knew her aunt well enough to know that she would never allow her face to give the wrong message. Aunt Mary was cunning, ridiculously intelligent, and believed that the result would also justify the means. If Aunt Mary was portraying a lack of concern about the weapon, she knew it wasn't loaded, and was trying to convey that information to Fiona without telling everyone else present.

To face down a killer who was pointing a gun your way was a gamble, a huge roll of the dice based on nothing more than the expression on an old woman's face. Such was her faith in Aunt Mary. Fiona stood her ground.

'Don't do it, Tom. Give the gun back to William.'

Tom's finger curled as he swung his aim from Fiona to Susie and instructed the weapon to deliver death. The shotgun made a noise; instead of a killing boom it gave an insignificant click.

Fiona was already launching herself forward as Tom's finger tightened onto the second trigger. Her arm swept upwards, directing the barrel at the ceiling as the firing pin struck nothing.

Now there was a boom. A huge one that made Fiona's ears go numb, and while she knew there'd be shouting and possibly screaming, she could hear none of it. She drove her knee towards Tom's groin as her hands grappled for the shotgun, but Tom was already twisting his body as he fought to retain his grip on the weapon, so rather than land square on her intended target, Fiona's knee thudded into Tom's thigh.

Fiona couldn't compete with Tom's strength and he ripped the shotgun from her grasp and thumped the stock into Leighton's face as he sprang to Fiona's aid. Leighton went down, and the hands he clutched at his face already had blood seeping between their fingers.

William wasn't so easily dealt with, as he grabbed Tom from behind in a bear hug that clenched his arms against his body. Fiona feinted another knee to Tom's groin and then threw a palm strike at Tom's nose.

Tom's efforts to free himself by butting the back of his head into William's face meant Fiona's aim was off and, instead of striking Tom's nose as intended, the heel of her hand slammed into Tom's chin. Because Fiona put everything she had into the blow, when it landed, Tom's knees buckled and she took the opportunity to wrest the shotgun from him.

To further incapacitate Tom, Fiona thrust the shotgun's stock into Tom's midriff, leaving him gasping for breath.

'Get me one of the ropes from beside the door, Susie.'

As Susie scrambled to where all their gear had been dumped, Fiona stood poised, ready to deliver another blow should Tom show any further signs of resistance.

Fiona's hearing was starting to return and she could hear crying from the two children Becky was trying to console. Behind her she was aware of Aunt Mary and Elsie fussing over Leighton; and the acrid smell of nitroglycerine from the shotgun cartridge filled the air.

When William released Tom so he could take the rope from Susie, Tom fell to the ground still dazed and hungry for oxygen. Fiona planted a foot on Tom's shoulder, pinning him to the floor as William used the rope to bind Tom's hands behind his back. From the savage way he yanked the knots tight and double bound the shepherd, William's thoughts on Tom's actions were there for all to see.

William didn't just bind Tom's arms, he also lashed his ankles tight. Once Tom regained his breath and senses, he'd maybe be able to find a way to stand and jump himself forward, but he'd be slow and ungainly, and that was fine by Fiona.

Fiona's heart eased to a more normal rate as she handed the shotgun to William and watched as he pulled a lever that broke it apart and removed the sole cartridge from its barrels.

William looked to his wife. 'Elsie, grab me a couple cartridges, will you?'

'Couple cartridges.'

'No.' Fiona pointed down at Tom who was shaking his head as if trying to clear cobwebs of the mind. 'He's going nowhere, and after all the arguments tonight, a loaded shotgun isn't something that should be around. If he tries moving, hit him with the stock again. If he speaks, gag him. And, William, check his pockets for your knife.'

Fiona trusted William to not pull the trigger, but Susie was of a different mind than the neighbour she despised. If she could grab the shotgun she might well blast Tom away and, after catching her first killer, Fiona wanted to make sure he faced justice. By capturing Tom the way she had, Fiona had brought Susie a closure she'd never found herself. George and Isla's kids would share that closure, and so might Becky, if Tom confessed to having a hand in Craig's fall into the swollen waters.

As for the deduction she'd used, Fiona felt no pride in threading the strands of information into a tapestry of evidence. Her former sergeant Dave Lennox or her best friend DC Heather Andrews would have got to the same point she had and probably sooner.

William looked at Fiona, the empty shotgun in his hands still pointing at Tom. 'What now?'

'We get ourselves as comfortable as we can and wait for daylight. Either we can hike down the road to get help, or there may be search and rescue helicopters flying over whose attention we can grab.'

From nowhere there was a thunderous crash that made the entire house shake. Even as her body was absorbing the reverberations, Fiona's mind was trying to identify the source of the crash.

Aunt Mary tugged Fiona's arm, her free hand pointing upstairs. 'That's the same as when the tree fell onto the roof.'

FORTY-FIVE

It was what Fiona feared. The candle flames were now writhing on their wicks as a fresh current of air swirled into the room. With the downstairs doors and windows all closed, it had to be the upstairs that had been breached.

Fiona grabbed a Tilley lamp and made for the door. 'I'll go up and see what's what.'

The second she opened the door to go upstairs Fiona felt a strong gust chill her face. There had only been a breeze earlier, as the tarpaulin was by no means enough to prevent all of the wind getting in.

At the top of the stairs she pushed the door open to see if her fears were justified.

They were. Another large part of the tree had sheared from the main trunk. While smaller than the previous branch, it had punched through the edge of the tarpaulin and slammed its way into one of the roof's main trusses.

A wrenching creak filled the night as gravity and the wind pulled at the branch. It moved a little and then stopped, its main bole entangled in the roof truss. The wind howled as it built itself up for another attempt to dislodge the branch – then it blasted. Fiona felt the gust thrash icy raindrops against her face as the wind lent its full power to the task of dislodging the branch.

Again tree and truss creaked together until a mighty snap rent the air. Fiona had to throw herself against the far wall as the branch twisted one of the mighty trusses from the other parts of the roof it was tangled in and toppled it onto its side. Decades-old dust dislodged by the sudden movement mushroomed into clouds only to be whipped away by the wind and rain.

Pressed against the wall, there was far less danger of anything falling onto Fiona, but she was trapped in the bedroom by a knotted mesh of broken timber.

Above Fiona, tatters of the tarpaulin flapped back and forth, and she could hear slates being riven from the nails fixing them to the roof timbers as the wind plucked at them.

Fiona's first objective was to escape the bedroom and get downstairs before more of the tree fell into the farmhouse or further sections of the roof collapsed. She held the Tilley lamp high and examined the mess of roof timbers holding her prisoner. In some ways it reminded her of the game KerPlunk she'd so often played as a child. Instead of removing a plastic straw with the aim of not releasing a marble, she now had to clear a passage through the debris that wouldn't collapse on her as she passed through. Around her the storm raged, its fury whipping her with icy rain as she identified which timbers to try and move, and which to leave as supports.

Fiona placed the Tilley lamp where it would be safe and set to work. Many of the smaller parts of the roof were easy to cast aside, but there was one that was pinned by a large part of the roof truss and she didn't have anything like the strength needed to move it. She grabbed a length of timber she'd already discarded and tried using it as a lever.

'Come on, move you stubborn, stinking pig.' Fiona heaved

with all her power, muscles straining and face reddening. The length of timber she was trying to clear from her path moved with the sloth of continental drift. 'If you don't get out of my way, I swear I'll smash this lamp onto you and you'll burn. How would you like that, eh?'

Threatening an inanimate object in this way was always going to achieve nothing, but the more exhortations came from Fiona, the more she felt anger boosting her strength. When she eased off the lever she'd fashioned, there was enough of a gap for her to get part way through the bird's nest of timbers.

It was tight, so tight there was little room to move without bumping into a piece of timber or one of the many nails that spiked from the shattered roof. Worse was the fear that at any moment the whole structure could give way and crush her, or another piece of the tree could land atop the pile, smashing her body.

Fiona's heart raced as her hands grasped at the timbers on the other side of the pile, pushing them ahead of her until they lay on the floor. After a minute's work, Fiona had cleared enough of the loose timbers for there to be an opening she could crawl through.

The Tilley lamp went first, and with it placed as far from her intended route as she could get it, Fiona fed her arms and head through the gap she'd formed. By squeezing her arms into the position of an Olympic diver and propelling herself forward with toes still in contact with the floor, Fiona was able to wriggle her shoulders between the two hefty beams that were once part of the roof truss.

When her belly button scraped its way over the truss, Fiona felt her upper body tilt towards the floor as she got past the point of balance, so she dropped both hands to the ground. The change in position meant she had no way of applying a forward force, her legs now hanging out behind her. She tried walking forward on her hands, but it didn't afford her the slightest advantage. Next she eased the tension out of her arms, lowering her upper body in the hope the weight of her torso would pull her hips free.

That didn't work either. And nor did any of the squirming twists she attempted.

Behind Fiona, there was a series of creaks as her weight created tension on an already fragile structure. Something fell onto Fiona's calves and, while it wasn't heavy enough to do any real damage, she felt the sharp prick of her flesh being pierced.

'Come on, you can do this. After all that you've been through tonight, you're not going to let a bunch of kindling get you.'

Fiona reached down and, with scrabbling fingers, snatched a grip on a piece of timber. Gripping the timber with both hands, Fiona summoned every morsel of strength her body could provide. Her back arched as she pushed the timber back against the truss with all her might. Slowly at first, she felt her hips scrape through, and then, with the suddenness of a released champagne cork, her legs slithered through the opening.

Such was Fiona's focus on her efforts that she never felt the hands on her shoulders or saw the boots beneath her face, until all she had time to do was close her eyes before impact.

FORTY-SIX

'Are you okay?' Leighton kept a grip on Fiona's shoulders until she'd planted her hands on the floor and had drawn her knees under her hips.

When she looked up at him she saw he was offering his good hand to help her up. She took it. 'Thanks, I was beginning to think I'd be stuck there all night.'

'No problem. You were almost free anyway, all I did was break your fall.'

Fiona didn't know whether Leighton was employing false modesty, or telling the truth. Either way she was glad he'd come to help. Someone had used Steri-strips to patch up his nose, which had taken the full brunt of Tom's strike with the shotgun. It would heal, but he'd need a damn good plastic surgeon if he wanted his nose restored to its former shape.

'Cheers.' Fiona lifted the Tilley lamp and made for the stairs. 'Let's get down before any more of the roof falls in.'

By the time Fiona got to the bottom of the stairs she'd worked out what needed to be done to transfer everyone to the barn.

Every eye turned her way when she entered the room, each one asking the same question.

'Another branch fell into the house, ripped the tarpaulin apart and smashed one of the roof trusses. The wind is starting to strip the roof, so we're all going to have to move to the barn.'

Fiona made sure her tone was assertive enough to back up her blunt words. There was no time for democracy or explanations. They had to get out of the house as soon as possible, as there was no telling how much damage it would sustain.

'What about *him*?'

There was no need for Susie to point at Tom. Her tone was layered with more than enough venom for it to be obvious.

Fiona had an idea for the best way to deal with Tom. If he was in the barn with them, there would always be a chance he'd end up as Susie's victim, and while Fiona believed Tom deserved everything that was coming to him, she wasn't going to allow any harm to come to him while he was her prisoner.

'William, your cattle trailer's up in the field, isn't it?'

'Aye.'

'If we put Tom in there and closed all the flaps on its sides, would he be able to get out even if he managed to free his hands?'

William squinted at the ceiling for a moment. 'No.'

'Good. You and Leighton untie his feet and put a rope around his waist.' Fiona turned to the women. 'You guys get yourselves ready to go out, and help Becky and the kids do the same. We'll take Tom to the cattle trailer then come back for you.'

The cattle trailer was a makeshift solution. It would be a cell in which Tom could be kept. According to protocol, there should be eyes on a prisoner at all times, but sometimes protocol wasn't always achievable. With his hands bound behind his back, Tom wouldn't be able to harm himself, and if they hooked the trailer up to William's pickup they could reverse it into the barn – she'd be able to monitor Tom at regular intervals.

Two minutes later Fiona was standing on the trailer with Tom's leash rope in her hands, watching as Leighton and William fed Tom through the window. She wasn't fool enough to try and restrain Tom herself; and to stop him barging her and trying to run off, she'd knotted the loose end of the rope around one of the trailer's hitching points, making sure Tom saw what she was doing.

Tom's face was twisted as he glared at her. It was something Fiona was used to. She was often verbally abused by those she arrested. Prisoners would comment on any aspect of her they thought would score them a reaction. She'd been called ugly, fat, a bitch, a whore and a whole raft of other insults she'd let pass her by, but this was the first time she'd looked into the eyes of a killer and known that he wanted to end her life. A chill ran through Fiona.

William and Leighton clambered their way through the window and joined her on the flat bed of the trailer. With both of them now holding Tom's leash, she released the other end and cast her torch past the trailer. The waters had risen enough that they would be six inches deep throughout the farmhouse had Tom's waterproofing ideas not worked so well.

There was an irony to Tom's efforts to protect the farm-house being so effective. He'd been camouflaging himself. By seeming the most willing and practical, he'd been trying to portray himself as the good guy who was doing everything he could without complaint.

Fiona went to the far side of the trailer, shone her torch past it and jumped down. She gestured at William to throw her the rope.

Leighton brought the rope with him as he joined her, but Tom was ready and, as Leighton landed, Tom barged into him, sending him sprawling. Fiona went to grab Tom only to receive a head-butt that sent her staggering backwards.

The head-butt wasn't anything like as destructive as it should have been, but it still did enough damage that Fiona had to shake her head clear before setting off after Tom. William had the good sense to direct his torch so it was illuminating Tom's back.

With his hands tied behind his back, Tom wasn't running at any great speed, so Fiona easily caught up with him. Torn between trying to grab the rope or a handful of Tom's coat, Fiona opted for a third option and kicked sideways with her right foot.

Fiona's boot connected with Tom's, sending it arcing left. Tom went down. Hard. His head twisted to one side as his face plummeted towards the rough tarmac of the road. For good measure, Fiona planted a hefty kick into Tom's midsection that left him doubled up and gasping. It was against the rules to beat up a suspect, but she knew she could always argue she'd used no more force than necessary to subdue a dangerous man trying to flee custody.

Together with Leighton and William, Fiona wrestled Tom towards the cattle trailer until the beam of her torch illuminated a sight that kicked her plan square in the teeth. The cattle trailer lay on its side, two of its wheels spinning in the wind that had toppled it over.

'Right. To the barn with him.'

Tom writhed and tried to kick out at them, but William had brought the shotgun with him, and, while it wasn't loaded, its stock being driven into Tom's kidneys was enough to take the worst of the fight from the shepherd.

At the back of the barn there was a stack of portable sheep pens. Each section would only weigh a few kilos, but Fiona laced Tom's rope leash through the whole pile, pulled it tight so Tom had no more than an inch or two of room to move, and

then lashed it together with a knot that was far more compli-
cated than necessary.

Even with Tom secured like this, Fiona wasn't taking any
chances, so she took the shotgun from William and handed it to
Leighton. 'You stay and guard Tom. We'll go get the others.
Come on, William. Let's put a few more bales round Pierce's
body so it's out of sight now Susie's coming, and then go get the
others.'

It grated on Fiona to leave a civilian guarding a murder
suspect, but she had to get Aunt Mary and the others out of the
house. By choosing Leighton over William, she had at least
selected a guard who had the least beef with the suspect.

FORTY-SEVEN

As they walked down the slope to the farmhouse, Fiona was still going over everything in her mind. For all she'd caught a killer, she still needed to make sure justice was done. She had to get Tom to a police station and into an interview suite. There was more than enough evidence and witnesses for him to be charged, but that couldn't happen until he'd been interviewed. At first light, she would have to find a way to make that happen.

Fiona boarded the trailer and banged on the window.

Aunt Mary opened it at once, her expression a mixture of fear and determination.

'Send Susie and Elsie out with the kids. We'll come back for you and Becky.'

Jamie seemed excited as he stood on the trailer between William and Susie. For him this would be a grand adventure. Aunt Mary had to help Elsie through the window; the shakes in the old woman's hand had little to do with the chill night. When Aunt Mary went to pick Adele up from where she was snuggled against her mother, there was an instant eruption of tears and screams. No matter what either of them tried as Aunt Mary handed Adele to Fiona, there was no appeasing the child.

Fiona hugged Adele tight and stepped from the trailer to the road. William helped Elsie, Susie and Jamie down, then with William and Fiona carrying the kids, they set off for the barn. Elsie tucked in behind her husband, at his direction, and Fiona saw the wisdom of it. William may be a year or two older than his wife, but he was a great deal more used to braving the elements, and still possessed as much strength as a man half his age.

Susie also saw the wisdom of William's idea as she moved in behind Fiona, the action causing Fiona to grind her teeth. Yes, the woman was older than she was, and was grieving the loss of her husband, but she was one of life's takers and, as exhausted as Fiona was, her first thought was that Susie's actions were typically selfish. It was a thought that passed as Fiona realised by Susie using her as a shield against the weather it was also an endorsement of her capability and toughness. All the same, if she hadn't knocked the shotgun barrel upwards, Tom would have killed Susie, so after saving the woman's life, Fiona felt Susie might have acted with less self-interest.

On and on Fiona trudged with little Adele wriggling to be free with every step taken. Let Susie trail in behind her, she could take care of the little ball of wriggles when they got to the barn. With luck, caring for Adele would provide a small distraction to her from both grief and her natural tendency to cause trouble. As sympathetic as Fiona was to Susie losing her husband and her home being destroyed, there was no escaping the fact that if Susie's bitchy nature hadn't compelled her to persecute Tom's daughter to the point where she took her own life, nobody in the Scales Valley would have died tonight.

To Fiona's eye, William was spent. Every one of his years showed on his face and it looked like someone had added another twenty for good measure. As well as carrying Jamie, he'd also lugged four of the black bags Elsie and Aunt Mary had stuffed with duvets, towels, blankets and dry clothing.

'William, you take over from Leighton. He can help me get Becky.'

William's mouth opened then something in his eyes changed and he dipped his chin. 'Aye.'

By the time Fiona was halfway back to the farmhouse she'd worked out how best to transport Becky to the barn. For the eighty-yard journey it wasn't worth the effort with anyone else, but Becky was lame as well as pregnant, and with only two of them fit to carry her to the barn, it would be a slow and draining process.

Fiona checked William's pickup and found what she expected: the keys hanging in the ignition. Farmers were lax about keys at the best of times. Doubly so when they lived at the end of a long valley.

With the pickup parked as close as she could get it, Fiona mounted the trailer. Leighton had climbed through the window and was in the process of helping Becky. It took a lot of grunting and a few pained grimaces from Becky, but they got her out the window and into a position between Fiona and Leighton, where she could hop across the trailer to the wall.

Fiona put her mouth to Becky's ear. 'We'll sit you on the wall then jump down to help you into the pickup.'

It was in Fiona's mind to bring Aunt Mary with them, but she wanted to grab a moment alone with her aunt. A lot of the information she had used to build her case against Tom had been based on information Aunt Mary had given her. Aunt Mary was a smart woman, who possessed more than enough intelligence to have worked out Tom had a motive for killing George and Isla. Fiona wanted to know why she hadn't made sure to tell Fiona everything she knew about Tom a lot sooner than she had.

Getting Becky to the pickup wasn't easy, but the pregnant woman was stoical as she did her best to help their efforts.

In the barn, Elsie was pulling faces to amuse the kids, but

there was no sign of Susie. As Fiona was about to ask her where-abouts, a muffled sob came from behind the bales shielding Pierce's body.

'You help Elsie and Becky look after the kids. I'll go and get Aunt Mary.'

With the instruction to Leighton given, Fiona set off back to the farmhouse. The pickup's lights illuminating nothing but rain and sodden ground, she reversed it into place ready for the trip back to the barn.

When Fiona got onto the trailer the first thing she noticed was that there were two slates lying on its load bed. The second thing she saw was Aunt Mary's fear-etched face at the window. With the wind now dropping slates over their escape route, there would be no time to grill Aunt Mary before transferring her to the barn. She had to get her out of the house before the occasional falling slate became a cavalcade of debris as the wind tore the farmhouse's roof apart.

Fiona crossed the trailer bed and reached through the window for Aunt Mary's hands. 'Quick. There's a two-foot step at the end of the trailer. Once you're down it, get in the pickup.'

Aunt Mary's jaw tightened and Fiona felt a pull as her aunt began to feed herself through the window. While not as sprightly as she once was, Aunt Mary was in decent shape and, when the weather was kinder, would often enjoy a long walk in the surrounding hills. This kept her fit, but there was no halting the ravages of time, and where once she would have trotted across the trailer, now her best pace was no more than a quick march.

As Aunt Mary dropped onto the roadway, a slate hit the trailer bed with a thunderous clang. It was enough to break both women into a stumbling run as they sought the safety of the pickup.

Fiona had twisted the ignition and was reaching for the gearstick when a slate hit the windscreen, starring it into a thousand prisms. She screamed at the suddenness of the impact and gunned the engine, causing the pickup to shoot forward. She dipped the clutch at once and dabbed at the brake.

With the windscreen shattered by the slate, forward vision was impossible. A mosaic of splintered glass allowed Fiona no clear section to see through. She let the pickup pull itself along in first gear without touching the throttle. What she did touch was the window controls.

By shining her torch from the driver's window, and using the fence as a reference point, Fiona was able to navigate the short distance to the barn without incident. When she pulled to a halt and cut the engine, she flicked the internal light on and looked across at Aunt Mary. 'We need to talk.'

FORTY-EIGHT

For the first time ever in all the years she'd known and loved Aunt Mary, her aunt couldn't make eye contact. It was a dagger to the soul, as she owed Aunt Mary so much. She was the woman who'd picked up the broken pieces of a girl whose life had been destroyed by indiscriminate violence. Without Aunt Mary having her back, Fiona would never have made it into Police Scotland. Nor would she have been able to finish school, run her own house, and in those first debilitating days after her parents' murders, get out of bed in the morning. Whatever was said before they left the pickup, Fiona would have to ensure both tone and vocabulary did nothing to damage their relationship. The toll of tonight's trials was already way higher than it needed to be, so for her and Aunt Mary to fall out was both unthinkable and unnecessary. Still, Fiona had to take deep breaths before opening her mouth. When she did, she aimed at an easy target.

'You thought the shotgun was unloaded, didn't you?'

'Yes.' Aunt Mary's head bobbed in eagerness at this soft line of questioning. 'You'd told me about poor George being murdered, so when I was in the pantry helping Elsie put some food together and saw the shotgun and the box of cartridges beside it, I took the cartridges and hid them, in case anyone went for the shotgun. I had no idea that there'd be a cartridge in it. I swear, Fiona, I would never have let you stand in front of it if I had known.'

'I know that. It was your demeanour that gave me the courage to face it. I could tell you weren't concerned and trusted that you knew it wasn't a threat.'

'I'm so sorry, Fiona. I guess I should have checked there were no cartridges in it. I just assumed there wouldn't be. I mean, who in their right mind leaves a loaded gun in a pantry?'

This last point was one Fiona had already chewed over. She knew guns were meant to be stored in a locked cabinet. That was a basic part of obtaining a licence. However, farmers who'd grown up with shotguns rarely obeyed such rules. William no doubt deemed the pantry both a secure and handy enough location to keep his shotgun and the cartridges it fired. In the greater scheme of things, it was a minor transgression, but it would still be a point the procurator fiscal would pounce on when reading her report of tonight's events.

As she reviewed Aunt Mary's words, Fiona found something of her own to pounce on. In the interests of familial harmony, she tempered her tone until it was as light as she could get it. 'You said you should have checked the shotgun wasn't loaded. I didn't know you knew about guns.'

That was as easy as Fiona could make it for her aunt. By not directly asking the question, she'd allowed Aunt Mary the chance to offer the information rather than be questioned on it. A nasty thought was trying to infiltrate Fiona's mind and, if her thinking was correct, the thought would forever torment Aunt Mary.

'A, err... friend showed me.'

The thought put out roots and pushed a sapling towards the sky in search of sunlight and rain. Fiona wanted to pluck it. To rip it clean from her head and discard it with every other distasteful thought she'd ever had.

Fiona said nothing. In an interview suite, silence was a detective's friend. A tool that was used to elicit chatter that would incriminate. Deep in her gut, Fiona felt nothing but roiling. An acid ball was growing and threatening to make her retch. Still she waited. If her relationship with Aunt Mary was to remain as strong as it had always been, her aunt had to tell her without the indignity of being interrogated. That would come. Detectives would cross-examine everyone who got out of this valley alive.

Here, alone with Aunt Mary, the conversation was about respect, love and understanding. Although if Fiona's thought was right, understanding would take a hell of a lot of doing.

'You know, don't you?' A tear ran down Aunt Mary's cheek and dripped from her chin.

To Fiona that single tear was a wrecking ball whose destructive force was attacking her life. The last time she'd seen Aunt Mary cry had been after her parents' funeral.

An immovable rock throughout that awful day, Aunt Mary had been at her side when she'd needed her to be, and distant enough that Fiona was given her own space when required. They'd returned to Aunt Mary's cottage after the wake and sat in silent reflection for hours. Fiona had gone to the bathroom and returned to find Aunt Mary sobbing as her boundless fortitude reached its breaking point.

'Know what?' Fiona was determined to let Aunt Mary confirm the wretched thought in her own way, but she already knew it to be true. The little glances she'd witnessed between Aunt Mary and Tom now made sense to her. As did her aunt's insistence that Tom was a good and decent man. All the clues had been there, it was just that it had taken a police officer's mind to interpret them.

The pain of self-recrimination on Aunt Mary's face, in her

voice, was more than enough to make Fiona's eyes prickle as tears eked their way to freedom.

'Don't play dumb with me, young lady. You know perfectly well what I mean.'

Fiona let the rebuke crash into her without comment. It was nothing more than Aunt Mary's guilt lashing out. By now her aunt had more than enough time to work out that, by not telling Fiona everything sooner, she'd allowed a killer to remain free long enough to add to his victim list. Whether true or not, Aunt Mary would always believe she had Pierce's blood on her hands.

'You're doing that cop thing of leaving a silence for a suspect to fill. Don't you dare treat me like a suspect, Fiona. I couldn't bear it.'

Those last four words rammed a knife into Fiona's heart and twisted it. She'd got her approach wrong. Instead of trying to tease information from Aunt Mary, she ought to have had the strength to approach the issue head on.

'You're not a suspect, Aunt Mary. Nobody would ever think that. A star witness, yes. Suspect, no.'

'Now you're humouring an old fool.' A sob. 'I know what I am, how things will look.'

It was time for statements. Damage control. 'Tom was the friend who showed you about the gun. I'm guessing you and he were more than friends.'

Aunt Mary turned her face away. It was all the confirmation Fiona needed. The full story would come out in time, but Fiona could easily put the pieces together. Aunt Mary's life would be lonely. She was a people person, and while she enjoyed a peaceful life in Scales Valley, Aunt Mary deserved to have someone in her life who made her feel special.

After years of putting her life on hold to rebuild Fiona's, Aunt Mary more than deserved the happiness that came with companionship. To Fiona's knowledge, Aunt Mary had dated once or twice, but had never found the right man to spend the rest of her life with. Tom may or may not have been that person had he not turned out to be a killer. Aunt Mary would feel a fool, and was sure to be filled with self-loathing and guilt.

Fiona reached across the pickup and rested a hand on Aunt Mary's shoulder. Gave a little squeeze. 'It's okay. You've done nothing wrong. Yes, you may have fallen for the wrong man, but show me someone who hasn't at some point in their life felt attracted to someone who was bad news, and I'll show you a unicorn.'

Aunt Mary's head turned back until she was looking at Fiona. '*You* haven't.'

Fiona's eyes closed. If only Aunt Mary knew the truth. She dated, but never for more than a month. As soon as Fiona felt herself getting close to a man, she broke it off. She didn't need to see a therapist to understand why. It was the fear of once again loving someone only to lose them.

'He told me he ended up in Scales Valley so he could catch them out when they ruined someone else's life. He made it sound like he was doing a noble thing, and... and all the time he was plotting this. Planning how he'd kill them. I'm such a fool, Fiona. If I'd only pieced everything together the way you did, Pierce might still be alive. Instead I believed his lies and, until Pierce was killed, I was trying to find reasons he was the killer. Even after that, I thought it must have been Leighton or William who was the killer. I swear to you, I never ever believed Tom would kill anyone. You should have seen him with William's sheep and lambs. He was so gentle with them.' Aunt Mary wiped her eyes. 'I fell for him, Fiona. I fell for a man who killed people. It's true what they say: there's no fool like an old fool.'

'Don't talk like that. Now, come on, let's go join the others.' It was a deflection and Fiona knew it. 'Since you're the one who's carrying all the guilt, I nominate you to tell William his windscreen's ruined. Think of it as atonement. And, Aunt

Mary, forgetting that I'm a cop, you do realise you're also in trouble for not telling me as your niece that you were seeing him?'

The wan smile that trembled its way onto Aunt Mary's lips told Fiona they'd be okay.

FORTY-NINE

Fiona curled herself tight and snuggled into the duvet. It made no difference to her body temperature, so she eased a leg out from under the duvet and clambered to her feet. Most of the others were awake, with only Elsie and Susie still motionless. Aunt Mary looked as if she hadn't had a wink, and that was no surprise. Not with everything that would be going round her brain.

Throughout the night, Fiona had shared one-hour guard spells with Leighton and William. Tom hadn't tried to make an obvious escape attempt and was now immobile against the sheep pens.

Daylight had come, but it was a murky winter morning half-light whose purpose seemed to be to shroud the world rather than illuminate it.

Fiona stretched and rotated her body to ease away the morning stiffness and get her blood pumping. Motion would be the only source of warmth.

Leighton was handing out biscuits as a breakfast substitute, and William was over by the barn door looking out. From the lack of pattering raindrops and tin clanking where the wind attacked the sheds, Fiona knew the worst of the storm had passed.

William didn't turn when Fiona got to his side. She didn't blame him. Not when she saw what he was looking at. Under the morning's grey blanket, the destruction of Scales Valley Farm was intimately visible.

The waters of the Scales Burn surrounded every building with eddies that swirled lazy circles. The farmhouse roof was a broken skeleton atop a lifeless home. Beyond the farm steading, the valley was now a fjord whose brown waters would leave a trail of destruction when released from their temporary home. It would be years before this farm could turn a profit again, if ever. To clear the debris and begin farming the land again would take months. The cost would run into hundreds of thousands, and the work and stress associated with getting the farm back on its feet would knock lumps out of a young man. William was ready for retirement, the farm was to be sold. In its current state, the farm was worthless. There would be insurance, but there was little chance of the insurers paying out before Tom had been tried, as they'd be looking for a loophole. One that would be presented to them by Susie's accusations of negligence regarding William's husbandry of the Scales Burn that flowed through his land.

Fiona didn't speak to William. At a time like this, words were useless. Even the ones said with the kindest of intentions would fail to provide even the merest hint of solace.

The rain was now a good Scottish smirr as tiny droplets fell to earth in a cluster so thick it was three parts mist.

A look at William's hands gave Fiona cause for concern. His knuckles were white as he held the shotgun. She could understand that, he was bound to be grieving for his farm. For Craig and all the others who'd died last night. For the lost vision of his future.

William's period of denial would be brief, as there was too

much evidence on show for it to be anything else. He'd now be feeling anger at the senselessness of it all. Fiona understood that. She was still angry about the murder of her parents almost twenty years ago. Back then she'd wanted to exact a personal revenge on her parents' killer. To hurt them as they'd hurt her mother and father.

William held a shotgun. It might not be loaded, but it was large and heavy. William was a man whose strength had been honed by a lifetime of hard work. In his hands the shotgun didn't need a cartridge to be a deadly weapon.

Fiona knew that she'd either have to keep William under constant supervision, or remove him from the valley lest he avenge his losses on Tom. She touched his arm. 'It's awful, isn't it?'

'Aye.' A look slid over his shoulder towards Tom. 'And it's all his fault. That thing you said about him chucking branches and treetops into the river so they'd block the heck, that's what's ruined my farm. That's what caused Craig to be swept away. He needs to be punished.' The shotgun trembled in William's hands to such an extent Fiona thought she'd have to remove it from his grip before he went back and used it to beat Tom to death.

'We need to get out and raise the alarm. We need a doctor for Becky and a full team of detectives. Most of us are bound to have mild hypothermia, or some form of exposure. And that's before you take into account all the bumps and cuts and bruises we have. Now I can see it properly, your face looks like the oil scalded it in a couple of places, as well as the back of your hands. That needs to be treated too.'

'It's not my face and hands that bother me.' The words came forth in a despondent croak.

Fiona draped an arm around William's shoulders and pulled him close. 'Oh, William. You'll get through this. I don't know how, but you will. You're too good a man not to.'

As Fiona released William, she felt the shotgun being pressed into her hands. 'Here. You better have this. I know you're a copper and everything, Fiona, but I'm telling you this straight. I need to get away from here because if I don't, I'll kill that Tom.'

'I know.' Fiona gestured out the barn door. 'Go and get your quad and the chainsaw; it's probably the best thing to get us out of here now it's calm and we've got some daylight. We should be able to use the road. And yes, I'm coming with you. One, because you may need help at some point, and two, as a police officer, me reporting the murders will get a much quicker response. While you're getting the quad, I'll let the others know what we're doing. Tom's tied up and if Leighton has the shotgun on him, he'll stay put. He doesn't need to know it's not loaded.'

FIFTY

When William didn't appear within a few minutes, Fiona went to look for him. She didn't think he'd go without her, but she wasn't sure enough to wait all morning. The shotgun had been passed to Leighton, and she'd had a quick word with Aunt Mary. If anyone could keep Susie and Becky calm, it would be Aunt Mary.

Fiona found William in the field bent over the quad bike. If she hadn't seen his shoulders and arms moving she'd have feared his heart had given out. William was working at the quad's engine, a can of WD40 in his hand. He straightened and Fiona saw his thumb go to the starter button.

The quad grumbled into life and William slung a leg over its seat, his thumb away from the throttle as he allowed the engine to warm.

Fiona climbed on and sat behind William, her fingers gripping the cold rack to stabilise her. William had placed the chainsaw on the front rack, and Fiona had a rope looped over one shoulder. Whether they were needed or not, they'd have them. There was a crunch as William kicked the quad into gear and set off.

William trundled the quad along at no more than ten miles an hour. In the smirry rain it was fast enough, but Fiona knew the reason for his sloth wasn't the driving conditions. William's head was corkscrewing back and forth as he surveyed the devastation of his farmland. What was once a fertile valley was now a horrible brown lake. Pieces of debris floated in the waters, each making their way downstream in a lazy drift.

Although it was daylight, the smirr was thick enough to act as a shrouding blanket that limited vision to no more than a couple of hundred yards. Even with this limited visibility, Fiona was scanning over the waters in the hope she'd see Craig clinging to a tree. As she expected, there was no sign of the man.

To their left, the grassy hills glistened dampness. Creeks formed in the gullies and shed rainwater downwards. Ahead of them a ditch overflowed across the road at a low point.

The quad's engine slackened as William dropped two gears and forded the water at a steady pace that didn't send up a spray of water. Fiona could hear the bulbous tyres crunch on the gravel that had been washed onto the tarmac. It was a familiar and yet unnerving sound.

When they rounded the corner leading to the bridge, Fiona could see where the newly formed loch had gouged a gap in the road. Contrary to what had been predicted, the gap was no more than eight or so feet wide, but the predictions about the water flow weren't wrong. It thundered through the narrow gap at a furious pace and gushed from the downstream side, where it fanned out before making its way to the river's natural course.

Along the farm side of the roadway, debris had been pressed by the waters until it formed a barrier that allowed a steady seepage through.

William stopped the quad twenty feet from the water's edge and looked over his shoulder. 'You'll have to get off first. Don't want to kick you by accident.'

Fiona did as he asked and took careful steps across to the

debris that had been washed against the bank and pulled out a long narrow branch. Maybe eight feet long by an inch and a half wide at its thin end, the branch would make a good probe.

Fiona took small steps towards the fissure in the roadway until she could test the water's depth. As soon as she'd lowered a foot of the probe into the fissure, Fiona could feel it being swept downstream by the raging waters. Such was the power of the flow, Fiona gave up on the idea at once. Even if the water was only a foot deep – and it was more, she was sure of that from the volume spilling out – there was no way they or the quad bike could pass through the flow without being swept away.

Fiona launched the probe into the water and turned her back on it as it was whipped away by the surging current.

This was a bust. There was no way they'd be able to get to the bridge, much less travel onwards towards the A7 and Hawick. They'd have to go over the hills. And that would likely mean hiking, as the ground was too steep and sodden for the quad's tyres to find any reliable traction.

Fiona turned her attention to William and what he was doing. Instead of testing the water's depth or trying to haul heavy branches from the pile of debris to form a makeshift bridge, William was just standing with his back to the loch watching the waters as they spilled across the downstream field on their journey back to the river.

'Come on, William. We can't get through here. We'll have to find another route.'

'Look.' A weathered hand pointed at the field, angry red spots decorating the skin where William had been splashed with the hydraulic oil. 'The ground there is level, so the water spreads out.' The hand moved across to the downstream side of the roadway near the bridge. 'The bank's not too steep there, and the fence is buggered. I reckon we could take the quad across the field and up the bank. Then we'd be able to get out.'

Fiona assessed William's idea with an equal mixture of excitement and trepidation. If it worked it'd be a lot easier and quicker than trekking over the hills. However, if the quad stalled or the power of the water was too great for it, they'd be swept away.

'What's the quad like in deep water?' Fiona pointed at its fat bulbous tyres. 'Won't they make it want to float? Wasn't the engine already bad to start because of damp?'

'It's never stalled before, but I'll give the engine another once-over with this.' William pulled the can of WD40 from his pocket. 'As for worrying about it floating, our weight will help and we can easy put some extra weight on it. There's a pile of stones by the gate.'

What William was saying made sense and Fiona could see the plan working. 'Then let's get going.'

William took the quad to the pile of stones and while he sprayed the engine with the entire contents of the can, Fiona loaded the largest stones she could onto the quad's storage racks. She was tempted to remove the chainsaw and leave it behind, but the memory of the tree blocking the road ahead made her work around it.

Fiona opened the gate into the downstream field and clambered back onto the quad. With the stones laden on the rack she had to wrap her arms around William to help her balance. It was reassuring as he trundled out on a wide arc so he'd be fording the flow of water at its shallowest point.

Down through the gears William went until the quad was moving forward at little more than a crawl. Before they'd gone ten feet into the water, it was washing over their boots as the quad ploughed onwards. William had picked a course that saw them cut through the water at a forty-five-degree angle to its flow. The front right wheel of the quad was leading, nosing its way through the brown murk.

Ahead of them the flow seemed more intense, so when

William pressed the throttle forward, Fiona gripped his torso even tighter. If they got through this part, they'd make it.

'William, stop!'

Fiona grabbed William's shoulder and pointed to where the water was streaming against the fence. Half hidden by the torrent of water passing over it, flashes of bright orange were visible.

FIFTY-ONE

As they entered the deepest part of the water Fiona could hear the quad's exhaust become muffled as it was submerged, yet on it forged. William had turned the handlebars to direct the quad more into the flow, as the vehicle was being pushed sideways.

William's tactic worked and the quad kept pushing forward. When the exhaust broke the surface and its roar became audible again, Fiona would have let out a whoop had she not seen what she suspected was Craig's body.

A minute later, the quad was parked on the bank of the roadway.

When Fiona climbed off to investigate the orange flashes she'd seen, William was only half a pace behind her.

Together they waded into the knee-deep water and reached into the murk. As she grasped the orange material Fiona recognised its texture as PVC waterproofs.

Fiona looked at William. 'On three.'

It took their combined efforts to haul Craig's body free and carry it up to the roadway, but neither of them uttered a word of complaint.

As she looked down on her friend's corpse, Fiona felt the prickle of tears for the first time in years. A look at William saw her own grief reflected back at her. William wasn't the type of man who'd shed a tear, but he was as close as he'd come.

Fiona knelt beside Craig and took a closer look at him. His skin was covered in the mud carried by the water, but when she wiped his face and neck clean she found what she was afraid of. His throat had been slashed. Next she turned her attention to his body. There was still rope that was around his chest and, a foot from the knot, there was a clean cut. This told her Tom had slashed Craig's throat, cut loose his line and pushed him into the waters. After that he'd tied the end of Craig's rope around a calf and sent it out in the waters, to back up his lies.

Tom's end game could have been to dump Aunt Mary then replace Craig in Becky's life thereby replicating the family he'd once had.

William's face was hard as he helped Fiona to her feet. 'Hanging's too good for that bastard Tom.'

'Agreed.' Fiona laid a hand on William's shoulder. 'Come on. Let's get going. There's nothing more we can do for Craig than make sure Becky and the kids get taken somewhere safe as soon as possible.'

Fiona kept her focus on the bank at their left side as they travelled along the road. She was hoping to find a trace of her car. It would be a write-off, but there was always a tiny chance she'd be able to get some of her things from it. Most would be ruined, but even if they were broken, she wanted her mother's Lladro figurines back. Try as she might, she could find no sign of it.

Her loss was far smaller than that of anyone else in the Scales Valley, but she'd always mourn the loss of her mother's precious figurines.

When William eventually eased off the throttle and used a

hand signal at the Mart Street roundabout, a rush of endorphins fled through Fiona's system as the tension she felt left her. They'd made it.

Outside the police station, Fiona gave William a quick hug. 'Let me do the talking, yeah?'

FIFTY-TWO

Fiona leapt from the Police Scotland helicopter and dashed across to the barn with her head only a few inches higher than her hips. There had been a three-hour wait to get the helicopter and another from the Air Ambulance. The time had been spent answering a detective sergeant's questions and sipping hot drinks as the duty inspector put a rescue team together. The only good thing about the delay was that Storm Odin moved on, and while the sky was a long way from cloudless, the rain had ceased and the clouds at the edges of the storm were much higher in the sky.

From the air, the sight of the Scales Valley flood was spectacular, in a morbid way. Two detectives from Hawick station were at her heel and she could hear the incoming Air Ambulance.

'That's Tom Urquhart there?' The direction was unnecessary, as Tom was the only person who was bound. Everyone except Becky was on their feet to greet the arrival of the helicopters, although Becky had risen to a sitting position with Adele cradled on her lap.

Fiona saw Jamie pulling her way as she went to hug Aunt

Mary, his voice high as he addressed her. 'Did you bring my daddy back?'

Becky's face crumpled as Fiona dropped to a knee so she was eye to eye with the child. 'I'm sorry, Jamie, I don't know where he is.' When she looked up at Becky, she saw the dairy-man's wife nod and a plea enter her eyes.

The breaking of bad news was something Fiona had been trained to do, but nowhere had that training covered how to tell a child their parent was dead. A faceless copper had been with Aunt Mary that fateful day she'd been taken to the Head's office after completing her History exam. The copper had stood mute while Aunt Mary took over and delivered the devastating news with compassion.

Fiona had been a hormonal fifteen year old then. More than old enough to understand the concept of death, if not yet adult enough to know how to deal with her grief. Jamie was an innocent five-year-old. Craig would be his hero. The man he'd want to grow up to be.

'I'm sorry, Jamie, but we think your daddy was washed away by the floods. We think he's probably drowned. What we do know is that he loved you very much. You and Adele and your mummy. And the baby in Mummy's tummy.'

'No.' The word was a shout. And then Jamie was free from his mother's grasp. His little fists lashing out at Fiona as he yelled 'liar' over and over again.

Fiona took every blow Jamie threw without once trying to defend herself. Aunt Mary scooped Jamie up and held him tight until his fury dissolved into tears and he reached for his mother.

Air Ambulance crew appeared with foil blankets and a stretcher for Becky. As they loaded her onto their stretcher Fiona saw her mouth the word 'thanks'. It was enough. And too much.

The detectives were leading a handcuffed Tom to the Police Scotland helicopter.

Even with the two helicopters, there weren't enough seats for everyone, so William, Leighton and Fiona stayed back to wait for one of them to return. The elderly ladies, the pregnant woman and her children had priority; and the detectives had been insistent they get Tom back to the station, as they needed to make sure he was charged within the twenty-fours that had started ticking when Fiona arrested him. Pierce's body would be taken with them.

Leighton came across to Fiona and laid a hand on her shoulder. 'I don't know how you did that. I couldn't have done it. Are you okay? You know, in yourself?'

Fiona turned away and walked to the barn door. She was okay, and she wasn't. Her life had been afflicted by grief since the age of fifteen, and on days like today she wondered if she'd ever escape it.

This trip to see Aunt Mary was supposed to be time off to recuperate physically and mentally from the trauma of losing a colleague, and it had turned into this, whatever this may eventually be called. She'd identified and caught a killer, nearly drowned, been chilled to the bone several times over and had to break the worst kind of news thrice over.

Attending a Friday night fight at the Rose and Crown was a piece of cake compared to this. The sooner Fiona could get back to her regular duties, the sooner she'd be able to piece herself together again.

But first, Fiona needed to have a long talk with Aunt Mary. Her aunt had held back on telling her about her relationship with Tom, and now Fiona couldn't help but wonder what other secrets Aunt Mary had kept from her. After what she'd just been through, Fiona was more determined than ever to uncover the truth behind her parents' murders.

A LETTER FROM G.N. SMITH

Dear reader,

I want to say a huge thank you for choosing to read *The Flood*. If you did enjoy it, and want to keep up to date with all my latest releases, just sign up at the following link. Your email address will never be shared and you can unsubscribe at any time.

www.bookouture.com/g-n-smith

For me, writing *The Flood* was hugely enjoyable, as I've long hankered to write a whodunnit-style novel with multiple suspects yet have never been able to come up with a plot and setting I was comfortable with. While I've always been somewhat in awe of the authors who write seamless whodunnits, I'd never dared try my hand at it.

However, when I saw a news article about terrible floods engulfing parts of the UK, the images shown sparked enough of an idea in my twisted brain for me to go ahead and write this style of novel.

The news article showed miles of flooded land with some roofs poking out of the water and one house on higher ground that was completely dry. It made logical sense the people who lived in the houses that were flooded would seek shelter with the neighbours whose house was likely to be unaffected. However, because I write crime novels, I couldn't help but think 'what if they all hated each other before the flood happened?'

This coupled with a couple of plot ideas that had never seen the light of day gave me the push I needed to write a whodunnit.

To suit my plot, I moved the action to a remote valley so as to limit the availability of outside help, while also making it more credible that mobile phones wouldn't work. This gave me what I really needed, a situation where the weather conditions offered a massive threat to the characters, and a killer with a clear target among their midst.

I have many ideas for Fiona MacLeish where she'll have to pit her wits against the elements and killers in future novels, so I do hope you'll stick with me and Fiona to see where her stories take us.

I hope you loved *The Flood* and if you did I would be very grateful if you could write a review. I'd love to hear what you think, and it makes such a difference helping new readers to discover one of my books for the first time.

I love hearing from my readers – you can get in touch on my Facebook page, through Twitter, Goodreads or my website.

Thanks,

Graham

www.grahamsmithauthor.co.uk

facebook.com/grahamnsmithauthor

twitter.com/GrahamSmith1972

instagram.com/grahamsmithauthor

ACKNOWLEDGEMENTS

My family have always been incredibly supportive of my writing so it's only fitting they get the first mention of thanks.

After my family, I have a wide circle of friends and colleagues who take interest in my writing career and spur me on to create ever more entertaining novels for my readers. I'm hugely lucky to be a part of the Crime and Publishment writing gang, and to them, I say thank you for all the pep-talks, brainstorming and constant support; you're a fantastic bunch, and without you guys, I'd never have the discipline to get my bum in the writing chair as often as I do.

My physio, Paula Morrow, deserves a huge shout out for torturing the kinks out of my neck and advising me on some of the realities of policing in Scotland.

Finally, but by no means least, I'd like to thank the whole team at Bookouture for the fantastic work they do on my novels and the wonderful opporchancities they've given me. My editor Isobel Akenhead deserves a special mention as she's a pedant's pedant who kills my darlings with a reckless lack of mercy, puts up with my bad jokes and sarcastic replies, and wields a red pen with a surgeon's precision. I can say hand on heart that working with her has improved my writing immeasurably. Thanks, Boss.

Made in the USA
Middletown, DE
27 February 2024